DEFINED BY DECEIT

A. E. Via

Defined by Deceit

Published By: Via Star Wings Books

Copyright © March 2015

Edited By: Ally Editorial Services

Cover Art By: Jay Aheer of Simply Defined Art

Formatting & Illustrations By: Fancy Pants Formatting

http://www.fancypantsformatting.com

Trademark Acknowledgments

The author acknowledges the trademarked status and trademark owners of the following trademarks mentioned in this work of fiction:

Back to the Future: Universal Pictures
BMW: BMW of North America, LLC.
Boy Scouts: Boy Scouts of America
Carhartt: Carhartt, Inc.
Chevy Blazer: General Motors
Cialis: Lilly USA, LLC.
Country Kitchen: Country Kitchen
Cracker Barrel: CBOCS Properties, Inc.
Days Inn: Days Inns Worldwide, Inc.
Diner Dash: PlayFirst Inc
Fisher-Price: Mattel
Ford F-350: Ford Motor Company
Ford Focus: Ford Motor Company
Forever 21: FOREVER21, INC.
I'll Be There for You: Jon Bon Jovi & Richie Sambora
iPod: Apple Inc.
Mercedes: Mercedes-Benz USA, LLC
NBA: NBA Media Ventures, LLC.
Patron: The Patrón Spirits Company
Playboy Bunny: Playboy Enterprises.
Polo: Ralph Lauren Coproration
Thermos: Thermos L.L.C.
Timberland: Timberland LLC
Town Car: Ford Motor Company
Transformers: DreamWorks SKG,, Paramount Pictures, Hasbro, Di Bonaventura Pictures
Tupperware: Tupperware
Viagra: Pfizer Inc.
Visa: Visa, Inc.
WWF Smackdown: WWE, Inc.

CONTENTS

ACKNOWLEDGMENTS

Writing Llewellyn's dramatic story was definitely my most challenging accomplishment. I couldn't have done it without the help of a very talented team and long list of friends.

I have to thank my family for all their support and understanding of the long days and nights closed up in my office. My husband is the most patient and understanding man in the world and I love him with everything I have.

Tina Adamski has once again done a fabulous job with editing my work and teaching me important lessons on writing in the process. I really appreciate you working so hard to make my words flow easily. Casey of Fancy Pants formatting, as always, thank you for coming through and putting everything together into a beautiful package.

An extra special thank you to Jay Aheer for the most beautiful cover I have ever had grace the front of any of my works so far. I cried out for help after putting myself in a bind regarding this cover and she answered immediately, pausing her own work load to help me. She designed the cover for DbyD in one draft and I was so floored when I saw it that I literally had to dab at the corners of my eyes. I feel my writing has advanced to a higher level of maturity and I'm so grateful that Jay designed a cover that reflected that as well. Thank you so much and I look forward to working with you a lot more in the future.

Thank you to my team on Facebook – headed up by Iris Pross and Barb Hicks - that constantly spreads the word of my work and takes time out of their schedule to post promo for me or to read and review. You are all very special and very important to me. Thank you so much! Especially to River Mitchell, Andrea Goodell, Jennifer Wedmore for all of your great advice on developing this storyline. Taking time to stop from your own schedules to read and dissect each part of this book. That was so very important to me and I love you for doing it. Thank you. Crystal Marie thank you for writing the blurb for me, I fear that's a talent I'll never possess so thank you so much for rescuing me.

Fans, I love you to pieces. I hope you will enjoy this book. I'd love to hear what you think. Drop me a line on social medias or leave me a review.

CHAPTER ONE

"Llew don't break anything!" Moss half-yelled, half-laughed while his boyfriend chased him around his parents' mansion-sized home.

"Your ass is mine when I catch you… literally!" Llewellyn yelled, as he rounded the large kitchen island. His boyfriend was his best friend as well as his lover. In the small town of Emporia, Virginia, they were likely the only gay students in their high school. That anyone knew about. A kid that moved there from Los Angeles a few years back was gay and unashamed of it. He was colorful and flamboyant because he felt free to be himself. The community had been so cruel to him and his family, that they were run out of town so fast Llew didn't remember the pretty boy's name. He did remember being envious, though.

It was by sheer accident that Llew and Moss discovered each other's sexual orientation in the first place. They were football teammates and both attended a party hosted by one of the cheerleaders during their freshman year. Rosie Jameson's parents were traveling salespeople who left her and her twin sister home alone every couple of weeks. So that meant at least twice a month the teenagers had something fun to do in their dreary-filled-with-retirees town. Llew and Moss got shit-faced drunk, and ended up alone in Rosie's father's den watching WWF Smack Down.

Moss couldn't hide his hard-on while watching the oily, ridiculously hot, and ripped wrestlers writhing and rolling all over each other in the small wrestling ring. When Moss looked horrified that Llew had busted him and was ready to bolt; Llew smirked at him, and pulled up the hem of his long hoodie, exposing his own erection. The conversation they had that night changed their lives. They didn't immediately fall in love, but things progressed fairly quickly from that point.

They were so young back then; they just wanted to be friends. They needed someone to talk with openly; a friend they could drop the mask with. The mask they had to wear twenty-four seven with everyone else.

When Llew got pneumonia in their sophomore year, neither his mom nor dad could afford to take time away from work to stay home with him all day. Moss was there every day before and after school, taking care of him the same way a significant other would. Llew knew then that things had changed between them. He suddenly saw Moss' blond shaggy hair as sexy instead of messy. He'd noticed that his friend's once scrawny frame had benefited from their hours in the weight room, after school. Now his best friend was seventeen-years-old, with fashionably tousled hair, bright blue eyes, and a tightly packed body.

"Stop chasing me, I'm tired." Moss rounded the corner of the media room, and hurdled the couch in the formal living room like the track star he was.

"Then stop running," Llew huffed back, quickly closing the distance when Moss slowed down. Llew tackled his boyfriend onto the plush carpet, pinning him beneath his much larger body. He gripped both Moss' wrists together above his head, and used his other hand to push back the long bangs that had fallen over those blue eyes. He loved Moss so much. They'd been inseparable from the moment they met six years ago. Seamlessly transitioning from friends to lovers, now all they talked about – well Llew talked about – was leaving for college where he could love on Moss freely.

When they first moved to Emporia, Llew's father owned a small landscaping business and was contracted to service the mayor's property. Llew was ticked off he had to help his father every summer. Kids would tease him when they looked out their windows or rode by on their bikes on their way to the YMCA pool. While he hauled away overflowing bags of cut grass, Moss had come out of his mansion and started shooting baskets at the hoop in his immaculately paved driveway, but not before giving Llew a bottle of water and extending him an invite to play along. Although Moss was wealthy; the son of the mayor and sixth generation heir to the McGregor Empire, he never looked down on the working class like his parents did.

The mayor and his wife weren't bad people; they were wonderful to the townspeople. In spite of that, they always felt that their son could do better than the company he chose to keep. After Llew's parents died last year in a car accident, they took pity and stopped giving him and his older brother dirty looks. His now twenty-six-year-old brother was his only living relative and had moved back home to take over their father's business and make sure Llew graduated.

"You get sexier every day, babe." Llew ground his stiffening cock into the hard thigh beneath him. "What time are your parents coming home?"

Moss opened his eyes. The usually bright blue irises were the color of the sky before a thunderstorm, dark and smoldering with lust. "Mmm. In about an hour."

"Damn. I could fuck you so hard right now." Llew spread his legs wider, and drove down hard, pulling a strained moan from his boyfriend.

"Would you throw me around first? Slam me against the wall and take it has hard and fast as you wanted?" Moss moaned, his hips rising up to meet Llew's punishing thrusts.

"Ahhh, god. Hell yeah, I would. You're such a fuckin' pain slut, babe." Llew groaned, pulling hard on Moss' hair. His guy was into hardcore fucking, and Llew couldn't deny that he loved that shit, too. It was smoking hot. Moss would scream his name, bite, and scratch him while he pounded his tight ass. No matter how hard he fucked him, Moss would beg for more. He loved being tied down, gagged and even slapped a little. Llew had almost twenty pounds on his track star, so he was careful with him, but oh, how he got a head rush from controlling him. They were limited to backseat fucks most of the time, but every now and then Moss' parents would be out late at a charity dinner, or some official function and they'd have well into the night to explore their ever growing need.

"I would love for you to be bad right now, Llew, but you gotta go. I don't feel like hearing my parents' shit."

"Damn. How come they think I'm not a good enough friend for you?" Llew sat up, turning his back to his boyfriend. He pushed his hand through his thick, brown hair. "I'm the fuckin' star running back on the football team, and I have the eighth-highest GPA in our class. Goddamn. You think they're setting the bar a tad high on who's worthy to hang around you?"

Moss rose to his knees and draped his long arms around Llew's neck. He kissed him softly behind his ear, whispering in that voice that always calmed him. "Soon we'll be away at college. I've already gotten into UCLA, and I know your acceptance letter is coming any day now. The scout couldn't say enough good things about you, right?"

Llew just slightly nodded his head.

"Okay, then. We'll be together. No one will give us a second look if we're holding hands there. Or kissing. Or touching." Moss punctuated each statement with a kiss to Llew's neck.

"What if your dad finds out we're seeing each other while you're in school? What if he stops paying your tuition, or rent, or some shit? Would you like… stop seeing me?"

"Stop worrying. Damn. You're driving me crazy with all these questions." Moss stood abruptly, walking further into the media room, fixing the pillows they'd knocked off the couch during their roughhousing. Eliminating any trace that Llew had been there.

Moss had begun to insist that Llew not be around when his parents were home, anymore. Said it was easier for him. How? Llew had no idea. As far as anyone was concerned, they were friends. Just like so many other kids at school.

13

"Hey. Alright, I'm sorry. You're right. Being together is all that matters. We'll always be together." Llew cupped Moss' cheek, tilting his head up to look at him. He didn't comment on the look he saw in his guy's eyes, but he noted something was off. *He's probably stressed with exams and everything coming up.* He didn't have time to think about it any longer, since the front door beeped to indicate someone was coming in.

Moss pushed him away, almost causing him to fall over the low coffee table in front of the couch. "Shit babe, calm—"

"Don't fuckin' call me that. Are you crazy? Hurry up! Get your stuff," Moss whispered harshly, his eyes wide and terrified. It wasn't like they were in there getting high or something.

Llew shouldn't have let Moss' words bother him, but they did. You would've thought he was on the Feds' most wanted list the way his boyfriend was acting. He yanked his backpack off the floor and slung it over his shoulder. When he got to the marble foyer, he tried to ignore the disdainful look Moss' father threw him.

"Good evening Mayor McGregor, Mrs. McGregor, how are you?" Llew said, in his most polite voice.

"Oh. Hello Llewellyn. I'm just fine, thank you. If you'll excuse me," Mrs. McGregor said, on her way past him. She never wasted time on pleasantries with him.

"What are you boys up to at this late hour?" Mayor McGregor stood eyeing them cautiously, one hand in the pocket of his dress pants, the other leaning on the mahogany foyer table.

Llew looked at his watch. *It's not even seven o'clock.*
"Um, I just stopped by to give Moss his AP History notes
back. He loaned them to me — "

"Why don't you have your own notes, Mr. Gardner?"
Mayor McGregor said, standing taller, and removing his
suit jacket, his face tight and impassive.

"Father. Remember I told you — "

"Mr. Gardner can speak for himself." Moss' dad cut
him off.

Llew looked back at his friend and saw how he hung
his head at his father's tone. "A couple guys on by
brother's crew caught the flu, so I missed my last two
classes on Monday to help out at the business."

"I see," Mayor McGregor said casually. "Why don't
you two step into my office for a quick chat?"

"Father, Llew's brother is waiting for him."

"Sir, I know you're extremely busy. I didn't mean to
infringe on your family's time."

Both of them were trying to avoid any type of chat,
conversation, pow-wow, or anything else, with Moss'
father. He was intolerant to say the least; but whatever he
wanted to discuss with them wasn't going to be fun.

"I'll be brief." His tone and his expression said that it
wasn't an option.

Moss sat ramrod straight in one of the two wingback
chairs facing his father's large desk. Llew placed his
backpack on the floor and gingerly sat in the other chair.
He wasn't slouching, but he wasn't about to sit at attention;
like he was in front of the President of the United States,
either. Although the design of Mayor McGregor's office
could fool you into thinking you were; it was even oval-

shaped. The American flag stood tall behind him, just in front of the royal blue curtains flanking the window. The wall was adorned with degrees from UCLA and Harvard. Expensive-framed pictures of Mayor McGregor with influential politicians were mounted on the adjacent wall, and sat on three large bookcases. Llew's head whipped around from the massive thirty- by twenty-inch framed family painting when Mayor McGregor cleared his throat.

"How's the business going for your brother, Llewellyn?"

Llew looked to his boyfriend, but of course, his head was tucked low, not meeting his father's eyes. Well this pompous bastard didn't intimidate Llew. His father had instilled good moral values in him and his brother, before his death. Llew had no reason to hang his head.

"Business is doing well, sir. Leslie's even picked up some commercial properties in Colonial Heights. He's had to hire a third crew to cover the demand," Llew said, proudly. His brother had really done well with his father's legacy.

"Are you going to be joining his crew after you graduate in a couple months?" Mayor McGregor inquired casually. He had dismissed Llew's proud statement, continuing to follow his own agenda, without bothering to look at Llew as he shuffled some papers around on his executive-style desk.

"Yes sir. I'm going to work for him like I do every summer. Then I'll be leaving for college in the fall," Llew said, trying unsuccessfully to meet Moss' eyes.

Mayor McGregor's bushy eyebrows shot up, almost to his hairline. "Oh, really. Ahh, yes. You probably got an athletic scholarship."

"Yes, sir, I did."

"What school have you chosen?"

"I haven't yet, sir. I'm still waiting to hear back from my first choice."

Moss finally turned his head towards him, eyes begging. *What the hell?* Llew looked tiredly at his boyfriend, knowing that he was pleading with Llew not to mention the possibility of him attending UCLA. Honestly though, how was that going to be a secret any longer, once he was accepted? Word traveled quickly in their parts. No doubt, his big brother would be bragging all over town, too. It had been his parents' dream for both of their sons to go to college. Unfortunately, Leslie had to leave during his second year in graduate school to bury his parents and take care of Llew.

"And your first choice?" he asked, impatiently.

Llew and Moss continued to watch each other. Moss' brows scrunched together with annoyance. Fuck that. Llew was pissed now. True, they were both in the closet; because it just wasn't worth the trouble to come out in their town. He hated when Moss made him feel like he wasn't even worthy of being his *friend*. Why couldn't they go to the same school? UCLA was ranked number twenty-three in the nation's top universities. It took more than just the ability to catch a football to get in. Moss should be proud of him, not only as his boyfriend, but as his best friend.

"Virginia Tech, sir."

"Mmm. They have a good athletic program. You should fit right in, Mr. Gardner."

Llew's jaw was clamped shut so tight, it ached. He released a calm breath before adding, "They have a top-ranked engineering program, sir; since I also have an academic scholarship." Llew held back his grin at the faint redness that was creeping over the mayor's pristine white collar. Llew had already been accepted to Virginia Tech, but he couldn't stand the thought of being twenty-four hundred miles away from his boyfriend.

If his father were here, he'd tell Mayor McGregor exactly what he thought of his son's athletic, *and* his academic accomplishments. He wouldn't let anyone talk down to him. He wanted to do his father proud, but he loved Moss, he'd do anything for him. They only had to endure this bullshit a little while longer.

"You know Moss will be attending the family alma mater, UCLA, to carry on the McGregor tradition. You boys have been inseparable since middle school and I've tolerated it because it—"

"I'm sorry, sir. Tolerated it?" Llew interjected, his anger quickly bubbling to the surface.

Mayor McGregor sat forward, his hand tightly gripping the polished surface of his desk. "Yes, tolerated it. Boys will be boys. Now it's time for Moss to grow up and be a man, leaving childish things behind. He has a duty and obligation to his family's name."

Llew didn't know why he looked at Moss then, but he did. How could he sit there and allow his father to degrade someone he loved like that? Did Moss consider him to be a "childish thing" in his life?

"I understand, sir. I best be getting home now, my brother and I have plans," Llew said, as respectfully as he could muster, already standing and slinging his book bag over his shoulder. They had nothing more to discuss.

CHAPTER TWO

The two-mile bike ride to his neighborhood did nothing to tamp down his fury. Llew burst through the door of the doublewide trailer he and his brother shared, slamming his backpack on the floor while he paced back and forth between the kitchen and the living room. After about thirty laps, he went to the refrigerator, yanking it open so hard, most of the contents of the door tipped over.

"You break it, you fix it," his big brother said, standing on the opposite side of the counter. Leslie's sharp brown eyes watched him for a few seconds, while Llew tried to calm himself. "What's going on, bro?"

"The damn mayor is a dick, that's what's going on." Llew plopped down at the small kitchen table.

"He is who he is, Llew. He's filthy rich, and thinks anyone that has to use their back and hands to work is beneath him. He's never going to accept you as Moss' equal, and he will definitely never accept having a gay son."

Llew dropped his head in his hands. Why couldn't people just be normal? The second his brother asked him if he was gay, he knew he didn't need to lie. His brother would love him unconditionally, just like their parents had. He did warn Llew frequently to be careful while dating the mayor's son. If anyone found out, it would be disastrous for all of them. Llew was eighteen, but Moss was still seventeen, so he had to be careful of that, too.

"Why don't you and Moss just take a little break and once you two are away at college… then you can do what you want. The mayor of Emporia can't control and monitor everything, especially all the way in California." Leslie came over and sat down in front of him. "Llew. I don't want to see you get hurt. Don't you think you're getting a little too serious about Moss? There's a great big world out there for you to explore. You have a lot to offer. I don't want to see you used as the small town flavor."

Llew's head shot up. He narrowed his eyes at his brother. The concern that he saw there made it hard for him to be angry, but Leslie's words were hurtful. "I'm not the flavor of the town, Leslie. Moss loves me."

"Are you sure?"

Llew stood up, looking down at his brother. "Yes!" he yelled.

"Hey! Sit back down and chill. I'm just having the same conversation Dad would have with you, Llew," Leslie said, pointing at the chair Llew had been sitting in. He dropped down tiredly, and pulled again at the long strands of hair at the back of his neck that needed trimming. He hated thinking about this. Hated thinking about the look he saw in Moss' eyes every time Llew spoke of their future together. The look of doubt.

"He's just nervous about exams and stuff. He has a huge track meet at the end of the week, in Gloucester. He has a lot on him." Llew tried to justify Moss' behavior.

"You didn't even have to take most of your exams because of your high GPA. Moss and his dad don't recognize that accomplishment. You deserve better Llewellyn, I'm telling you this because someone has to. Moss McGregor the sixth seems fickle to me, even more so as he gets older and more like his father."

"He is not fickle. Can you imagine how much pressure it is to have to take over for your father?" Llew pleaded with his brother.

"Actually. Yes, I can Llew," his brother said, sadly.

"Damnit. I'm sorry, Leslie. That was stupid. Taking over our dad's business wasn't any easier than Moss taking over as CEO for his father."

Leslie waved his hand dismissively. "Yeah, it is a big difference. Moss is expected to be a certain way, Llew. Gay is definitely not an acceptable part of that. Not now, not in college, and for damn sure not after college. He'll be the owner of one of the nation's largest heavy machinery distributors, and he'll never make it in a corporate environment with a man on his arm." Leslie tapped Llew's arm to get him to look at him. "Be his friend Llew, please. Don't try to keep this up. I know you love him, but you're young, you will meet new guys."

"I don't want new guys." Llew got up again. This time he really was done with this conversation. He'd love Moss forever, there was no getting around it. "I got work to do."

"Alright." His brother sighed.

Llew was almost to his room when Leslie called out to him. "Hey, you wanna go bowling with us in downtown Norfolk this weekend? A few of the guys are heading down there to get away, have a little night-life fun. Bill's mom has a condo she's letting us stay in for a night. Whaddya say? That sounds like fun, right?"

"I'll think about it."

"Fine, go cry about it, punk. You're such a little girl, *Llewellyn*," his brother said, playfully accenting his name when he said it, his voice taking on a lilting tone.

"You're the one with the bitch name… *Leslie*," he shot right back.

"We both have bitch names, then." His brother joked, following him down the hall to his own room.

Llew laughed hard, his bad mood already lightening up; his brother had always had a way of doing that for him. "Why'd Mom do that to us?"

"She wanted girls." Leslie shrugged.

"Well she got one when she had you. Why didn't she leave me out of it?" Llew joked, running to slam his door when he saw his brother turn around and sprint towards him.

Llew closed his bedroom door and locked it, just before Leslie's shoulder slammed into it. "You ass!" he yelled.

Llew grinned, looking around at the small space of his bedroom. A sad sigh left his chest at the thought of how different it was from Moss' large bedroom, with a sitting area and his own en suite bathroom. He frowned, unable to remember the last time Moss had been over to his place. Did he not want to be seen in this neighborhood anymore? Had his father told him not too? Fuck! This was driving him crazy.

His brother's logic rang in his ears. Leslie always had Llew's best interest at heart; he would never want to see him hurt. So, he was going to have a serious conversation with Moss real soon. He needed to know where he stood. If he had to only be Moss' friend, and not his *boy*friend, it would hurt like a son of a bitch – but he'd accept it.

He'd been working on his model house for the next couple hours, when his phone rang. He looked at his watch before answering Moss' call with a curt, "What."

Moss used the sexy voice that always made Llew bend to his will. "I know you're not mad at me."

"Then you don't know shit," Llew answered, curtly.

"Come on. You can't blame me for my father's ignorance." Moss huffed.

"Is it only your father's?"

"What the hell does that mean?"

"You're smart Moss, figure it out."

"Llew this is bullshit, man. What's up with you?"

"You sit there and let him talk to me like I'm shit. Like I'm nothing. If you love me like you say you do, then that would bother you. I'm still your friend, too… right?"

"Yes, you're my friend. You're my boyfriend. You're the one I love," Moss said, quietly.

Llew rolled his eyes. "Words, Moss. Those are just words."

"Goddamnit, Llew. I said just chill out for the next few months, until we leave for school and we can be together like you want us to – "

"Like *I* want us to? Are you saying you don't want that?"

"Why are you picking apart every fuckin' sentence I say? You know I want that, that's all we ever talk about."

He heard Moss let out an exasperated breath. Usually that made Llew back down, not wanting them to have an argument, but he wasn't going to this time. As much as he hated to admit it, his brother had made a damn good argument.

"Moss. Are you gonna run your father's company as a gay man?"

Silence.

"Moss?" Llew looked at his phone to see if he'd lost the connection. He saw the seconds continue to tick past, when he finally heard a tired sigh. "Moss?"

"What?"

"Are you gonna answer me?"

"That's so far away, Llew. How can I answer that?"

"This is so fucked up," Llew growled. "You have no intentions of really being with me, do you?"

"That's a crock of shit and you know it. What's going on? Is your brother telling you not to trust me again? He barely knows me," Moss argued, weakly.

"This isn't about my brother. Who by the way, is the only one that knows you're gay, and hasn't violated your trust. So don't talk bad about him. He's my family and he accepts me for who I am. Will your family ever do that?"

"So your family is better than mine?"

"You can't be fuckin' serious. This is so stupid. I gotta go, Moss. I'm working." Llew was poised to hang up when he heard Moss yell his name.

"Don't go, Llew. Look, I'm sorry okay? That didn't make sense. My dad has just been riding my ass this last year, so I've been under a lot of pressure, babe. You know what I have to put up with."

Llew rubbed his thumbs into his tired eyes, and saved his work in his building design software. He powered off his laptop, moving over to look out over the rundown neighborhood. He couldn't wait to live in his dream home. He'd already submitted the blueprints for his final exam in his Design and Building class, now he was adding to it. He'd build it himself when he started his own construction company. This trailer would all be a distant memory. He and his brother had a plan. Llew would get his degree, while Leslie worked hard and saved their startup money. It was an unfortunate necessity that they'd had to sell their parents' home after they died, but he and Leslie just couldn't afford the taxes and utilities. It was either the home or the business.

"Llew, come over this weekend. Friday my parents are going to a campaign dinner for some senator in Richmond, and they won't be back until Sunday. We'll have the place all to ourselves." Moss whispered, seductively.

Llew cursed his eager dick. The thought of fucking Moss in a bed all night had his cock leaking almost immediately. When you were eighteen, and your boyfriend offered up his ass on a silver platter... refusing was not so easy. He let out an irritated sigh, he wanted to fuck, but he also wanted some answers. Moss was avoiding providing them.

"You have no intentions of being with me at UCLA, do you? I'm just what's convenient here. Some sex is better than no sex." Llew rubbed his chest as the pain, the reality sunk in. How the hell could Moss not love him? It made no sense. He'd given him everything it was within his power to give. Treated him like a king. Hmmm... maybe that was it.

"Llew, I'm going to be with you, and only you. I love you. You're it for me. I can't see myself making it there without you, I just can't do it. Please, don't start doubting us. I'm not my dad, isn't that why you fell in love with me?" Moss' voice was soft and sexy again.

Silence.

"Come to me so I can make love to you; show you how I feel about you."

CHAPTER THREE

Moss had insisted that Llew not come over until after nine o'clock. He knew it was because he didn't want the neighbors reporting that they'd seen him over there. Llew propped his bike in the backyard, up against the house. Moss was standing in the side door, waiting on him. He tried not to show how much he appreciated the way Moss was dressed.

His black tank top molded to every hill and valley of his abs. The frayed, well-worn jeans hung low on his narrow hips, tempting Llew's large hands. He wanted to grip him there and yank him against his body, squeezing hard enough to leave beautiful, purple bruises on his pale skin. He was sure he failed miserably at appearing impassive.

"What's up, dude?" Moss said casually, as if someone was listening.

"Hey." Llew eased past him into the kitchen, placing his book bag on the kitchen island. "Something smells good."

Moss stalked over to him and hopped up on the hard surface, spreading his legs in invitation. "Come over here. I don't like what's been going on with us lately."

"I don't either," Llew said, still not moving from his spot on the other side of the kitchen.

"Llewellyn. Come. Here."

29

"I don't even know why I'm here. We need to go back to being just friends, Moss. This isn't a good idea. We're not gonna be together in college, so I think it's best we just stop doing this." Llew's throat was closing up with every word he spoke. He didn't want that. God knows he didn't. He wanted forever, but he knew deep down that Moss didn't... or couldn't.

They remained on opposites sides of the kitchen, the heaviness of their reality weighing in on them. Llew bent to pick up his bag. "Um. My brother went to Norfolk, so I think I'm gonna go join him for the rest of the weekend. Give us some time to get used to this."

"Then let's have this last night," Moss whispered, his eyes glassy with emotion. "Give me that, Llew. One last night with you please, before you end us. Before you walk away from me."

Oh god. Llew was between Moss' muscular thighs before he could even finish the last word of that sentence. Fuck yes. He'd give Moss one more night. He'd make it the best they ever had, he'd make it so that Moss never forgot the one that loved him first. Never forgot the one that gave him everything, wanted everything with him. He understood why Moss couldn't promise him forever; but that didn't make it hurt any less.

Moss wrapped his legs around Llew's waist. "Take me upstairs."

Llew's strong hands were everywhere. Massaging and grinding against his boyfriend's hot ass. It was as if his cock knew this was it, the last time he'd have this beautiful specimen.

"Do it like I like it, Llew. Make me feel you for days, and remember you forever."

Llew squeezed his eyes shut at his lover's words. He'd hoped that Moss would've put up more of a fight for them, but he was going to take this like a man, and he'd decided that Moss was going to take this fucking like a man.

He burst through Moss' bedroom door, not bothering to close it behind him. They had the house to themselves for the next twenty-four hours. Every second was going to count. He threw Moss on his king-size bed. "Take your goddamn clothes off, Moss."

Moss scrambled up on the bed, slithering out of the shorts and tank top. "Oh god. Yes, Llew. Be bad, please. Show me what I'm miss—"

"Shut the fuck up," Llew growled, shoving Moss' discarded tank top in his mouth. "Turn over and spread your legs."

Moss whined as he obeyed Llew's orders. He went to the large walk-in closet, and got four neckties, he pinched the base of his cock when he thought about how hard he was going to fuck his best friend, his lover, this one last time. He climbed back up on the bed and slapped his palm down on Moss' pale ass, where a bright red handprint appeared almost immediately. He tied both of Moss' wrists to the large posts at the head of the bed. Llew leaned down and bit the back of Moss' damp neck, feeling a surge of power flow through him like never before. Whatever Moss mumbled wasn't clear, but he honestly wasn't all that interested. He licked and traced the soft skin down the ridges of Moss' spine. He paused when he got to the top of his ass, his heart clenching at his soon-to-be loss. He nuzzled the soft hairs there, gritting his teeth against the anger now starting to vibrate through him.

He slapped Moss so hard on his other ass cheek it made his hand sting. "Selfish little bastard," Llew grumbled, kneading over his handprint. He leaned down and ran the flat of his tongue over the burning flesh. Moss lifted his ass up, begging for more. Of course he was. This was the real him… the real both of them. He quickly tied each ankle to the bedposts at the footboard. He stepped back, admiring Moss McGregor the sixth, stark naked and spread-eagle. His ass was red, his hips grinding his cock into the plush comforter. Llew yanked the fabric out of Moss' mouth.

"What do you have to say, huh?"

"Fuck me. Fuck me hard. Right now, Llew."

Llew slapped Moss' thigh, his ass; alternated between cheeks. He aggressively pulled him open and dove in. Stabbing his tongue inside him, giving him little time to adjust before he lubed up two fingers. He rubbed them around Moss' clenching hole, while whispering harshly in his ear. "No one will ever fuck you like me, will they Moss?"

"No, Llew. Never."

He saw his boyfriend raise his face for a kiss, but he turned his head and bit him hard on his shoulder, down his arm. He climbed back up and licked behind his ear. "You ready?"

"Yes! Yes! Fuckin' do it."

Llew pushed in one finger, quickly following with the middle finger, too. He pumped in and out of that tight channel, his balls drawing up against him already. *Fuck.* He wanted to calm down so he could draw this out, and then he didn't. He wanted to lose control, stay in that crazy frame of mind so he didn't end up begging Moss not to leave him.

Llew spanked and fingered until his hand stung too much to keep going. "I'ma' fuck you now. Wanna hear you scream my name, Moss. Wanna hear you say that no one will ever know you like I do."

Moss' "Yes." came out like a sad sob. "Do it, Llewellyn."

Llew slicked up his hard cock, the ache in his balls had nothing on the ache in his heart. This really was it. He guided himself to Moss' raised ass and pushed in fast and angry until his balls slammed into flesh. "Ugh. Fuck!" He yelled at the grip on his naked flesh.

"Llew! Hard! Harder!" Moss begged.

Llew knew Moss didn't like a lot of preparation, he liked it when his body was bombarded with sensation, his mind barely able to handle the sensory overload. So he quickly pulled out and started up a brutal pace. He would usually lean in and bury his nose in the back of Moss' damp hair, but he didn't this time. Instead, he reared back and slammed both hands down on those scarlet red ass cheeks and thrust his cock in until he couldn't get any deeper.

"Oh fuck, oh fuck, oh fuck." There were no other words. When they'd fucked in the past, Llew would lay over Moss' back, and whisper his love for him while he tore his ass apart. He just couldn't... not now. Not and still be able to walk away.

"Oh my god. Llew, please! Please!" Moss shouted.

Llew growled and hooked his arms under Moss' armpits and back over his shoulders to gain more leverage. He was about to come. He could feel it building in Moss, too; could feel his body trembling with restraint. "Come with me," Llew hissed. He had barely enough breath to get out those three words; he was fucking Moss so fast and hard.

Moss' screams of bliss were louder than ever before. It was like Llew had lost his mind. He hammered away, determined for Moss to feel him for as long as possible. He wanted to see him hardly able to walk on Monday, and know that his ex-boyfriend was still thinking about him... he had no choice. Llew slapped him, and yelled for Moss to shut up and take it.

"Auuugh. Fuck!! Llew, goddamnit!"

He was about to come, he was there. Moss was screaming for his life, screaming for him. Lighting shot down his spine, and his balls drew up almost inside him when a shrill scream pierced his brain, making his hips falter and his heart rate skyrocket.

"What the hell are you doing to my son, Llewellyn?"

Oh god no!

Llew scrambled off the bed, his chest still heaving from exertion as he turned and faced a seething Mayor McGregor and his pale-as-a-ghost wife. They stood, stunned in place, still wearing their formal wear. Llew put his hand out in front of him, while crouching low to cover his deflating cock. He yanked up a couple of pillows that had been tossed to the floor.

"No! No way!" Mayor McGregor yelled.

"I-I can e-explain. We w-were not—"

34

"Father, help me, please. Help me!"

Llew looked over at Moss, his own heart about to beat out of his chest. He scurried to untie Moss from the bedposts, surely he must be mortified to appear like this in front of his parents. "Baby, I'm sorry. I'm gonna—"

Moss' next words brought Llew's world crashing down around him.

"Father don't let him touch me anymore! Help me!"

Mayor McGregor charged into the room, shoving Llew away from the bed; sending him flying across the thick carpet. Mrs. McGregor finally snapped out of her shock just long enough to yell that she was calling the sheriff.

What the fuck? The sheriff. "No, no, no. Wait a minute. Mayor McGregor, it's not what you think. Moss and I—"

"Dad, help me," Moss cried out again, drowning out what Llew was trying to say. Large tears were streaming down his face as he lay there, shaking as if he was truly afraid. Mayor McGregor looked back and forth between them and Llew saw the exact moment that he noticed the welts and marks all over his son's body. His blue eyes widened and his mouth twisted into a snarl more evil than Llew had ever seen on any movie villain. He came and towered over Llew, his entire body shaking uncontrollably.

"You raped my son, goddamn you." Llew was so stunned, that he didn't have time to prepare for Mr. McGregor's stocky frame crashing down onto him. The first punch caught him just under his jaw, but the next one was clean across his cheek. He put his hands up, after the third punch drew blood from over his brow.

"No! No! I swear. Moss! Moss!" Llew yelled for his friend. He needed to stop this craziness right now. Rape

35

wasn't something you used to cover up being gay, or getting caught having sex. They were talking about a serious crime. Mrs. McGregor was calling Sheriff Bailey. He'd been his dad's best friend. Moss couldn't do this to him. He screamed louder, "Moss, tell them the truth!"

Llew finally used his strength and pushed the mayor off of him. He ran over to the bed and began untying one of Moss' wrists. Maybe he was just too embarrassed, and once he got out of the compromising position, he'd be able to think more clearly. As Llew hurriedly raced to the other side of the bed to untie his other hand, he looked into his lover's eyes, not liking at all what he saw. Sheer terror and panic. "Moss don't do this. Are you crazy? You can't let them think I was raping you." He snarled angrily, "Tell them right —" Llew flew into the wall with the force of the mayor's body.

"Leave him alone. I'll kill you, goddamnit!"

Llew was able to block a few of the wild, out of control swings that Moss' dad was taking at him. He pushed the mayor off him, and when he saw him stumble and fall over one of the gaming chairs, Llew took the opportunity to grab his bag and jeans, and get the fuck out of there. He got to the door, and turned back to look at Moss. He was just lying there curled in on himself like a truly traumatized victim.

"Damnit, Moss. Don't do this! This is my fuckin' life we're talkin' about! Moss, look at me!" Llew saw Mayor McGregor working his way back up and heading towards him. Llew took off down the hall, frantically stuffing one foot into his pants leg, just barely getting the other one in as he took the stairs four at a time down to the bottom floor.

Mrs. McGregor screamed when she saw him, her hand shaking as she yelled into the phone.

"Mrs. McGregor. I wasn't raping him! I swear! Moss is my boyfriend! You have to believe me!" He yelled at her. "He invited me over here!"

Her frantic scream for her husband meant that he wasn't getting through to her. How could this be happening? They'd known him since he was in middle school. Did he all of a sudden look like a crazed rapist? Maybe so, with his entire body flushed and sweaty, wearing nothing except his inside-out jeans. Llew took off for the kitchen, grabbing his backpack on the way. He shouldered the back door open so hard that the glass pane shattered when it connected with the brick. He didn't bother going for his bike, he could hear the police sirens in the distance. He took off at full speed through the McGregor's backyard, hurdling the low picket fence and sprinting into the woods. The bushes and untamed branches bit at his bare chest while he tried desperately to distance himself from the wails of the cavalry coming after him. His feet took the worst of it. God only knew what was on that forest floor that dug into the tender skin. His head pounded while he pushed further towards his home. After a few more minutes, he had no choice but to stop. He doubled over, completely out of breath. Gasping and spitting as his lungs tried to get their fill of oxygen. *This can't be real, this can't be real. Can't.*

He needed help. He reached at his pocket, but of course, there was nothing there. Damnit, his phone was at Moss'. The sirens grew louder, and he was sure the whole town would be on high alert soon, especially if Moss didn't man the fuck up. He felt around in his book bag for his extra hoodie, quickly pulling that over his head and slinging the hood up. He had about a mile to go before he got to his house, then he could call his brother.

He figured he'd go down Baylor Street, since the lighting wasn't as good, cut through the back side of the athletic field, and that would bring him to his neighborhood. Llew took off again, thinking to himself that this is what fugitives must feel like. It felt like shit. He got his back door open, and he swore that the sirens and screams were just outside his front door... or maybe it was the panic in his head echoing in his ears.

He locked his back door with shaking hands. He didn't turn on any lights as he darted into the kitchen and yanked the receiver off the wall. It took four tries to get his brother's numbered entered. The darkness of his small kitchen lit up with bright blues and reds. *Oh no. Leslie please pick up.* If he was at a club somewhere then he wouldn't be able to hear his phone. "Leslie, pick up the fuckin' phone!"

The voice mail clicked on and Llew thought he was going to have a panic attack. He heard voices and car doors slamming out front. He hit the redial and waited what seemed like an eternity before he heard his brother's voice after the fifth ring.

"This better be good, Llew."

"Leslie, help me! You gotta help me! I think I'm getting ready to get arrested!"

"Whoa, whoa, Llewellyn, slow down!" Llew ran to the living room and peeked out the curtains. "Oh my god! Oh my god!" Four sheriff's cruisers were out front along with the mayor's black BMW. He was screaming and pointing at Llew's house, probably insisting they open fire on it.

"I can't hear! Turn that fuckin' music off now." Llew heard his brother yelling in the background. There was scuffling and static as his brother probably tried to get to a quieter place to talk. "Llew! Llew, what's going on?"

Llew ran his hands through his hair while he paced in his living room. "We got caught, Leslie. Moss' parents came home while we were doing it. They caught us." Llew was sobbing now; he couldn't hold it back any longer.

"Okay, Llew calm down. It's gonna be okay. The mayor can be mad all he wants that his son is gay but there isn't—"

"Moss said I raped him, Leslie! His dad went crazy. I had to fight my way out of there and I ran home half-naked! Now there's four sheriff cars out front with the mayor. Oh god. They're gonna take me to jail, Leslie!"

"That fuckin' bastard! I knew he wasn't shit. I'm gonna call Sheriff Bailey, Llew." Leslie was winded, sounding like he was running.

"I don't see him. I don't see Sheriff Bailey out there. None of them are gonna listen to me, Leslie."

"He might still be on vacation. Llew, don't worry. I'll straighten everything out. I'll call his cell, okay? He'll come get you until I can get there. I know everything. I know you and Moss have been dating. It's going to be fine. I'm going call him, too. I'll threaten his little ass and he'll tell the truth. Can you hear me, Llew? I'm coming—"

His brother's words were cut off by the hard pounding on his front door. "Leslie, I'm scared. Come and get me, please. You know I didn't rape him."

"Of course I know that. I'm on my way, okay? I'm leaving right now; I'll be there in a few hours!"

"Llewellyn we know you're in there! Open the door!"

"That's Deputy Jamison," Llew cried. "He hates me. He's going to put me in jail, Leslie."

"Open the door or we'll kick it in! Three! Two! — "

"Leslie!"

"Llewellyn!"

The front door shattered around the knob as Deputy Jamison and two other deputies burst through the door, their guns pointed at his chest; yelling for him to get down on the floor. Llew didn't think he'd ever been so terrified in all his life. Even his parents dying wasn't this frightening, because Leslie had been right there by his side the entire time.

Now he could just barely hear his brother's panicked yells through the fallen receiver over the deputies' orders.

"Get down on the ground now! Right now, Llewellyn! Don't make me tase you!" Jamison yelled.

"Llew do what they say!" Leslie screamed through the receiver. "Don't resist, Llew. I'm on my way to get you! Can you hear me?"

Tears streaked down Llew's cheeks from his wide eyes. He weaved his hands behind his head like they barked at him to do. He dropped down to his knees just as Deputy Jamison rushed over, pushing him face first to the hardwood floor. He yelled out in pain at the rough way his arms were twisted behind him while a two hundred fifty pound man put all his weight down on the knee in the center of his back.

"Llewellyn Gardner, you're under arrest for the rape of one Moss McGregor the sixth. You have the right to remain silent; anything you say can and will be used against you in a court of law. You have the right to an attorney. If you cannot afford an attorney, one will be provided for you. Do you understand the rights I have just read to you?"

Llew heard Jamison talking, but he couldn't wrap his around the reality. He'd just been placed under arrest and read his rights. As clearly as he knew everything was a big mistake and it would all be worked out soon, he was still scared shitless.

"Do you understand? Yes or no, Mr. Gardner?" Jamison screamed at him.

"Y-yes, sir." Llew finally stammered. He was yanked up to his feet, and he got a look at the other four officers inside his home, rummaging through their belongings. *Oh my god. They're searching my house.*

While Jamison dug his hands inside his hoodie pockets and his pants, searching for god knows what, he eyed him with a look of pure disgust. "I always knew you were a piece of shit, Llewellyn. You and your brother. I should've run you guys out of town years ago, but Bailey insisted you two were good. But when he sees that poor McGregor kid and what you did to him, he'll know."

Llew could only shake his head back and forth. They'd been looking at Moss' body. Saw the marks and welts. "No. Deputy Jamison, sir, I promise. I didn't rape anyone. Moss asked for that."

Officer Jamison cocked his fist back and hit Llewellyn so hard in the mouth, he was sure that a few of his bottom teeth were knocked loose. Llew hit the ground, crying out

41

again from falling with his hands tightly cuffed behind him. He rolled to his side, spitting out the blood that had built up in his mouth. His bottom lip had a deep gash in the middle, and the blood flowed from the cut, down his chin onto the floor. Llew looked around at the other officers, all of them with their backs turned like they hadn't just witnessed him being assaulted.

"No one would ask for that, you sick bastard. But you just keep talking, asshole. That's the more we can use against you in court," Jamison snarled, tugging Llew back up.

Shit. Llew was led out of his home, and blinded by the camera flashes; his ears assaulted by curses, slurs, and gasps. Oh god, he needed his brother right now. This was getting realer by the minute. He squinted his eyes, and noticed that everyone was out of their homes watching him, and the ones that weren't there were watching the one news channel they had in their town as they recorded his walk of shame.

CHAPTER FOUR

"Gardner!" The corrections officer yelled his name, startling him awake. He hadn't thought he'd be able to fall asleep. His fight with Moss' dad, the run through the woods to his house, the scared to death moment of his arrest, and finally the entire procedure of being fingerprinted and searched before having been thrown into a small cell, had left him unable to keep his eyes open another minute. He was just glad that there wasn't anyone in the cell with him. Emporia didn't have a high crime rate, so the small jail in Lyon County was for people awaiting trial, or going through the transition to another prison.

"You got a visitor."

Llew looked at his wrist before he realized they'd taken his watch. It must be his brother here to get him. The guard motioned for him to put his hands through the bars. Once cuffed, the loud clanking sound of the metal locks to his cell disengaging made his eyes flinch. That wasn't something he could get used to. He breathed a sigh of relief that he was finally getting out of there. As he walked through the dank corridor, he noticed through a small, high window that daybreak was approaching. When all this mess was cleared up, Llew vowed he'd never live a life of crime, because this was all too much. A man shouldn't live like this, in a six by eight foot cage… it was inhumane.

The guard led Llew down another long hallway, and he tried not to make eye contact with the few inmates that were walking single-file down the opposite side. He didn't need to, he was sure he didn't know any of them. Impact with a hard shoulder that felt like he'd hit a tree trunk made him stumble backwards. He looked up into dark brown, angry eyes. "Rapist," the man growled.

"Keep it moving!" the guard barked. The inmate glared at Llew for a few extra seconds before he kept walking in the direction he was headed.

"Jesus," Llew whispered. The guard came to a stop at another set of doors, and grabbed his elbow. Llew turned and faced the way he was told, and when the doors opened, he saw his brother waiting there with a man who looked to be in his early thirties.

His brother stood and rushed to him when he walked in. They'd just barely embraced when the guard yelled at them not to touch. His brother stepped back quickly, looking over Llew's shoulder at the guard before focusing back on him. He could only imagine how he looked right now with his cut eye and busted lip. But his brother looked in pretty bad shape too. Leslie looked like he'd been up all night. His face was heavily shadowed with whiskers, which perfectly matched the dark bags under his sad eyes. He had on the same clothes he'd left home wearing the day before. It was clear that his brother had been going nonstop for him. Emotions welled up inside of him and he turned his head to try to get himself under control.

"Its okay, Llew." The roughness of his brother's voice broke his heart. Tears flooded his eyes and poured over more quickly than he could stop them. His brother gripped his wrist but quickly pulled his hand away, remembering not to touch him. "Hey, look at me. We're gonna get through this, Llew."

Not trusting his voice, he nodded his head to show that he was listening.

"Llewellyn, I'm Jason Whitland. I went to school with your brother; I've known him a long time. He called me and told me your situation, so I came to see if I can help. Leslie has asked me to be your lawyer; is that alright with you?"

Llew's eyes went wide. "W-why do I need a lawyer?"

He watched Jason look back and forth between him and his brother, the frown on his face evidence of his confusion. "Llewellyn, you've been charged with aggravated sexual assault. That's a very serious crime and it carries a possible sentence of life in prison."

"What? I didn't rape anyone! I had sex with my boyfriend. This is freaking crazy." Llew scrubbed his hand over his now-dry face. "When can I get out of here? All I need to do is talk to him. Moss is just scared because he thinks his dad will disown him if he knows he's gay. He's not thinking this through is all. Once I talk to him he'll — "

"That's not possible, Llewellyn." Jason cut in. "Any contact with the victim is strictly forbidden."

Llew stood up and slammed his still cuffed hands on the metal table. "Victim! He's not a victim! Moss McGregor is my *boyfriend*. He asked me to come over, and we were having sex. He wanted me."

"Either calm down or this meeting is over," the guard said from right behind him, a heavy palm on his shoulder slamming him back down in the chair. His brother's fist clenched on the tabletop, and Llew could see he was fighting not to jump in and protect him.

"Okay. I-I'm sorry." Llew stammered. His head had begun to throb again. The idea of anyone believing he had raped Moss was unthinkable.

"Llewellyn, I'm on your side. Please stay calm so I can talk to you."

He nodded again and waited while Jason pulled a mini voice recorder and a manila file from his brown leather messenger bag. He watched him read over some scribble he had on a legal pad. Llew looked to his brother. He hated the sadness he saw on his face, but what was worse was he hated that he hadn't listened to him, hadn't gone with him to Norfolk, instead. While he waited for Jason to get his papers in order and set up his recorder, he figured he'd talk about something positive.

"Leslie what time am I leaving today? I'm supposed to be talking with a recruiter on Monday after our game, remember? We don't want to miss that. You wanted me to go to Virginia Tech, right? Screw UCLA, their team sucks this year anyway." Llew tried to joke.

"We can talk about that later, bro." His brother's forced smile didn't fool him. Did he think he wasn't going to college anymore?

"Llewellyn."

"Call me, Llew," he answered his lawyer, turning his attention back to him.

"Sure. Llew. Can you tell me how Moss McGregor got these marks and bruises?" Llew's hands began to shake harder with each new photo Jason pulled from his folder. Eight by ten inch photos of his best friend's ass, his thighs, back, chest, neck, his... *oh my god*. Bite marks and hand prints all over him. Llew choked on his startled gasp. There was a picture of Moss' anus... his red, stretched, and bruised anus. When he looked up, his brother was looking away from the pictures, moisture building in the corners of his eyes.

"Um. I um. I probably did it when we were having sex," Llew said, now more terrified than ever. He was so humiliated he thought he'd be sick. But he had to tell the truth. "Consensual sex, I mean. Moss likes for me to be rough with him. It wasn't the first time he's wanted me to mark him. If you just talk to him away from his parents then you'll — "

"I did talk to him," Jason interjected.

Time seemed to slow to a standstill as he watched the disappointing, hopeless looks play across his own lawyer's face. When he finally spoke, Llew thought he was going to faint. "Moss McGregor went to the hospital to be treated for his injuries, which primarily consisted of superficial bruising. Nothing broken or permanently damaged. A rape kit was done, and traces of your DNA were found inside him and on his body. He says that you came over, uninvited, after he'd told you that he wasn't going to stay friends with you once he left for college. He says that you confessed that you loved him, and forced yourself on him. Said that you tied him up, beat him repeatedly and then raped him. His father and mother were both witness to his tied up, beaten body."

The edges of Llew's vision blurred and he could've sworn the floor was rising up to meet his head. His brother's strong arms were on his shoulders tilting him back up. "Llew! Llew, wake up!" his brother called out, shaking him in his strong arms. When he looked up, he realized for the first time that this was all really happening. It hadn't hit him until right at that moment, when his lawyer said "rape kit" and "DNA." Moss was trying to have him sent to prison. Here he was thinking about not missing his game on Monday, when he should've been asking when his bail hearing was. *Shit, bail.*

"When can I get out of here?" Llew said, trying to take a few breaths thorough his nose.

"It's Sunday, so your arraignment will be scheduled on Monday, in General District Court, since you're eighteen."

Llew's heart rate jacked up again and he had to fight the nausea. He didn't even know he was shaking his head until his brother started saying, "Yes you can."

"Do you hear me, Llew? You're stronger than you think, bro. You can make it."

"No. No."

"Yes, you fuckin' can. You're my brother, you're strong. We're gonna fight this all the way, but I need you to get your armor on, bro and get ready to fight."

Anger and fear were warring inside of him. How had his life gone from full of promise to walking through the gates of hell? He was so afraid, but he was going to try to be strong for his brother. They were all they had. He wasn't going to give up. Again, he took a deep breath and blew it out slowly. He looked to his too-young lawyer. "What's first?"

"The arraignment is where we'll hear the official charges. I'm going to ask for bail at that time. You're a first-time offender, upstanding member of the community, a good student with scholarship offers. I think we'll have a good chance of getting bail." Jason smiled at him. "However, it might not be cheap." He looked to Leslie.

"I'll put the business up if I have to," Leslie said, determinedly.

"Goddamnit," Llew grumbled.

"We'll do what we have to, Llew. I'm getting you the fuck out of here."

"One thing at a time. Even if you get bail, we need to mount a defense to present at trial if Moss doesn't accept responsibility and drop these false charges. But, after what I heard from the investigators in this case, he and his parents are pursuing this prosecution fully. So we need to be prepared," Jason said, loosening his top button, his pen poised to write.

"I didn't rape my boyfriend."

"I believe you." Jason looked at him a long time, and Llew saw that he wasn't lying or blowing sunshine up his ass.

"Thank you," Llew said quietly.

"Start from the beginning."

CHAPTER FIVE

Llew had sweated through his suit while he waited for the jury to deliberate their verdict. His young lawyer had done all he could possibly do in the three-day trial, but even Llew had to admit that the evidence against him was overwhelming. The jury had looked mortified by the graphic pictures of Moss' injuries.

The opposing counsel ate his brother up on the stand; accusing him of lying when he insisted Moss and Llew had been in a gay relationship since they were freshmen. The schoolmates the prosecution had called rebutted Leslie's testimony, assuring the jury that Moss McGregor was not gay.

Llew's testimony was honest, but it didn't make him look like the Boy Scout his lawyer tried to sell. Attempting to convince some older men on the jury that his boyfriend liked hard sex, and wanted to be marked by his mouth and hands wasn't easy. He didn't know which hurt worse through the whole process. That Moss hadn't come to face him since his daddy had made it easy for him not to. Or that not one of their classmates was on Llew's side. Only his brother was seated on his side of the courtroom.

His brother awaited Llew's fate in the small conference room with him. Leslie had gotten a loan against the business to post his one hundred thousand dollar bail, but Llew hadn't been able to do anything other than remain in the house while awaiting trial. He'd longed to talk to Moss, but he'd been forbidden to do so. Moss' testimony was taken in the mayor's mansion, because the judge ruled in favor of the prosecution's motion that facing his attacker would be too traumatic for him, and that Moss had already sustained irreversible psychological damage from suffering an attack at the hands of his best friend.

"The jury's back, Llew," his lawyer said, peeking in the door.

His brother squeezed his hand, turning to look him in his eyes. "Little bro, whatever they come back with…." Leslie eyes flooded with tears, and it was at that point Llew realized he was going to prison. He'd have to leave his brother. "I love you Llewellyn. So very much. I know you're innocent, whether they can see it or not. No matter what happens, you'll get through it. Be strong. Be the man Dad raised you to be."

Llew bowed his head. He had no words.

"Will the defendant please rise?" Llew heard the Judge's order, but he wasn't sure if his legs would work or not. Surprisingly, they did.

"Has the jury reached a verdict?"

The older gentleman in a bowtie and sweater-vest that'd been selected jury foreman stood and replied, "We have, Your Honor."

The judge leaned in. "What say you?"

The foreman turned to face Llew. "We the jury, in the case of The State of Virginia versus Llewellyn Mark Gardner find the defendant guilty of the charge of sexual assault in the first degree."

Llew clutched his chest. The whole scene that played out was like something out of movie. His brother was cursing and pointing his finger at the mayor, calling him a fool and an in denial son of a bitch. Llew didn't even have a chance to say goodbye to his brother, he had been apprehended by a couple bailiffs.

"If you don't talk to me, Llewellyn I can't help you. Are you thinking of ending your life?"

Everyday. Every minute, Doc.

"Inmate. Do you want to stay in the hole? No visitors, no rec, nothing."

As long as I'm in the hole, no one's able to kill me.

Llew had been in the hole for two months before he couldn't take it anymore. He had to see his brother. He hated for Leslie to see him like this. He knew he looked like hell, since he could only sleep a couple hours a day. His cellmate had told him he'd better not sleep, or else he'd do to Llew exactly what Llew had done to Moss. Anytime Llew opened his mouth to say he didn't do anything, he was punched in it. He'd learned to keep his mouth shut, because the alternative was losing teeth.

He was learning fairly quickly how to dodge certain people and situations, but some things just couldn't be avoided. The main things were the gangs and the crews. There were so many, but the first thing he learned was which ones were the most violent. Llew was in a three-tier, maximum-security prison, which didn't house the friendliest group of men, but at least there were few lifers in the unit. Everyone there had a release date, and therefore, something to lose. Llew didn't want to be on anyone's side, he didn't want to be in anyone's clique. Not that cho-mos – prison term for child molesters – were ever invited to join a crew, but he still tried to stay out of their way.

It was required that everyone worked a job: in the kitchen, landscaping, trash removal, or library, whatever. Llew would have preferred landscaping, especially since he would be outdoors every day, but he couldn't do it, because there were too many ways for him to get cornered out of sight of the guards. He petitioned for the kitchen, but that would soon turn dangerous as well.

Llew was in his cell, drawing a blueprint for a model home, trying to remember his design and build software when the guard came to let him know he had a visitor.

His brother stood when Llew walked in, but the guard quickly reminded them not to touch. That was the easiest way for outsiders to bring in contraband, and slip it to inmates. So the "no touching" rule was strongly enforced.

"Hey, Llew," his brother whispered. "How you holding up, bro? How they treating you in here?"

Llew barked an incredulous laugh. Could his brother really not see his busted lip? "Let's just say, I'm not getting the respect a rapist deserves."

"Llewellyn, you're not a rapist."

Llew tried to run his hand through his dirty, tangled hair, but his fingers ended up getting snagged. Since he had to avoid the showers most of the time, his hair was in dire need of a good washing. "Bro, please don't come here anymore. I can't handle this."

"What?" Leslie choked.

"I don't want you taking a six hour drive just to come here and look at how fucked-up I am now. My life is over."

"It's not over, Llew." Leslie shook his head sadly.

"Ten fuckin' years, Leslie! Ten! They threw the fuckin' book at me. I'm gonna fuckin' die in this place. I can't do ten years in here, especially as a child rapist."

"Child rapist." His brother looked confused.

"Some fuckin' way, everyone knows that my so-called victim was a minor. So now I rape little boys."

"Oh god." Leslie looked sick, but he had no clue.

"My back is against the goddamn wall, man. I ain't gonna survive this place." Llew squeezed his eyes shut. This was the hardest thing in the world to do, but it had to be done. "Don't come back, Leslie. It's over for me."

Tears streamed down his brother's cheeks.

"Guard, I'm ready to go back to my cell."

"Llewellyn don't do this. You can make it."

"Not ten years, I won't."

"You'll be out in eight with good behavior."

"Leslie I'm not gonna make another eight days."

"Llew don't talk like —"

The guard was behind him, and Llew stood to leave. He could hear his brother calling him, but he ignored it. On his way out, he saw an inquisitive pair of bright blue eyes locked on him. The man watched him like Llew was the most interesting thing he'd ever seen. The guy was another inmate who was visiting with someone too. First thing Llew noticed was that he was absolutely stunning, but Llew couldn't think that way, especially not in here. The man regarded Llew with a quick dip of his chin before turning back to his company. Llew caught a glimpse of the King,

Queen, and Jack playing cards tattooed on the man's neck, the Ace of Spades the largest of them all.

CHAPTER SIX

Llew served the inmates on the chow line with his head down, refusing to make eye contact with anyone. He'd scooped a helping of mashed potatoes on the tray that had appeared in front of him, but when he pulled his serving spoon back, the tray didn't move.

Here we go. After a few more tense seconds, Llew's heart rate kicked up.

"Look at me," the deep voice demanded.

Llew slowly looked up and saw it was the man he'd seen in the visitation room. He had at least twelve, hell maybe fifteen guys standing behind him, all of them big and angry-looking. This man was holding up the chow line, but not one person uttered a word or a "move the fuck on." Llew figured this had to be a bad motherfucker. Once Llew looked in the man's crystalline eyes, he saw something there that he hadn't seen in a while; decency, maybe kindness. "My name is Ace. Remember it. You're gonna need it." And with that, he was gone, leaving his tray behind.

Fuck me.

"So, you going to talk this time or just stare at me, Llewellyn? I think you might feel a little better if you let out some of that pent-up stress."

I don't.

"Are you afraid to talk to me? Nothing you say goes past these walls, Llewellyn."

Yeah sure, Doc. You work for the state.

"You think you're the first innocent man to go to jail? Hmm? You're not the first and you won't be the last."

Llew's head shot up, his eyes had to be the size of saucers; but he had to see if the Doc was just pulling his chain, a ploy to get him to talk. Was it possible that someone in here actually believed him? The counselor watched him back.

"I'll see you next week, Llewellyn."

Llew got up and walked to the door. His scratchy polyester pants irritating his skin.

"Unless you want to see me before then. You're able to request to see me anytime, you know that right? I can help you get through this, Llewellyn."

Llew walked back to his cell. He'd decided to forgo chow and eat a cup o' noodles instead. The chow hall wasn't the safest place for him. Eating a metal tray didn't sound too appetizing. After he'd finished his meal, he stretched out on his bottom bunk and opened up the new book his brother sent him. His throat formed a lump when he thought of his brother, just like when he read his many letters. Llew still hadn't agreed to see him again.

"Well, lookie here. You enjoying yourself?"

Llew's repulsive cellmate had come back to their cell with disgusting red sauce around his mouth and on his shirt; as if he'd eaten his food like a two-year-old. He jumped up off his bunk, too vulnerable there. His cellmate was usually in the rec room after chow, until lights out. What the fuck was going on?

"Ya know, Damon will let me join his crew if I deliver you to him on a silver platter. Grab your shower shit and let's take a walk, tree-jumper."

Llew steeled his spine. He wasn't going a damn place and he certainly wasn't going to be given to Damon and his crew. He'd fight to the death before that would happen. All they'd do was beat the shit out of him, rape him, and then beat him again. Rinse and repeat.

"Let's go," his cellmate growled. The West Coast gang tattoos bulged on his thick neck, and Llew wondered if a guard would bother to come if he screamed loud enough.

"I ain't going nowhere."

"Dumbass cho-mo." His cellmate pulled out his state-issue toothbrush, and Llew frowned at him wondering what the fuck that –

"I'll cut your fuckin' throat out," he snarled, turning the toothbrush around revealing a razor-sharp edge on the other end.

Fuck. The big bastard was going to try to cut him with that thing ,and Llew had been in long enough to see what kind of damage a rigged-up shank could do.

"Freeman. You ain't got to do this. We gon' end up in the hole, man. Chill out."

"Get your shit and let's go."

Llew shook his head. Trying to fend off one man was better than going up against Damon's entire crew.

"Big Waldo. Big Waldo walkin'," a loud voice yelled outside.

"Shit," his cellmate growled, shoving his shank under Llew's mattress.

Oh fuck no. Big Waldo was prison speak for the warden or the guard's captain: the highest ranked prison official. If either one was on the floor, it wasn't going to be good. Llew was pretty sure it wasn't the warden, so it was probably Captain Jessup. Llew sprang into action, pulling the shank out from under his thin mattress and throwing it back at his cellmate. Freeman flew at him, throwing a wild punch that Llew tried to duck, but that meaty fist still half-connected with the side of his jaw. If it had been a full-on hit, Llew's jaw would be shattered.

"Fuckin' fucker," Freeman snapped, going for Llew's throat.

"Freeman! Gardner! Against the wall!" A guard shouted, turning into their cell; accompanied by three more, all with clubs drawn. "Get your asses over there!"

Llew quickly went to the wall; not wanting to be slammed against it, but Freeman needed a little convincing. One of the lieutenants put his baton against the back of his cellmate's neck and slammed him against the unforgiving concrete wall, yanking one of his thick arms behind his back. Freeman yelled out when his wrist was pulled upward. Llew winced, turning his head away from the scene. What the fuck was going on? There's no reason for them to be here. If Llew lost his good behavior or got a write-up, his good time would be reduced. Although he'd told Leslie he wasn't going to make it, he was trying.

Llew heard Big Waldo's smooth, confident voice, but refused to turn and look at him. "What's going on, gentlemen?"

Gentlemen. Is he serious? Llew hadn't had the unfortunate pleasure of meeting Big Waldo, and from what

60

he'd heard, he didn't want to. Him being in your cell meant shit was fucked.

Waldo came over, close to his side, to face him. His eyes were dark and full of warning; but while the other guards were grilling his cellmate, and their cell was completely tossed, Llew got a slight smirk and a wink from Captain Jessup before one of his lieutenants called him.

"We got a shank."

"It ain't mine," Freeman growled.

Llew leaned his head against the rough brick. *Why is this happening? Why can't everyone just leave me the fuck alone to do my time?* His fingers dug uselessly at the brick, desperately wanting to reach over and slap the dog shit out of his cellie. *Motherfucker.*

"Is it yours, Gardner?"

"Tell the truth or you're a dead man walking," his cellmate yelled.

"Shut up!" Waldo snapped, his cool resolve slipping for only a second before it was back again. "Gardner is this yours?"

Llew didn't speak. He hated that fear had consumed him. Was he really about to take the fall for his punk cellmate, who only moments before the guards came was going to turn him over to the devil himself? He was going to lose some of his good time. *Fuck.* Llew watched Captain Jessup. Big Waldo's eyes moved to Llew's hands; still spread against the wall, and noticed their shaking. No matter how much he tried to calm himself, he couldn't. Fuck, now he couldn't breathe. Llew turned his head, gasping for air, and coughing hard. He wanted to crouch down to clutch the pain in his stomach, but he wouldn't move in front of Big Waldo, didn't want to disobey orders. His vision blurred around the edges and he felt the strongest arms in the world catch his body before he hit the concrete. Boots clattered and hard, sharp commands were made, but Llew couldn't make out what they were saying. He thought he was dying, he wasn't taking in oxygen, and he couldn't see anyone. Maybe this was for the best. He stopped fighting it and closed his eyes.

CHAPTER SEVEN

Llew rolled over on the soft bedding, the sound of elevator music reaching his ears. For a minute, he thought he might be in heaven. It felt like he was floating, like all was right with the world. It felt so damn good. He blinked a couple times before his eyes adjusted to the dim lighting. Although he was in a partitioned area, it wasn't long before reality hit him, and he realized he was indeed still in prison. He closed his eyes, mildly disappointed that he was still alive. Why couldn't the good lord just put an end to all this? He'd only done ten months, and it felt like ten years already.

"How is he, honey?" Llew heard a male voice asking next to him. *Who is that?* He didn't know, and he kind of didn't want to know.

"He's gonna be fine, Ace. It was a panic attack," a woman answered. "I gave him a mild sedative and—"

Ace. What the hell is he doing here?

"Thanks Anne. Let me talk to him alone, please."

"Of course."

Llew heard footsteps and the scraping of a chair, but he still hadn't opened his eyes. He didn't plan to, not until he was asked.

"Open your eyes, Gardner. I know you're awake."

Llew opened his eyes, stunned by how close Ace was to him. Leaning over him, his mouth only inches from his own. When the gorgeous blond man spoke again, his minty breath fanned across Llew's chin. "You're in the infirmary right now. I'm not gonna keep helping you, Gardner. Are you listening to me?"

Llew didn't speak, but his brow furrowed. *How did he help me?*

Ace caressed the side of his face, and Llew's first reaction was to jerk away, leery of trusting anyone. One minute it'd be a caress and the next he'd be strangled. But it'd been too long since he'd felt any contact. "Your eyes will give you away every time, Llew. I'm surprised you're even in prison. But anyway. You've been blacklisted, Gardner."

Oh god. They're gonna kill me.

"Believe it, handsome. You gotta choose, man. I won't keep helping you and you won't claim my set."

Llew's voice cracked when he finally spoke. "You sent B-big Waldo?"

Ace didn't respond. He knew the guy had enormous power but, Jesus Christ. If he did go with Ace's crew, what in the hell would he have to do for them? He wouldn't jeopardize his good time for anyone, not even for the kind of protection he knew Ace could offer. Or was it something else Ace wanted from Llew? Something he wasn't giving anyone in here.

"Easy, handsome. I'm already taken. I don't need that, and neither does anyone in my crew. I'm not gonna pimp you out, man. But I believe you can help me. I believe we can help each other." Ace bent down and pressed his forehead to Llew's. "We can help each other."

Ace stood up, smiling down at him; a warm inviting smile. "Think about it."

"What's going on Ace? Captain Jessup said you needed me."

"Yes. I think Gardner would like to talk to you. He had a panic attack in his cell."

"Really," Doc said, his thick gray and black eyebrows raised in curiosity. He pulled the thin chart off the end of Llew's bed.

"I'm not in the mood to talk," Llew said grudgingly. He was starting to feel his life was no longer his own.

"In my set everyone sees the Doc. Twice a week individually and we have weekly group sessions. It's not debatable," Ace said with finality. Llew narrowed his eyes, but Ace simply winked at him before pulling out a small cell phone. "Hey Tank. Yeah, I'm ready to go. Make sure everything's set up."

He couldn't believe Ace had a cell phone, but he couldn't believe all the other shit the man did either.

"I got a surprise for you when you get back to your cell, Gardner. I'll come check you out when you get back on the unit. I'll also be expecting your final decision. For now, just rest up." The two men who walked in looked like they belonged in the extreme fighting hexagon with their bulging arms, and necks as thick as fucking car rims. Ace gave Llew one final look before he left with his own personal guards.

"I heard some of what happened. Do you want to tell me your version?" Doc said, breaking into Llew's musings. The older gentleman pulled up a chair, smoothing his hand over his checkered sweater. "You think I leave pot roast night at home for just anyone, Llewellyn?"

For some reason that made Llew smile. He thought of his brother's pot roast.

"What's funny?"

"Pot roast," Llew croaked. "It's my favorite. Leslie makes it just like my mom used to." That was the most Llew had said to the Doc in ten months. But over the years, he would say so much more. Without the Doc, Llew was sure he wouldn't have survived.

CHAPTER EIGHT

Llew walked through the unit, noticing that a couple guys were walking behind him. They kept their distance, but were definitely following him. He'd had two whole days in the infirmary with the nicest nurse in the world, and he hated when she said he had to go. It was unbelievable that a nurse with the best bedside manner in the world worked in a place like this. She belonged in the pediatric oncology ward at Cedars Sinai.

Llew hoped those men behind him weren't his cellmate's friends or Damon's guys. He couldn't deal with them right now. One session with Doc wasn't gonna cure him. Llew got to his cell and gasped at the changes. He had a television, a radio, tons of books; ranging from Modern Architecture to mystery novels. He thought for minute that maybe he'd been moved to another unit, but he saw his pictures still hanging on the wall by his bunk. His immaculately made-up bunk. He had commissary items, too. Noodles, drinks, soups, and peanut butter and jelly, he had a whole damn pantry. *Oh my god a coffee pot.* Like the ones in hotels.

"You like it?"

Llew spun around. Ace stood there in jeans and a starched white t-shirt. His blond hair was styled with product and his blond beard was streaked with black. Damn, he was spectacular, standing in Llew's cell, backed by ten men, two of which were the men who had been following him.

"Ace. What is all this? I can't pay you for this." Llew flopped down on his bed. *Is this thing softer?*

"You know that we would've negotiated that first if it was intended to be a loan."

"Well, then I can't accept your gifts. My cellmate is going to take it all anyway."

"Your cellmate's been reassigned. You don't have a cellmate any longer." Ace's clear, take no shit glare told Llew that it wasn't a coincidence.

Ace stepped in farther and squatted to look in his eyes. "All I need is your eyes, Llew. I don't want you doing anything to jeopardize you getting out of here. But you can't join my crew and not do shit. All you'll do is watch my back. How hard do you really think that is, huh? I just want you to watch shit, and when I ask you about what you saw, you tell me."

Sounds easy... too easy.

"Don't ask me why, Gardner. You just remind me of someone I had a soft spot for once. Nothing hidden in my agenda. But you watch my back and I'll watch yours. Simple as that. Whatever your decision... enjoy the stuff."

Ace got up to leave. "Rivers and Detrix will stay with you for a couple days, because you're still blacklisted. I'll be back then for your decision. If it's no, I won't bother you again. But I suggest it be a yes. I can help you survive this place, Gardner."

The guys had stayed with Llew like Ace promised they would; and Llew was able to come and go as he pleased. He'd worked out in the yard without any problems, no one even made eye contact with him. He went to chow and didn't have to sit in a corner against the wall. It was nice to sit with Ace and actually laugh with the rest of the guys. It's when he'd told his guards to leave him alone for a while and Llew went to the shower room thinking it was empty that he was cornered by Damon. He called for his guys but they must've been taken down by Damon's gang, who were just as big, if not bigger than Ace's.

He fought with everything he had, but it wasn't enough. As he was beaten and pummeled, he prayed for his brother, that he would go on and live for him.

Llew woke up who knew how many days later, in the infirmary, to Ace yelling into his cell phone. He knew it was him without even opening his eyes, because Ace's voice held a growl that made you pause and cringe.

"Those motherfuckers should be brought up on attempted manslaughter charges, babe! They almost killed him and my men. I want those bastards in the hole for a goddamn year. Leave 'em in there until they can't fuckin' think straight!"

Who is babe? Did Ace have a fancy lawyer as a boyfriend? Is that why he got so much done? Llew tried to stop his mind from thinking, because his head was pounding harder than a jackhammer on concrete. He reached down and could feel the heavy bandages around his hips. *What the fuck? What happened to me?*

"Gardner, hold still man. I'm gonna get Anne, she'll get you something for the pain. Are you in pain, Llew?"

Can a bull buck? "Yeah, man. Hurts like hell, Ace. What happened?" Llew kept his words to quick sentences, the thundering in his head growing in intensity with each word he uttered.

Ace's voice had gone soft and sympathetic, and Llew wondered just how jacked up he was. Was he paralyzed? Because it didn't feel like he could move. *Oh no. No. No.* He didn't know what was happening to him but his entire body felt like it was on fire, and he couldn't breathe.

He heard the fear in Ace's voice. "Gardner calm down. Llew! Llew! Can you hear me?" There was nothing else after that except silence, darkness. His last thought was that he should've chosen Ace a long time ago.

When he woke up, it was dim in his area, and a large but gentle hand was rubbing his thigh.

"You awake, Llew? Open your eyes."

His eyes opened in more ways than one. Ace was there, and so was the Doc. It took him a long time to come to terms with what was going to keep happening to him if he didn't get with the only person that had shown him any decency since he'd been there. He had counseling and therapy, then more counseling. But nothing prepared him for the aftermath of surviving the attack. Absolutely nothing. Regardless, he knew he wouldn't physically survive another like it. Even with Damon's gang gone, there were more waiting to take their place. So joining Ace's crew was the best thing for him. When he'd recovered from his surgeries, he left the infirmary to begin to really live and breathe prison life.

CHAPTER NINE

"I can't believe how big you are, Llew. Jesus. Did you do anything else in there besides lift weights, man?" Llew didn't answer his brother. He'd only been home for a few hours. Just long enough to take a shower and look through his bedroom. Everything was still the same. His full-size bed and two dressers full of clothes that were now four sizes too small. He'd always been big and tall, but now he was extremely big and tall. All the tools he'd worked long summers to be able to pay for were still in the closet, neatly tucked into his canvas bag. The only things different were the brand new laptop still in the box, and two new design and building software packages. His brother knew it was what he'd use to cope with the changes in his life. He'd build.

His brother scooped a heaping spoonful of pot roast and potatoes into a bowl and set it in front of him. "My pot roast is still your favorite, right?"

Llew's answer was to shove a huge spoonful into his mouth. His brother appeared to be waiting on some type of response… but he didn't have one. He'd been taught to keep his mouth shut and only speak when he absolutely needed to. "Does it taste alright?"

Llew nodded his head once.

His brother breathed a soft sigh. "Llew, please say something. You haven't said more than ten words since I picked you up. Are you mad at me?"

Llew looked at his brother with eyes that he'd been told were intensely emotion-filled. "I'm not mad at you, Leslie."

Leslie nervously twisted his hands together. "The counselor said that you may need some time to adjust again, but I want you to know that I missed you very much, and I'm going to help you as much as I can to get back what you lost."

Llew slowly wiped his mouth with his napkin. He stood and came over to his brother, looking down at him now that he was bigger and a lot wider than him. He put his large hand on his shoulder. "You can't give me that, Leslie. Eight years of my life are gone. I have to think ahead, think about what I want to do in the future. I won't be one of those angry men who goes out here and fucks up because they feel someone owes them something. No one owes me anything. Especially not you. Your letters and visits, Leslie." Llew scrubbed his hand over his face. "They got me through, bro. I could never be mad at you."

His brother's emotions quickly surfaced, but he didn't wipe away the tears, he let them fall. Leslie pulled him in close and Llew allowed himself contact with another human being. It felt... different... foreign. He slowly put his arms around his brother and hugged him back. Before he knew it his brother was coughing and tapping him on the shoulder. "Llew. O-okay. I can't b-breathe."

For the first time in what seemed like years, Llew laughed. Genuinely laughed, then smiled. "Now let me finish my roast, it's definitely still my favorite. You'll have to teach me how to make it soon."

Leslie finally looked happy with Llew's answer. He quickly scooped some into his own bowl and joined him at the small kitchenette table. "You want to take a couple weeks to get acclimated, or do you want to start working with me this week?"

He finished his last bite of the tender meat, wanting some more but not used to asking for seconds. His brother seemed to sense it and swiped his bowl from in front of him, quickly filling it again. He sat back down, looking at him expectantly. "So."

"How does your crew feel about me working with them?" Llew's deep voice filled the small kitchen. "You said there are some guys I went to school with that work for you now."

"I don't give a damn how they feel. It's my business. If they don't like it, they can quit." Leslie fumed.

"I'll start whenever you want me to."

"My guys are paid the standard right now and that's what you'll be paid too. Which is sixteen fifty an hour; I start everyone at that rate. I know it's not much, but after ninety days you'll get a—"

"Leslie. For the past eight years, I've been working manual labor for thirty-two cents an hour. I'm okay with your starting rate."

A collage of emotions passed across his brother's face: sympathy, outrage, compassion, and a few others that he didn't quite recognize since he hadn't seen those feeling directed towards him in almost a decade. "I'm sorry, Llewellyn."

Llew stood abruptly, his chest heaving with restrained anger. "I don't need any apologies, Leslie. Understand that." He took his bowl and carefully placed it in the sink. "I'm gonna go for a walk, okay?"

Leslie kept his head lowered, but the nod let Llew know he'd heard him. He knew his brother meant well, but he didn't think he could handle being treated like a pussy. This was his life. He'd accepted it long ago. He didn't need anyone's pity or apologies. His pulled his coat tighter around him as he walked up the quiet street. Dusk was approaching quickly and Virginia in November definitely required something heavier and more well insulated than the windbreaker he was wearing. That would be added to the growing list of things he needed to get. He had four hundred thirty-two dollars that he'd saved; all he'd earned working the past eight years. It may seem like crumbs to some; he understood that most men made more than that in one week, but Llew was proud of it.

He walked down the cracked sidewalk that led out of the large trailer park as memories of his youth flooded him. Memories of him running or biking to school. Sprinting to football practice. Playing touch football under the streetlights. Late night walks with Moss. Stolen kisses under the moonlight. Llew closed his eyes and accepted the rage, let it invade his mind; but not control it. He'd learned it was alright to be angry, alright to be mad; but he wouldn't allow himself to hate. Hate was a poison that caused a man to act desperately. He didn't hate Moss McGregor the sixth. Didn't hate that he'd gone on with his life, his career; gone on like Llewellyn Gardner had never existed to him.

He'd been walking for well over an hour when the abrupt chirp of siren brought him to an immediate stop. He turned around, squinting his eyes at the bright spotlight beamed at him from a deputy's cruiser.

"Get your hands out of your pockets, now!"

Fuck me. Deputy Jamison. He didn't think it was possible for him to forget that voice… now *that* was the sound of pure hate.

Unfortunately, Llewellyn was no stranger to following official orders. He slowly pulled his hands out of his pockets, spread his thick fingers, and with his palms facing out, raised them to shoulder level.

"Well look at what the dirty, filthy rat dragged out," Jamison snarled. "Keep your hands up."

Llew didn't speak, didn't argue, he just watched as Jamison got closer. The deputy's hair was shorter, with a few streaks of gray mixed in. His face was clean-shaven, and it looked like he'd done well with staying fit for his job. But, when he got right in front of Llew, he didn't miss the way Jamison swallowed upon getting his first good look at Llew's size. He glared down at the shorter man, his eyes surely screaming his anger, but his voice deathly silent. With Llew's hands linked behind his head, the windbreaker he wore did little to hide his large biceps.

"Don't move." Jamison went behind him and dug into his pockets, yanking out the wallet his brother just let him borrow. He threw it to the ground after rummaging through it, finding nothing but a few bills, his state-issued prepaid Visa with his entire life savings on it, and his expired ID. A rough hand dug in his back pockets. The papers from his release were still tucked in there, folded neatly. Jamison pulled them out and looked at them with his flashlight.

"No shit. Just got out today, huh? I thought you had ten years."

Good behavior, shithead.

"They just let anything walk the streets these days. Now I got a fuckin' rapist to deal with in my town." Jamison threw his papers down on the ground, coming back around to face him. "Why are you over here by the high school, huh? You have no business over here. Feeling nostalgic, Gardner?"

He still kept his mouth clamped shut tight. Guys like Jamison loved to abuse their authority. Llew wouldn't give this prick the satisfaction of seeing his fury. "I'll be calling your probation officer first thing in the morning, let him know I caught you out here prowling the streets. I swear if you even jaywalk, I'm hauling your ass in, Gardner. I'm going to make sure you're on the sex offenders list too. No one will hire you here. Don't know why you came back in the first place." The menacing snarl on Jamison's face made it look like he was really getting ready to go off on him when his radio chirped on his shoulder, the dispatcher sending units over to the Okey Doke pub for a disturbance call. Jamison pulled out his baton and pushed it under Llew's chin, raising his head higher. His eyes squinted at being touched by him, quickly remembering the cheap shot he took at him when he was arrested. "I'll be watching you, punk. You better believe it. When you fuck up, I'll be there, motherfucker."

Llew waited until Jamison burned rubber away from him before he clenched his fists and brought his hands down. He sucked the cool night air in through his mouth and blew it out through his nose. He stood on the dark street, doing that repeatedly until his body stopped shaking.

"It's okay to be mad. It's okay to be angry. You have every right to be. But don't let it control you, Llewellyn. I don't want to see you back here. You don't belong here."

His counselor's words rang peacefully through his mind, quieting his rage. He squatted and picked up his wallet, aggressively brushing off the dirt. He squinted at the multitude of instructions on his release papers, his vision still blurred from his ire. Folding and tucking them back into his pocket, he figured it might be a good idea to head back towards home. Home. Not a cell.

He was four units down from his trailer when the door to a single unit sprang open and a man about his age bounded down the steps with a large bag of trash in his hand. Llew kept up his pace, but ended up meeting the man at the end of his driveway. He tried to move around the trashcans without acknowledging him.

"Llew. Llewellyn Gardner. Is that you?" The man dropped his bag in one of the cans and took a couple tentative steps closer to him.

Llew lifted his head higher, letting his old football teammate get a look at him.

"Holy shit, dude. When did you get out?"

Silence.

"Do you remember me? Jace Skeeter. I was a corner on the team during your senior year."

Llew just nodded his head once, his dark eyes boring into the guy's skull. He wasn't in the mood to have a chat about the good ole days. Jace probably took Llew's glare

and silence as hostility, because he backed up with his
hands out in a pacifying gesture. "Sorry, man. Didn't mean
to bother you. I, uh. I don't want any problems ya know?
All that shit you did, I don't give a damn. I live here now
with my wife and two boys; so long as you stay down
there, and away from my kids… we're cool."

Away from your kids. Llew shoved his hands back in
his pockets and kept walking to the end of the cul-de-sac.
He saw Leslie sitting on the steps watching him walk up.
"What did that asshole say, Llew?"

Llew ignored the question, brushing past his brother
into their trailer, not stopping until he was in his bedroom.
He closed and locked the door, sliding down the hard wood
until his ass hit the thick carpet. He dropped his head in his
hands, pushing his thumbs into the throbbing at his
temples. *Fuck. Fuck. Fuck.*

"Llewellyn. Are you alright?"

Silence.

"Llew it's gonna take some time. Don't let the bullshit
of these petty-minded people get to you."

Silence.

"Llew, please. Talk to me."

Silence.

He heard his brother sigh just outside his door. "I'll be
out here watching the game if you want to watch it with
me. Otherwise, we leave for work at six. Okay? Wear
something warm."

Silence.

"Llew, I love you, bro, and I'm glad you're home."

Llew's throat felt like it had a boulder lodged in it.
Even if he had wanted to respond, he couldn't. Finally, he

heard footsteps retreating down the hall. After sitting there in the dark for a couple hours, Llew undressed down to his briefs and climbed into his bed. The mattress was soft and plush, almost folding in on him. He didn't remember it feeling like this when he was young. He reared up and pulled back the fitted sheet, squinting in confusion at the thick foamy cushion on top of his mattress. *What the hell is that?* Llew pushed into the soft material and watched in awe as the foam molded to his palm, then went back to its original form when he removed it. He shook his head, tucking the sheet back under the mattress. He glanced over at the small alarm clock on his nightstand – two fifteen in the morning – he flipped from side to side on the unusual surface before he finally pulled the comforter off his bed and stretched out on the hard floor. Sleep came quickly.

CHAPTER
TEN

"Um, Llew. You going to work today?" Leslie asked, uncertainly. At five fifteen in the morning, he looked uncomfortable standing just inside the back door, watching Llew work out in the freezing cold in only a pair of worn cargo pants and a sweaty tank top. He had each forearm linked through a cinderblock while he alternated lifting them to shoulder level.

He answered by dropping the concrete blocks onto the ground, then stacking them back with the others against the shed. "Yeah," he said brushing past him to hurry and get changed.

"Here's an extra pair of gloves, Llew. You'll need them. It's getting cold now, and we're pruning back rose bushes this week." Leslie held the synthetic leather gloves out to him and he reluctantly took them. They looked expensive and unnecessary. Gloves were a luxury that the state couldn't afford its laborers. His brother went about preparing two large thermoses of coffee, using a fancy-looking machine. Even the creamer looked expensive. It said vanilla, caramel, macchia — something on the container. Oblivious to Llew's discomfort, Leslie continued. "I know you did primarily construction when you were in prison, but I still do the same things you used to help me with during your summer breaks. You remember? Hedging, pruning, mulching."

When Llew didn't respond, Leslie stopped what he was doing and turned to him. "You remember?"

A simple head nod was all he gave, making his older brother shake his head at him. "A man of few words, huh."

Llew smirked. He knew Leslie wanted him to talk, but it just wasn't him anymore. But his brother had missed him. Being apart had hurt him just as much as the distance had hurt Llew. Leslie had felt like he'd failed him, like he'd should've been here the night he was arrested. But Llew really didn't see how anything would've been different.

"I remember how to do it, Leslie. If there's something else you want me to do, just tell me. I was on the landscaping crew for three years before there was an opening in construction. So I think I can handle it." Llew grinned, and held up the gloves. "And I did it without these pussy-ass gloves, too."

Leslie busted out laughing, reaching up to pull Llew into a headlock, like he used to when he was younger. He easily maneuvered out of it, playfully jabbing Leslie in his side, but his brother actually grimaced and clutched at his ribs. "Jesus, Llew. Your freakin' fists are hard as shit."

Llew covered his grin, his heart warming just a tad. "Oops. My bad. I didn't know you'd gotten that soft, bro."

"Fuck you. I'm not soft, man. I just don't lift fuckin' thirty pound cinderblocks for fun." Leslie shoved the thermos into Llew's broad chest, shouldering him in his upper arm as he went by.

They were still smiling when they climbed into Leslie's work truck. Things almost felt like they used to between them. But, when Leslie pulled up to their first job site, Llew was thrown back into his reality.

The twelve men that sat and stood around the two other work trucks eyed them skeptically as he and his brother approached. Surely, Llew's size left an instant bad taste in most of the guys' mouths, the slight curls of their lips was evidence of just how much. "Everyone. I told you that my baby brother was coming to work for me this week or next week, but anyway. He's home now." Leslie slapped Llew on his shoulder, a proud smile on his face. "He'll be on my crew for the duration of his probation period, then he'll head up Darren's crew when he leaves in February."

Llew snapped his head around at his brother's words. *Heading up a crew.* It wasn't only him that was shocked at Leslie's words, either. A man in khaki brown overalls about half Llew's size, with shaggy red hair sticking out from under his skullcap, hopped off the back of the trailer, slamming his metal lunch pail down on the ground.

"What the hell you mean, Darren's crew? I'm up next for that position, Leslie. You know that."

Not backing down an inch, Leslie stepped closer to the fuming man. "What I know is that my brother owns half this company. I never said that position was yours, James. No one is entitled to shit around here. Positions are earned. Calling off work at least five days a month sure as hell ain't earning it. Now Llew will do the ninety days under my supervision, but if he's even half as good as I think he is, the position is his. Does anyone else have a problem with this?"

The guys all turned around and finished packing the gear on the trailers. Llew quickly jumped in and helped, mostly with the heavier items. When they were all packed, he went to Leslie's side of the truck, where he was going over the specs for the day's jobs.

"Hey, bro. We set to go?"

Llew rubbed the back of his neck. "Yeah, all ready. Uh, Leslie. Why didn't you tell me about putting me on as head of a crew?"

His brother turned to him, clicking the end of his pen as he regarded Llew's concerned expression. "Llew. This is your business too. That logo says Gardner Boys. That's me and you. It's always been about me and you, since Dad started this company." Leslie huffed out a puff of cold air, turning to face him. "I know we had a plan, bro. You were going to be the architect and we were gonna mold our businesses together… but… sometimes you have to go to your back-up plan. With you and me together, we can still build this company to something huge. You were always the visionary, Llew."

"I'm not the same, Leslie." He grimaced, turning to walk away.

Leslie grabbed him and yanked him back to face him. His face was angry, and although his words were hushed, they were just as powerful as he meant them to be. "You're right. You're not the same. You're stronger, smarter, a survivor, Llew. The sooner you accept that… know that, the sooner we can move forward. Just like you said. Focus on the future."

The first week went by without incident. Llew didn't have much to say and the guys had even less to say to him.

But he worked hard and enjoyed it. By the middle of the second week, Leslie had to let the guys go home early because they didn't have their last two accounts to do. By Friday, they only had two accounts, both of them commercial. The six residential accounts had terminated their contracts.

Leslie was quiet on their way home, and Llew dreaded having this conversation with him, but it had to be done. His brother was losing his accounts all over town because of him. If they continued like this, the business would go under. He was going to have to stop working for him. They quietly retrieved their lunch containers and thermoses from the truck, and tiredly dragged themselves up their driveway.

His brother threw up his hand in greeting to his seventy-year-old neighbor Mr. Healy, but the gesture was not returned. "Old geezer," his brother grumbled, dropping his bag just inside the front door.

Llew sat down at the kitchen table, picking at the dirt under his nails. "Les. We need to talk."

With his brow scrunched in concentration, his brother rifled through the bills as he sat across from him. "About what?"

"Look. I know what's going on with the accounts, Leslie. You can't hide it, and the guys are talking. Actually, more like bitching, about it."

"Speaking of accounts. Here you go." His brother interrupted; a wide grin on his face. "It's payday."

Llew took the folded envelope his brother pulled from his pocket and laid it flat on the table. "Keep it."

"What?"

"Keep it." Llew slid it back across the table to him. "For the accounts you lost because of me."

"I didn't lose any —"

"Don't lie. I'm quitting, Les."

"The hell you are. You can't quit a business you own."

"The business is yours. I'm gonna apply for some construction jobs I saw in the paper last week."

"No, Llew!"

"I'm sorry, Les. I won't let you, or the guys who depend on working for you, suffer because of me. They have families to take care of. I'll find something."

His brother put his hand over the envelope and slid it back to him. "Let's not make any rash decisions right now. I have a date tonight, I'm going to go and unwind from a very long workweek. I'll be staying over at her place tonight. Maybe you should ummm… go to that new club over in Petersburg."

"I'm good," Llew said, getting up to avoid a very uncomfortable conversation. His brother trying to send him off to a gay bar to get laid was not even a little okay.

"Llew, don't walk away." Leslie got up to follow him.

"I'm not about to talk about this with you, dude."

"Why not? We're brothers, man."

"Exactly."

"Llew."

Leslie came and sat next to him in the living room. He tried not to make eye contact, as he repeatedly clicked the remote to find a distraction. His brother's eyes bored into the side of his head.

"It's been two weeks, Llewellyn. Don't you want to have a little fun? You know... make love to someone? Or is... is there... m-maybe someone you miss from —"

Llew bolted up off the couch, his eyes blazing with anger. "For fuck's sake, Leslie. No! I didn't fall in love while I was in prison with a bunch of other criminals. I didn't even —" Llew threw the remote back on the couch and left the room. He heard his brother's quick footsteps behind him, then a light tapping on the door.

"Llew that was stupid of me. I'm sorry. I'm gonna head out after I shower. She lives in Gloucester, so I'll be back about noon tomorrow, okay? Okay, Llew? I'm sorry."

Llew stood silently as he stared out his small bedroom window overlooking a vacant lot. It's how he felt inside. Vacant, desolate, like no one had time to be bothered with him. He was sitting on his bed in the dark, his eyes still focused on nothing, when he heard the front door open and close. Falling back on the bed with a resigned exhalation, he thought about what his brother said. *Make love to someone.* God, yes he did want that. He'd love nothing more. To just hold someone close to his chest, feel a man's hot skin against his. His strong muscles; and hard thighs around him. Someone to simply whisper something... anything sexy in his ear. He brought his watch up to his face. It was a little after seven. He could be showered, changed, and in Petersburg in a couple hours. *No, this is crazy. Who'd want to get in bed with a rapist? Hmm. Petersburg. No one would recognize me there. In a gay bar, almost an hour from town. I wouldn't run into anyone I know, and it's just one night.*

CHAPTER ELEVEN

He'd been sitting in his brother's truck outside The Brickhouse Run for almost an hour. The bright red brick building sat off Cockade Alley, and Llew had actually chuckled when the GPS announced the street. *Typical,* he'd thought. The surrounding area looked fine, not much else located around this part. He'd watched the party goers enter and exit the large building, too unsure to go in himself. He figured he was dressed okay judging by what others were wearing. He'd stopped at the outlets on his way there and bought a couple pieces, so he wouldn't stick out like a sore thumb in clothes that didn't fit. His charcoal V-neck sweater clung nicely to his broad chest, the saleswoman saying it brought out the mysterious darkness in his eyes. The black jeans had also been suggested by her. He'd closely shaved his cheeks, trimmed his goatee, and left a nice bit of length on his beard. He fingered the course hair as he watched another couple of guys walk into the dimly lit club. *Okay, I look like a fuckin' creep sitting out here.*

Llew got out the truck and walked as casually as he could to the door. The doorman was a big guy, almost as tall as Llew's six foot three, but not as muscular. "You here to take my job, buddy?" The man smiled, bearing stark white teeth at him, but Llew didn't return it. The bouncer's eyes lost their humor at Llew's seriousness. He didn't want the big man to think he was a trouble maker, but he knew any smile he tried to muster would fall way short.

"ID, please."

Llew handed over his expired license but the guy didn't seem to notice it. He stepped aside and let him in, not wasting any more niceties on him. As soon as he walked inside, he squinted at the sudden change of light. The place was so damn crowded, it was amazing people weren't running into each other. After standing against the side wall closest to the door for a few minutes, his eyes adjusted and he was able to see what was around him. Men. Plenty of men. The room was oddly shaped, almost like an oval. The oblong bar was accessible from all sides. Tables lined the large dance floor, but they were all just about vacant, since seventy percent of the people in the place were on the dance floor.

Llew watched two young guys saunter past him, wearing clothes that had to be too tight to allow them to breathe. The one in black leather and a white tank top with pink rhinestones on the front shaped like the Playboy bunny dragged his finger across Llew's chest as he went by. *Oooookay.* He figured he'd need a drink to get through this night. Nightclubs weren't his thing. But, in actuality he hadn't had a chance to get to know what his thing was. Hell, maybe he would like clubs. His twenty-first birthday was spent in a prison library, reading the latest Stephen King novel.

A guy with black hair and a blond Mohawk wiped the bar top with a rag as he asked him, "What can I get you?"

Llew nodded his head in the direction of the taps. "Budweiser."

"Regular or tall?"

"Tall." Llew watched the man pull his drink and set it in front of him. He looked up at Llew for a split second before dropping his eyes. "Four fifty. Or do you want to start a tab?"

Setting a five-dollar bill on the counter was Llew's answer. He turned and looked out over the dance floor, watching the men move about in the most carefree nature he'd ever seen. Men free to live and do as they wanted. Not a problem in the world. *What the fuck am I doing here?* Just as Llew was going to down the last of his beer, a small hand brushed over his bicep. He looked down at the fair-skinned fingers before looking up into beautiful green eyes.

"Hello."

Llew looked at the man who was standing close enough for him to smell his sweet perfume. He wasn't as young as lot of the guys there. Probably early thirties. He wore a preppy gray and green sweater and blue jeans. His smile was wide and genuine as he slowly rubbed his hand up to Llew's shoulder.

"My name is Gene. My friends and I saw you come in, and you know what I said as soon as I saw you?"

Llew continued to watch this man, not responding to his questions.

"I said I thought you could use a hug. You look so serious. My friends said I'm crazy, but I have a gift for reading people."

You don't want to read my story.

"What's your name? I've never seen you here before." The guy had moved in even closer to Llew's side, and was practically whispering in his ear so he didn't have to yell

91

over the annoying techno music blaring from the five thousand speakers all over the building.

His eyes had seemed to slip shut on their own as he turned his head into the silky skin brushing against his beard. "Llew," he said, hoarsely.

"Lou… just Lou." The guy looked at him disbelievingly.

"Llewellyn." He clarified, his eyes scanning over the lithe chest beneath that sweater.

"Oh. Okay. I gotcha. So how about it, Llew?" Gene brought both hands up and draped them on Llew's shoulders. "Can you use a hug?"

He let the man pull him closer; his long arms completely over his shoulders and linked behind his head. Llew had to admit it was a really nice hug. It wasn't the type you'd give a stranger. It was intimate and suggestive. Llew brought one hand up and slid it around the guy's trim waist. "There. How's that feel?" Gene's lips were pressed against his ear while he talked, his hot breath fanning over the side of Llew's neck. Instead of pulling back and ending the hug, Gene kept him wrapped up. "You're a very handsome man, Llew. Do you hear that a lot?" Gene chuckled. "Probably all the time."

No, not really.

"Well, even though you look like you want to be left alone, I had to come over here and say something." Gene rubbed his creamy cheek against Llew's neck. "Do you want me to go?"

Llew's strong arm tightened and he pulled Gene closer to him. The breathy moan was evidence that Gene approved of his nonverbal response. "Ummm. I have a place just down the way, Llew. I wouldn't mind a little company. How about you?"

Gene finally pulled back and Llew stared back at his now-date. "Let's get out of here." Gene smiled again.

Llew stood up from his stool and Gene's eyes widened with shock. "Good lord, you are tall. Oh my god. You don't look that big when you're sitting."

Llew quickly sat back down, his eyes scanning the bar for anyone that was watching them. Gene looked almost scared. He didn't want to give anyone the wrong idea. *Shit.* He knew this was a bad idea. Gene shook his head. "No. No. That's okay. I like it." He purred, pulling on Llew's hand. "Come on."

Llew followed Gene out of the club, his pounding head immediately thanking him. He was fairly sure now that he wasn't a club person. His temples had throbbed to the tempo of every song. The only good thing about that was that Gene had had to practically sit in his lap for Llew to hear him.

"My car is right there." He pointed to a black Ford Focus. "You can follow me. I'm only fifteen minutes from here." Gene flashed that beautiful smile again, and Llew nodded once before he turned to go to his truck.

He followed the taillights up the dark street, while thinking the entire time that he was ready for this, he just had to jump in with both feet. He deserved this. He just hoped that... fuck... he hoped it would be okay now.

"It's all psychological, Llew. You're not a rapist... believe you aren't and you'll enjoy the company of a man again."

Llew again thought of his counselor's comforting words. He'd helped Llew so much, he didn't know if he would've made it without killing himself in that hellhole. He turned into a small condominium complex and weaved through a few turns until he saw Gene point towards a visitor's lot. He turned into one of the empty spaces, took a couple deep breaths, and climbed out of the truck. Gene was waiting there for him on the sidewalk. When he reached him, Gene stuck his hand out for him to hold as he lead them to the downstairs unit.

Gene unlocked both locks and let them into his warm apartment. There was a dim light filtering in from the kitchen and Llew could see that Gene probably made a pretty decent living, since his house was nicely furnished. Deep blues and chestnut browns decorated the large living room and it put Llew at ease that he was with someone that was definitely a fully grown adult. His date turned to him and slid back in to close the distance between them. His head was tilted all the way back as he looked up into Llew's eyes. "Do you want something to drink? Or I can fix us something to eat. You look like you like to eat." Gene chuckled softly, and Llew thought it was the sweetest sound he'd ever heard.

Instead of answering, Llew ran his calloused thumb over Gene's soft cheek, his eyes focused on the bobbing of Gene's Adam's apple as he caressed him. No, he didn't want a drink, and he didn't want any goddamn food. He needed to feel some intimacy with another man. He wanted to be the aggressor and just go for it, but he couldn't. His head raced with indecision and his heart bled with hurt.

"Come here," Gene whispered, pulling Llew's head down to his. Sure fingers weaved through his thick dark hair, while satiny lips brushed over his mouth. Llew kept his eyes open, watching the serenity on Gene's pretty face. He tried to remember to kiss back, but he was stunned into stillness. *Damnit.* Had he forgot how? That's not possible. He loved kissing; it had been his favorite thing to do with Moss. *Shit.*

Llew pulled back, his last thought almost paralyzing him. *Don't think about that... not now.*

"You're okay. Its okay, Llew. I told you, I can read people. You need this right now. It's okay." Llew was slowly led down a short hallway and into a cozy bedroom with a wonderful king-size bed in the middle of it. He didn't look around very much, trying not to miss how Gene was seductively removing his clothes in front of him. Llew backed up and sat on the edge of the bed, his knees suddenly weak at the thought of having sex again. He was actually going to see a naked man, a man that he *wanted* to see naked... not that he *had* to see naked.

Gene pulled off his jeans and Llew sucked in a breath at the sexy black and red briefs his date had on underneath them. Instead of pulling them down too, Gene toyed with the waistband before dropping his hand inside to massage his fully erect cock.

Oh god.

"Lean back. Let me undress you." Gene crawled up Llew's long torso, gripping the bottom of his sweater, tugging the soft fabric up to just above his nipples. "Oh man. Your chest is fuckin' fabulous. You got muscles for days, babe."

He kept his eyes focused on Gene's petite mouth while a warm, pink tongue snaked out and laved over his nipple.

Jesus. Llew groaned low in his throat. It felt like he'd been hit by lightning. His back snapped straight when Gene bit down firmly on the perky bud, swapping between nibbling and licking. He wanted to grab Gene by his neck and hold him down on his chest, make him alternate between his nipples, before he pushed his head down his hairy abdomen and ground his pelvis into his fancy face. But he didn't. Llew kept his hands locked at his sides. He didn't want to make Gene do something he didn't want to do. Although it was against his nature, he'd let his date lead. Didn't want there to be any room for confusion. If he didn't want to lick his cock, he wasn't going to make him... didn't want to force him. *Fuck.*

Gene's moans and whimpers had his jaw aching to release his own sounds, express his own desires. But his voice was scary sometimes, it was deep and growly – he'd been told. He tried not to make people feel intimidated or frightened around him. Damnit, why was he thinking like that right then? *Just focus on this insanely sweet, beautiful man, trying to make you feel good.*

A rock-hard cock ground against his thigh while Gene moved down his body. Nimble fingers fumbled with his belt, then the button of his jeans. "Let's get these out of the way, sexy. God, your size is turning me on so much, Llew. Got me about to come right now." The breathy confessions were enough to have any man leaking in his own pants. He was tapped on his hip, and Llew lifted up so Gene could pull his pants off him. He was afraid to look down. Afraid to see beautiful green eyes full of disappointment. When all movement ceased, and Gene's moans no longer filled the room, Llew glanced a look down. Just as he'd thought. Fuck! He scrambled to pull his sweater down, already trying to sit up and tug his jeans back up. His limp cock lay flaccid against his thigh while he had the sexiest man he'd seen in eight years writhing all over him.

"Hey. Calm down, babe. It's okay. Lay back down. I know exactly what to do," Gene murmured against his groin, his hot breath blowing on his sack.

Llew's breathing fluttered as Gene tried to lessen his embarrassment. He had one arm slung over his forehead, shielding his intense eyes. Again, he didn't want the small man to think he was getting angry at him for this. He took some deep breaths like Gene said, and held in the last one when his dick was surrounded by the most delicious warmth.

A winded "ahhhh" escaped from him before he knew it. Oh, hell it was good. Soft, hot, and wet. It felt like Gene was making love to his dick with his mouth. The sucking wasn't urgent and fast, no; it was sweet and gentle. Gene worked his cock like it was a sensitive, timid appendage that needed to be broken in gently. "Fuck," he moaned. He liked this a lot, but he didn't want to be treated like a job. He was man, not some female that required a shitload of overtime and for his date to jump through a bunch of hoops just to get him off.

"You're thinking too hard, Llew. Just relax and let me do all the work, okay?" Gene's mouth was flushed a deep crimson, his bottom lip swollen and raw from his efforts. He'd switched it up from gentle and calm, to wild and urgent, then back again. Any man would've come down that tight throat by now, but Llew's cock was just as soft as if he was about to get a vasectomy. An exasperated breath had his date looking up from between his legs with concern. *Oh no. Not that look.* Maybe he needed to try something else. He sat up, cupping Gene's blotchy cheek. He nuzzled against the side of his face, placing soft kisses on his neck. He could see Gene's small hand back inside of his briefs, jerking his own neglected cock while Llew sucked harder on his neck. But still, nothing happening down south for him. "Let me suck you," he whispered into Gene's damp skin.

The slight upturn on his date's jaw was the answer he'd hoped for. Gene stood up, simultaneously tucking his tight underwear under his drawn-up sack. Llew stared at the tempting piece of man meat. His mouth watering at the way it bounced against his chin in anticipation. He was going to savor this. If anything was going to work, it'd be this. Gene's cock was long and slim, not as thick as his, but not too shabby at all. It had a slight curve to the left, and Llew was going to love how it poked his cheek when he swallowed it down. He wasn't afraid of the possibility that his skills had gotten rusty. True, it'd been a while. But sucking cock was like riding a bike.

He grabbed Gene's dick around the base, and rubbed the sensitive head against his scratchy beard, making his date moan at how much he loved it. He called Llew's name, told him how gorgeous he was, how sexy he was. That no man had ever turned him on more. Llew groaned around the hard flesh and reached down to stroke his own. He winced at just how fuckin' soft he was. Not even a quarter of an erection. He sunk his mouth onto that tempting cock, not stopping until the groomed stubble on Gene's groin tickled his nose. He pulled back, letting the silky hardness slide along his tongue. Gene pumped his hips forward, and Llew had the urge to hold his hips in place, only let his date get as much as he wanted to give him, but again he kept his strength out of it.

While the pretty man fucked his face, Llew's hand flew over his own cock, pulled hard on his balls... and still nothing. Not even a twitch or pulse. He dug his blunt nail into his slit, yearning for his pre-cum. He could feel Gene's body tensing up, the vibration coursing through his abdomen, settling in his balls as they drew tight against his bottom lip. Gene was getting ready to come. If he didn't already know the signs, the increased curses and moans coming from above him were all the proof he needed. Llew squeezed his eyes shut and worked double-time. He used both hands on his cock and balls while his face was fucked with wild abandon. Gene needed to be controlled. Damn, how he wanted to tame this wild tiger, but his brain was telling him he should behave, he didn't want to get in trouble again. *Get out of my head.* He pulled off for a split second and spit in his palm, needing some lubrication. His head was yanked back in place, and the throbbing cock pulsed on his tongue. Gene yelled out Llew's name, his hips bucking hard against his chin when the first blast of spunk hit the back of his throat. He could only imagine how good his date was feeling right now. The euphoria that came with a good release. Damn, if he didn't need it too. Gene milked his cock, flooding Llew's mouth with all he had. Not stopping until he was completely drained.

"Fuck yeah, Llew. Oh my god, that's fuckin' good, babe." Gene's sated cock slipped from his lips and Llew almost roared in protest. This couldn't be fuckin' over. Not yet.

Llew leaned his forehead against Gene's lower abdomen, continuing to jerk himself anxiously. *Please*. His biceps flexed with exertion as he hunched in on himself. He felt his date lazily rubbing his shoulders, probably too drunk with post orgasmic bliss to do much else. He felt worthless right now. He yanked on his balls again, cursing at them to do something… to give him something. He needed the pungent smell of his essence to be added to Gene's, or else it'd be like he hadn't even been there. His cock was starting to burn, he was fuckin' chaffing himself. He growled angrily at his epic failure. He held on to the edge of the bed with one hand, while he brought the other to a regretful stop. With his head still bowed and leaning against Gene's bony pelvis, he peeked one eye open to look at the useless hunk of flesh between his thighs. It was lying down over his balls, irritated and flushed red, not from the flow of blood to it, but from the punishing effort of trying to get it hard. After a couple of slow tugs, he rested his hand on his sweaty thigh. *Goddamn useless*. He felt like a Silverback gorilla that couldn't beat on his chest in victory. He wasn't the alpha anymore.

CHAPTER TWELVE

"Llew, you don't have to go," his date said, from the middle of the bed. "We can talk, you know."

Llew fastened his belt, not taking his eyes off Gene's unsure ones. He was being nice. Although he thought Llew was hot, good-looking, mysteriously sexy... he was fucking impotent. That wasn't a good characteristic when searching for a life partner. He cleared his throat. "I appreciate it, Gene. But, um. I think I'm gonna head home. I gotta early day tomorrow," he lied.

"Okay," he said, quickly. "I did have a good time, though."

"Sure thing." Llew's smile never appeared, even though he'd wanted it to. He grabbed his jacket, and his long strides had him at the front door in seconds. By the time he'd unlocked the door, Gene was there with a shy hand on his shoulder. He turned, looking back down at eyes that were full of empathy, which – although it was nice – wasn't wanted.

"I hope you find what you're looking for, Llew. I think tonight had a lot to do with me."

Llew shook his head.

"It's okay. I'm just not your type, Llew. That's what all this was about." Gene gestured lower. "Either that, or you weren't being yourself. I noticed you barely touched me, so it's probably more me."

"It's not you. I promise, Gene. Thank you for tonight."
Llew turned and left. He wasn't going to explain anything
else. He was fucked up in the head, and whatever defect he
had up there was directly hardwired to his cock. There was
no Viagra in prison; he just had to deal with it in there.

*"A lot of men don't get erections in prison. That's not
as uncommon as you may think, Llew. "*

Llew had hoped it'd been restricted to that
environment only, but obviously it wasn't. During the
forty-five minute ride home, he contemplated what he was
going to do about his brother and the business. It was
painfully obvious he couldn't stay and work for him, or any
business in Emporia, for that matter. He thought again
about Henderson, NC, and all the new developments his
brother had mentioned going up in the fast-growing town.
While it was still a relatively small area, it was still larger
than Emporia, and most importantly, no one knew him. He
could apply at some construction companies, hardware
stores, or whatever. Happily, it was only an hour and half
away from his brother so they could visit often. Llew
pulled into the only twenty-four hour gas station in town to
refill his brother's truck.

He'd just come out from paying the clerk when his
eyes locked on the regal figure standing at the pump behind
his. *Jesus Christ*. He was taller. Still lean and fit beneath a
tailored, black pinstriped suit. He was facing away from
him, watching the tally of his gas dispensing, but Llew
knew without a shadow of a doubt that it was Moss
McGregor the sixth. He hadn't seen him since that night.

His chest constricted and his steps faltered. He realized
he was standing in the middle of the lane when a loud car

102

horn yanked him out of his shocked state. Moss' head spun around, and eyes that used to stare at him with adoration locked on to him. Fear danced across Moss' handsome face, and Llew knew he had to get the fuck out of there. He hurried across the street, back to his pump. He wanted to run like hell, but he'd paid his fifty bucks to fill up. He kept his back turned to Moss, but he could feel those bright blue eyes boring into his back.

"Honey, who is that?" The sharp female voice could be heard over the loud ringing in Llew's ears.

He'd heard Moss had gotten married to a debutant from Richmond, like his father had always planned. Llew's body burned all over when he head Moss' response of, "No one."

His fuckin' hands shook so hard he could barely keep the nozzle inside the tank. He wasn't supposed to be in the vicinity of his victim, according to his probation documents. He looked up at the dispenser when it clicked and saw the numbers slow down, as he got closer to his prepaid amount. *Hurry up, goddamnit.*

Screeching tires and the chirp of a siren made Llew close his eyes and pray for god to just take him now. "Get your hands up, Llewellyn Gardner!" Deputy Jamison yelled, bounding from his cruiser after was just barely throwing it in park. Another sheriff car raced up, slamming on the brakes; blocking his truck's exit.

Llew gritted his teeth, finally turning to look at Moss. He'd thought he didn't have tears anymore, having cried them all out the first two years he was in prison, but of course he was wrong again. His own dark eyes burned with moisture when Moss' sorrowful ones finally met his. Bright blue eyes that were once so vibrant and full of life were now as dreary as a polluted pond. Moss looked absolutely miserable, his face contorted into what looked like pain when he saw Officer Jamison slam Llew into his truck, yanking his hands behind his back. The unforgiving metal of the handcuffs pinched his flesh when they locked closed. He didn't resist it. He grunted and flinched at the harsh treatment, but he didn't fight it. Llew's head was pressed against the cold, hard door, but he was determined to keep his eyes locked on Moss'. *Are you going to let this happen to me again? Did you really never love me, Moss?* Llew was finally able to face his accuser after all these years. Moss couldn't hide this time. What Llew was trying to convey with his eyes must have been received; because Moss' face twisted into anger, and he barged past the deputy that was asking if he was okay, storming up to Deputy Jamison. He was close enough that Llew could smell faint traces of his cologne.

"Let him go, Jamison!" Moss yelled.

"He's violating his probation. He's not supposed to be around you or your family," Deputy Jamison snarled, pulling Llew by his collar.

"Stop it! He's not violating anything. I pulled up after him. He didn't even look at me. Release him immediately!" Moss' voice was strong and confident; nothing like the weak boy he'd been eight years ago.

Deputy Jamison looked back and forth between them, obviously stunned that a victim would be sticking up for his attacker. That had to appear odd. But he reluctantly unlocked the cuffs. "We got a call from Janie saying that you were cornered by him, sir."

Llew rubbed his wrist, looking up through the convenience store window at the girl in a paisley smock, who used to be the captain of the cheerleading squad, as she wrung her hands. He thought she was acting weird, but he'd shrugged it off. Everyone in this goddamn town acted weird. He hadn't uttered one word to her though, and she'd called the cops. Yeah. He had to leave.

"This is your final warning, Gardner." Deputy Jamison pointed his finger at him. "You stay away from Moss McGregor, his parents, or his lovely wife. If I get one more call regarding you I'm — "

"That's enough Jamison." Moss ordered.

Llew opened the door to his truck, but he couldn't help but look back at his old lover one last time. Most likely the last time. He whispered only for him to hear, "Why couldn't you say that before?"

Instead of waiting on a response that he knew wouldn't come, he got in his truck and carefully drove off, extra cautious not to go over the speed limit, since Jamison was right behind him.

CHAPTER THIRTEEN

Llew's couple of bags were packed and waiting by the door of their trailer when his brother got home the next evening. His smile dropped and his shoulders slumped as soon as he saw them. Llew appreciated that his brother didn't try to talk him into staying. He knew this had to be done, too. It was either him or the business. As soon as Leslie went back to work the next day, he would surely hear what had happened between him and Moss, so he needed to tell him now. Tell him the truth. This town was not gonna give him a fair shake. It never had, and it never would.

"So, where you gonna go?"

Llew was stirring his spaghetti sauce when he answered. "Henderson."

He heard the shattering of the glass vase that sat on one of the bookshelves, making him turn sharply. His brother's face was a dark red, his hands balled into fist. "This fuckin' sucks, man! You just got home, Llew. They can't force you to leave."

This is what he understood more than anything in the world. He understood unfairness. His brother had a right to be angry... he was, too. He'd lost so much time, time away from the only family he had, but this was the hand he was dealt. He wasn't folding, but he knew when to hold. He and

107

his brother would have their time, but first he had things to do.

He still didn't speak as he let his brother kick the bags that sat against the wall and throw magazines across the room. When it looked like he'd calmed down and gotten most of it out of his system, Llew set their two plates on the table. His jaw was clamped tight while he waited for Leslie to join him. They ate in silence, the reality of Llew having to leave again heavy on their hearts. After they were done, instead of Llew going to his bedroom to explore his drafting software like he usually did, he decided to sit with his brother and watch the game. While he didn't yell and bitch at the television, he did quirk his mouth up and smile as his brother hollered enough for both of them.

The game — and then of course, the post-game show — didn't end until after midnight. Llew left his snoring brother on the couch, as he made sure everything was locked up and turned off. He'd thought about going outside to work out, but knowing how his late night rituals concerned Leslie, he chose to wait and do it in the morning, instead. He showered quickly, and sans any nightclothes or underwear, he stretched out on his floor. His thoughts went to a pretty blond, with green eyes and a beautiful smile. He wished he could've fucked him. Ate his hole until he couldn't take it anymore, then sank deep inside him. He probably would've only lasted two minutes, but he'd be damn if it wouldn't have been the best two minutes he'd had in years. Gene had been so eager to please, but deep down Llew knew it was because the man had no idea who he was with. He'd said he could read people. Was that why he'd taken Llew home? Because he knew Llew wasn't a rapist, a bad person, someone who got off on hurting people? Well… he did love to give his lovers some raw passion, a bit of dominance, because there were some kinds of pain that were good. Gene probably would've welcomed it. He would've begged for it.

"You think you could avoid me forever, bitch?"

"Look man, I'm just here to do my time. I'm not trying to be in anyone's gang." Llew slung back at the big bastard *that had been harassing him to join his gang for the past ten months. Llew didn't want a gang, especially Damon's. He didn't want friends. Ace had flaunted his wealth and power at him, but he still didn't want a goddamn thing but for eight years to go by as quickly as possible.*

"I don't give a fuck what you want. But you are gonna give me what I want." The man sneered. His bald head *glistened from the constant sweat that seemed to cling to his massive body.* *"I could use a hot rapist like you on my team. A few of my guys have a problem with using that type of force."* Damon released an indignant snort. *"But obviously, you don't."*

"I'm not a rap —" Before Llew could finish his *sentence, one of Damon minions took him out from behind. Hitting him in the back of the neck with a fist that felt like it was made of stone.*

"Yeah. And I'm not a murdering psycho. We're all goddamn Mormons in here." Damon sneered, crouching *down where Llew knelt holding the back of his head. Everyone knew Damon was serving a life without parole sentence for murdering his boss and his boss' family for firing him two days before Christmas. The stories Llew heard about the man had him hiding from Damon in every*

way he could, but he'd known it was only a matter of time before Damon became more forceful and more violent towards him. Why not? The man had absolutely nothing to lose. "Now, what's it gonna be handsome? You with us or what?"

If Llew joined Damon's crew, he could forget about getting out on good behavior. He'd always be knee deep in shit and probably spend half his time in solitary for getting busted doing the shit work Damon would insist he do. He got up on his knees, his face contorted with pain and anger. "Fuck you. My answer is still no."

"Ace! Ace!" he screamed. Nothing. No one came.

His predator slammed his fat hand over Llew's mouth so hard he thought he may have knocked a tooth out. Damon narrowed his eyes in anger. "You stupid bastard, you can use this cock to rape a fucking boy, but you can't put it to good use in here." Damon looked up at the three men behind him and barked a simple three-word order that had Llew wanting to continue to scream uselessly for help.

"Hold him down."

Llew jerked awake, clutching his balls. He tried to control his urge to vomit. He could still clearly remember the insurmountable pain he'd felt when three men stomped his groin until he'd passed out. He'd woken two days later in the infirmary, wishing he was dead. While there hadn't been any permanent damage, the fractured pelvis was the most excruciating pain he'd ever felt.

Even months after he'd healed, he still hadn't been able to obtain an erection. His counselor explained to him that being called a rapist and trying to be forced into raping other inmates while being assaulted in the groin had done him serious psychological damage. Like Llew recognized his cock as being the cause of all of his turmoil. So his mind was blocking his ability to use it. It all sounded like a bunch of crazy, psychoanalytic bullshit to him, but Dr. Jackson said he could help him, and eventually Llew had learned to trust him and Ace's crew.

He groaned, getting up from the floor. He still hadn't been able to sleep in his bed, the firmness of the floor more like normal to him than that weird foam thing. His back was drenched with sweat and his balls ached from his clutching of them. The flashback dream was just as real as when it'd happened. *Get out of my fuckin' head.* He propped himself up against the small dresser that sat along the opposite wall and stared out at the dark sky. In a few hours, he'd be leaving for a new town; new start, and hopefully a new beginning. His probation officer was coming at nine to bring him the relocation request forms, and of course, the goddamn sex offender registration, since he had to register in any city he would ever reside in. It would be public knowledge, but how many people checked that list anyway? Although he hated to leave Leslie, he was actually pretty excited about going someplace where people hadn't already labeled him. Here, he couldn't even pump gas without the authorities swarming in and throwing him against the hood of a car. But most of all; he never wanted to see Moss McGregor the sixth again.

"What time you getting on the road?" His PO asked him, tucking the forms back inside his leather brief case.

"Well it's only an hour and a half away. I'll probably leave in a bit. It'll give me time to look around, maybe find a few construction sites and apply."

111

"I'm gonna talk with Deputy Potts this afternoon."

"Who's that?"

"The Chief Deputy of Henderson."

Llew stood so fast, he knocked his small chair over. He scowled down at his PO, who'd already skidded his chair back, putting some distance between them. "Why are you talking to him? About what?"

His PO stood up, putting himself almost eye level with Llew. He wasn't a small man by any means, but he was definitely smaller than Llew. He could see that the officer was trying to keep the situation under control by not stepping closer to him. But, the frown-lines on his forehead and the throbbing at his temples clearly said he was pissed. "I'm going to give him your sex offender registration paperwork. You're in his county, and I have a legal obligation to let him know."

"I'm going there so I can start fresh, man. How the hell am I supposed to do that if the cops are already on alert?" Llew ran his hands threw his hair, dropping back down into his chair. "Fuck!"

"Here."

Llew looked up and saw the man was holding out a plastic cup in his direction. "Piss, so I can go. Then you can finish your tantrum." The look he wore said that as a PO, he'd heard it all, seen it all.

Llew left immediately after his PO. He didn't want to stick around just in case his brother swung by on his lunch break. Leslie was still fuming over him having to leave, and he couldn't bear to watch it anymore.

He threw his duffle over his shoulder, and hooked his backpack on. He only had to a quarter-mile walk to the bus stop, not too bad. His brother insisted he take his truck, and he would use his work truck as transportation, too. Although Llew had agreed, he'd only done so to avoid continuing the discussion. He had no intention of taking his brother's vehicle; of making him have to use a truck with a huge trailer hitched to it to make a simple grocery run. When the time came, Llew would buy his own car. His brother couldn't keep coddling him, trying to eliminate every obstacle thrown his way. He wasn't eighteen anymore, he was almost twenty-seven, he'd been a man for a long time.

Llew abandoned his musings when he saw the sign that said "Welcome to the City of Henderson, North Carolina." He sat up higher in his bus seat and looked out at what was to be his fresh start. There was nothing to be seen but trees on the interstate, but when the bus pulled into the small station, Llew caught a glimpse of the rural town rich with history. It looked like the set of the movie *Back to the Future*. If he was a smiler, it would've shown, but instead he smiled on the inside. He'd loved history, enjoyed watching movies that depicted old-style living. *This will be fine.*

He grabbed his bag from the luggage compartment beneath the bus and fastened his backpack on his shoulders. He needed to walk and look around before he decided on a place to crash. Maybe he'd check out the town center first, most likely there'd be job postings and room vacancies listed there. He walked into the building and was surprised that the outside had a vintage rustic look, but the inside had been remodeled with marble floors and tall hand-sculpted columns. It looked too expensive and it didn't fit. He hoped

113

all the buildings weren't like this… an illusion. He wanted small-town Americana on the inside as well as the outside. *I'm already thinking like this is my city.*

Llew picked up *The Daily Dispatch* – the local newspaper, a couple brochures from nearby attractions, and a flyer for a town meeting tomorrow. Soon he was trekking up the cobblestone sidewalk along Garret Street on his way into town. There weren't very many people out and about when he arrived. Only a few older couples; most likely retirees, everyone else was probably at work in the middle of the day. His head was buried in the paper when a woman carrying three grocery bags piled high in her arms and a toddler at her side bumped him hard enough to drop his paper. One of her bags crashed to the ground.

"Oh my goodness lordy. I'm sure sorry. I didn't see you," she said hurriedly, shuffling the other bags in an effort not to drop them too. She looked up at him when Llew hadn't said anything. Whatever she saw in his eyes must've made it okay. She smiled sincerely, the laugh lines that crinkled next to her brown eyes said she did that a lot. "I really apologize."

Llew shook his head, hopefully relaying that it was okay. He squatted and picked up his papers, tucking them in the side pocket of his duffle and hefted the woman's bag back up in his free arm. "I'll help you, if you want," he said quietly, not wanting his deep, growly voice to scare her.

"That'd be right nice of you. As usual, I picked up more than I meant to at the market." She pointed behind him. "I'm up the way there, off David Ave. I'm the Victorian on the right." With a simple nod at her, he gently extracted another bag from her arm and carried both on his strong forearm. He began walking in the direction she'd indicated.

After she'd secured the little boy with her one free hand, she turned to look at his bags. "Are you new here? Just arrived? Must be, I've never seen you."

Head nod.

"Are you here to visit someone, you got family in Henderson?"

Llew cleared his throat. "No ma'am I've just relocated here. I'm from Em—" Llew stopped abruptly, switching his answer. "E-east of here; in Virginia."

"Oh okay. So what brings you here to our little neck of the woods?"

Again, he was smiling on the inside. To some it might have appeared like she was nosy, but growing up in a small town, he knew that's what people did. It was called good ole' Southern personality. Gotta love it.

He shrugged and said honestly, "Looking for work." Saying he was looking for a fresh start, would've only prompted more questions. Questions he didn't want to answer.

After passing a few nice homes, she turned; unlocked a short metal gate, and led him up five wooden steps that creaked angrily under his weight. Hearing them, she explained, "Yeah, those rickety things need to be replaced. I've been saying I'ma' get to it. My son is so busy all the time with work and his own home, I can't seem to get him over to do anything."

She opened her door, still rambling, and held it open for Llew to squeeze through; letting him right inside her empty home. And again he smiled inside. She wasn't the slightest bit afraid of him. Most country people trusted you until you gave them a reason not to.

The home was a nice size, with plenty of antique furniture, some restored and some not. He ducked under the low doorframe into the kitchen. She pointed to the table that sat off to the side, just in front of a bay window. After telling "Jimmy Jr." to go play in the sunroom, she turned back to look at him. "Wow. You don't look as tall when you're outside. In here you look like a Jack the Giant."

Llew quirked his mouth to the side. That was actually pretty cute. Sounded like something his mom would've said. "Have a seat there. Take a load off, honey. Least I can do is give you a glass of iced tea for your help."

"That's okay ma'am. I best get going. Got some ground to cover and find a place to stay before evening," Llew said, adjusting his duffle bag on his shoulder. He admitted to himself that he didn't want to go. The three and half hour bus ride had his back cramping. More than that, he was starved. The warm kitchen he stood in smelled like fresh baked pecan pie.

"Oh. Do you have a place in mind?"

"Um. No ma'am not yet, but—"

"Call me Ms. Pat, if you wish. But stop ma'am-ing me. I'm not that old." She cut in, swatting him on his arm before pulling more of her groceries out of the bag. "I'm only fifty-two. Save that ma'am for my momma when you see her." She admonished him, placing a couple boxes of cereal in the large pantry off of the kitchen.

"What's your name?"

"Llew," he said, deliberately not giving his full name.

She nodded her head, seeming okay with that response. When she took the canned goods from another bag and went to open another cabinet, it came apart at the top hinge, falling off to the side. "Oh, gosh darnit. This place is falling apart on top of my head."

Llew dropped his bags and rushed over to relieve her of her canned goods. She banged the side of the cabinet with her petite palm, trying to get the pieces of the broken hinge to connect. He stepped to her side and used his large palm to push the pieces back together. It was missing a screw at the top, that's why it kept coming apart.

"You got a toolbox, Ms. Pat?"

"Sure, hon. In the garage, through that door."

Llew tried to keep his usually heavy steps light in her quiet home while he moved across her large kitchen. He easily found the rusty, once bright red toolbox and shuffled through it. He found a nail that was probably not the exact size he needed, but it'd be a temporary fix. He came back in and easily tapped the nail into the hinge. He tested it, pulling it open and closed, before turning back to her. "It'll hold," he said.

"Very well." She smiled broadly, setting Llew's iced tea on the table with a huge hunk of sweet potato pie.

He knew something had been baked recently. He wouldn't be rude. He washed his hands in the sink and sat down to enjoy his desert. After a few moments of silence, Ms. Pat asked her question again.

"So do you already have a place in mind, Llew?"

"No ma'am, I mean um, no, Ms. Pat. I don't. My bus just came in. I was looking through the classifieds for rooms when we met."

She sat down with her own glass of tea. "You mean when I 'bout knocked you down." Her smile was infectious. But he ducked his head and ate his last bite of pie. "Well, since you're looking for rooms… fate just knocked you upside your head, honey. Because I have a room for rent. It's not a lot, but I'm proud of it. It's over the garage, newly finished."

Llew looked up at her with shock and confusion. How could she possibly offer him a place to stay when— His stomached dropped, and even though the pie was delicious, he wished he didn't have it in his stomach right then, because it was turning over. He felt sick inside. She was only offering because she didn't know who he was. An ex-con, a just-released convicted rapist. As soon as she found out, she'd have him out on his ass before he could say he didn't do it.

"Well, don't look like that, dear. It may not be what you had in mind, but at least take a look at it first," she said softly, patting his hand. "Let's have another piece of pie and then you'll look." She was nodding her head while she cut them both another piece.

After Ms. Pat tucked Jimmy Jr. in for his nap, she took Llew to see the room. They walked through a door to a small space before she unlocked the second door. While he walked up the back stairs, she told him that the room was just done and she hadn't even listed it yet. He almost dreaded it. He was sure he'd love it, but when it was ripped away, it was going to hurt.

She unlocked and opened the door. "You'd have your own set of keys. No one would be able to enter but you." The smell of fresh paint assaulted his nose as soon as he stepped into the wide space. It was a completely open floorplan. On one side was a small L-shaped kitchenette on a square of tan linoleum; a small, two-burner stove with an oven. The counter was just big enough to hold a microwave, and maybe a toaster. On the opposite side of the stove was a pretty nice-sized mini refrigerator. On the corner was a single sink.

"Go on dear. Have a good look." She beamed. Was the look in his eyes already saying how much he loved it?

Llew walked all the way inside. His boots making large prints on the brand new tan carpet. He looked out the window at the quaint neighborhood first, and then opened one of the three doors in the room to see a decent size walk-in closet. He'd never have enough belongings to fill it. He closed the closet door, walking back across the room to open the other door, which led to a small bathroom. There was a small oval mirror with a pedestal sink standing beneath it. An organizer caddy for storing personal items sat on the floor between the sink and toilet. The standing shower looked barely big enough for him, but he'd lived with worse. Llew found that the last door led out to small landing and a staircase leading out to the side driveway.

"That way you have your own entrance. You don't have to use the front door, ya know, and come through the house," Ms. Pat said from where she stood with her hands on her ample hips. "I knew you'd like it. It rents for three-fifty a month, all utilities included. You'd have access to the washer and dryer in the garage. There's a doorbell at the bottom of the stairs. It was my son's idea. If you want to come into the house, just ring it, and I'll open it up. My son's a stickler about things like that. Privacy and all."

Llew didn't quite know what to say. He did like it and it was well within his price range. He still had some money on his card and his entire paycheck, which Leslie had practically forced him to accept. Hopefully, by the time his next month's rent came due he'd have a job. Hell, even if it was fast food, he'd do it. Llew looked up at her and nodded his head; telling her, "Yes, I really do like it."

"That's great. There's no security deposit. Just the first month's rent to move in."

Llew tucked his thumbs in the pockets of his jeans. "Um. Don't you have an application or something to fill out?" *A credit and criminal background check.*

"I hadn't even gotten around to making one up." She tilted her head as if thinking about it. "But I get a good vibe from you, Llew. Not too many young men would offer to help carry a strange woman's bags for her. The way you up and fixed my cabinet, just because it needed fixin' and you were there. I can already see from your manners that you got good family upbringing. That's what I'd like to have in a tenant. Not just some information on a piece of paper, that don't mean diddly-do."

Llew hinted at another smile. "Thank you," he said, quietly.

"Oh you're welcome, honey. If you like it, and it's in your range; then it's yours, Llew. Save me the trouble of running an ad," she said, her eyes crinkling again with her sweet motherly smile. Come on down and we can talk some details while I start dinner. My grandson has quite an appetite and gets right fussy when he's hungry. And after his nap, he'll be hungry as a bear."

Llew stepped back into her home and sat at the table, not knowing what else to do. She went about pulling some kind of stew meat and some vegetables out of her refrigerator. Llew's stomach liked the idea of possibly having homemade beef stew. After setting another glass of tea in front of him, she went back to her stovetop.

"I'm really excited, Llew," she said, chopping up vegetables. "I think you're gonna love the town. What type of work do you do?"

Llew cleared his throat again. "Um. I can do 'bout anything. But I wouldn't mind working in construction."

She frowned slightly, her eyes cutting up and to the left like she was thinking. "Hmm. My boy does construction, but he's downsizing at the moment. Poor thing. Also, there's a huge company based here that does a lot of the town's construction. Big Daddy Smith's son – my god-baby — took over the company when his daddy retired last year, and now they do construction in a few neighboring states, too. That boy of his is so smart, and sweet as pie. It was his guys that did your room for me. Didn't they do a great job? Smith's usually only does commercial stuff, but he insisted on doing it for me. He could probably use a strong man like you, Llew." She seemed to say all that in one breath before adding, "Oh by the way, what's your last name?"

Llew tensed before he could stop himself, glad that she had her back to him. He really didn't want to answer that question, but there was no point not answering. She'd find out eventually. He just hopped he was able to prove he was a good guy before word got to Ms. Pat about who she'd just invited into her home.

"My name is Llew Gardner. Um, Llewellyn Gardner."

Still adding numerous ingredients to a large pot. "That's a lovely name, Llewellyn."

"Thank you."

She finally turned to him, wiping her hands on a small dishtowel. "So are you gonna say 'yes' to the room?"

Llew nodded his head. "Thank you very much. I sure appreciate it."

She took the two keys out of her apron pocket and clasped his hand, placing them in his thick palm. Llew reached in his back pocket and retrieved his wallet, unfolding the right amount of cash to pay his first month's rent. He slid it across the table towards her and she beamed with delight. "You can take your stuff up, Llewellyn." She paused. "Do you mind if I call you, Llewellyn instead of Llew? I really like that name."

He simply nodded his head again.

"You just don't talk much do you, Llewellyn?" She swiped her hand in the air. "That's okay, honey. I can talk plenty enough for the both of us."

Llew gave her a small smile when she laughed at her own joke. "I'll have dinner ready in a couple hours. You can make your own meals or if you want what I cook, all you gotta do is ask. I babysit my grandson during the day, so I'm always fixing something. It's nice to have someone to cook for."

Llew picked up his bag. He turned back before he got to the door. "I think I'll go into town for a little bit and look around. See if I see any construction sites."

"Sure thing, dear." She went about what she was doing and before Llew could close his door, he heard her say on a soft sigh. "Such a sweet boy."

CHAPTER FOURTEEN

Llew kept on his jeans, but pulled on the charcoal sweater he'd worn out the night he'd met Gene. Made him look like he cared about a first impression. Which he did. Although he'd only seen a few help-wanted postings in the paper, neither for Smith's Construction, he'd go by there anyway and fill out an application.

It was four p.m. and the town was a little more alive now. He'd been walking for forty minutes, choosing not to take the local transportation, so he would o be able to go in someplace if he saw a "help wanted" sign. He didn't go in any of the shops, but he did wonder about the large Farm and Home Supply store that sat at Beckford and Raleigh. It took up the whole corner. He could stock shelves or something there. He went through the automatic doors, and it felt to him like all the people that were in view of the front entrance turned to face him. He looked up for a sign that pointed to customer service, wanting to apply and leave as soon as possible. The store was full to the rafters with everything from bulk-style family food staples to farm supplies.

"How can I help you, son?"

Llew stepped up to the counter; holding his hand out to the older man, his nametag indicating he was the general manager. He looked at Llew's hand for a brief second before grasping it and giving it a firm shake. "Good evening, sir. My name's Llew Gardner, and I just moved here. I was wondering if you had any positions open or are taking applications."

Llew watched as the man shifted to pull a binder from underneath the counter. "Let me see here. I was thinking of hiring someone at night to put up the deliveries. It's the only thing I need right now, but I haven't been able to fill it because it's only Monday and Thursdays from ten to two. It requires some pretty heavy lifting; no one jumping up to do that job, especially teenaged boys." The guy laughed.

Llew shrugged. True, he would like something full-time but he'd take what he could get. "I'd like to apply."

The guy's bushy, grey eyebrows rose up in surprise. "Well, alright then." He handed Llew an ink pen and single page application on a clipboard, telling him he could fill out over at the other side of the counter. Unfortunately, as he scanned over the application he realized there was going to be one helluva gap in his work history. He listed his brother's crew leader as a job reference and his counselor from prison as a personal reference. That was really all he had. He breathed a sigh of relief when he got to the section that only asked if he'd been convicted of a crime of moral turpitude. He checked no. Surprisingly, he found out early on that rape didn't fall under that category. It seems that this store was only interested in knowing if you were a convicted thief.

He signed his application and gave it back to the manager. He stuck his hand out again offering a confident shake. "Thank you, sir. I hope to hear from you."

The man nodded. "I'm Mr. Graham by the way. Give me a few hours to check your references and I'll get back to you."

He left the store feeling quite pleased. This was going better than he thought. The job probably only paid around ten bucks an hour, but something was better than nothing, his dad always said.

He walked further into town as dusk descended and more people took to the quaint streets. It wasn't the busy scene you'd see in New York, but it was more than in Emporia, for sure. It looked as if it was the town movie night. There was a small cinema that sat at the corner of Rose and Chestnut. Llew looked up at the dimly lit marquee. He had no clue what the listing was, but he figured he'd check it out soon. He hadn't been to a movie in… well, yeah.

"Thinking of going in? Or are you just gonna block the entrance?"

Llew turned at the sound of the sure voice behind him. Since he seemed to tower over everyone, he automatically looked down at the pretty brunette with dark brown eyes to match. "Um. Sorry," Llew mumbled, quickly moving out her way.

"Well don't be sorry shuga, just escort a lady inside." Llew couldn't even blink as he watched the lady stalk towards him. Her full chest sat above an extremely narrow waist. It almost looked unnatural. She was dressed and made up like a grown woman. She looked maybe thirty from a distance, but her smooth skin and awkward approach screamed her real age. She was jailbait if he'd ever seen it. Llew gave her a slight head nod and had turned to leave when his elbow was hooked.

"I saw you in the general store applying for a job. You musta jus' got into town, because if not, I'd have known, honey. So, you got kin here?"

Silence.

The laugh was an all-out girlish giggle, and it grated on his nerves. "Cat got your tongue, darlin'?" She moved in even closer and dragged a long red nail down Llew's arm, tilting her head back to look up at him. "You want me to beg, huh? Come on now, handsome. Escort a lady to a movie... then maybe — "

"Maybe when he sees a lady... he'll escort one."

Llew diverted his attention away from the overzealous minx that was practically humping his leg, and focused on the beautiful man approaching with another guy in tow. The man's voice wasn't overly deep like his own; it was smooth and melodic. Sounded like he could be a singer or a poet. He walked with an unhurried gait that was a mixture of "I'm in charge" and "You're on my time, not the other way around," and Llew found it sexy as fuck. His tall friend chuckled behind him, sauntering over to purchase their tickets. *Is he on a date?* No, their demeanor definitely said friends.

"Mind ya own business Smith Jr., I saw him first."
Smith Jr.

The man hooked one thumb in his pocket, not the slightest bit fazed at the remark. But Llew was thrown. Was this guy actually gay or was she being a smart aleck? He came even nearer to them and Llew got a nice whiff of his spicy, bold cologne when a cool breeze blew his way. It was an interesting contradiction, because the man's entire persona gave off a cool and composed vibe.

"Mosey along, Sallie Ann. Don't make me ring ya daddy. He told me keep an eye on you while he's gone, and I agreed. He'd be rather put out if I didn't follow through on my promise."

She reluctantly let go of Llew's arm, letting loose a long drawn out huff of childish annoyance. Llew didn't bother watching her walk away. She was irrelevant. He tucked his hands deep in his pockets as he eyed the man in front of him with a strange fusion of curiosity and wistfulness.

"Sometimes a person has gotta run interference with that girl. She's usually not that bad, but her daddy is outta town, so ya know how young girls can be."

Actually, not really.

"Hi. I'm Shane Smith Jr." He stuck out a large, calloused hand, and it took Llew a couple seconds to process the information that he was going to touch him. Llew shook his hand and watched the man's eyes; his own mouth still shut tight. They were light brown and full of humor and amusement. Right away, he figured this was obviously a guy who had few, if any, worries in his life. *Wait a minute... Smith... Jr. Is he the owner of...?* He released the strong grip he had on Shane's hand and wished he'd held it a little longer.

"And you are?"

Llew swallowed before answering. "Llew."

Those eyes twinkled again, and dark brown brows rose up in question. "Llew... just Llew."

It was humiliating when a man was ashamed to tell someone his full name. But doing so meant that they would soon be able to figure out who he really was. Know what he was classified as. He didn't want this man to know, god help him he didn't. But lying wasn't an option. *Fuck it.* "Llewellyn Gardner."

So many broke eye contact with him at that point in the conversation, and Llew was more than intrigued that Mr. Shane Smith Jr. was staring at him just as hard as before, and he was returning the stare. He didn't know why he was looking at him that way, but he sure didn't mind it.

"Now that's a name." Smith smiled beautifully.

"Movie's already started, Shane. You coming or what?"

Llew looked up, having already forgotten that Shane wasn't alone.

He cleared his throat. "Um. Nice meeting you. Don't let me hold you up."

"Did I hear you was looking for work?" Shane drawled, ignoring his friend.

Llew turned back towards him. "Yeah. I just got into town."

He smiled that beautiful grin, reached into his back pocket, and pulled out a worn brown leather wallet. "You don't look like a stranger to labor." He aimed a simple white business card at him and Llew quickly read the elegant script:

Smith Construction ~ One Plaza Way
Shane Smith Jr., Owner & Operator
252-636-9999

"Come on by." He paused and grinned at Llew again before adding. "If you're interested, of course. I'm actually in the process of hiring some additional crew. I gotta lot comin' up here soon, gonna need some tough guys to get it done."

Llew wasn't sure if this guy was flirting or not, he'd been in a place for so long where flirting didn't exist, he'd forgotten what it looked like… what it sounded like. The way Shane Smith Jr. was smiling at him, it sure seemed like flirting. Llew could imagine himself with a strong man like this. A man who was gorgeous, but didn't know it. Not overly fashionably outfitted in fancy clothes; he was dressed like a working man, but he wore the look well. He was simply confident, followed his own counsel, and not easily persuaded. But Llew wouldn't dare get his hopes up. As soon as word got out that there was a newly registered sex offender in their quaint little town, Smith Jr. might be leading the lynch mob to run him out of there.

CHAPTER FIFTEEN

Good heavens above. Who is this man? Shane thought
when he pulled up to the movie theater. He had been in
construction since he was knee high to a grasshopper and
following Big Daddy Smith around the job sites with his
little Fisher-Price toolbox. Shane had never, in all those
years, seen a man so broad and masterfully built; he
apparently lived and breathed physical fitness. A man that
looked as if he was chock-full of a double dose of
testosterone, but oozed a type of sensitive masculinity.

"Who the hell is that?" he said, to himself more than to
his best friend and foreman; Jack Hammond.

Jack peered up the sidewalk and nonchalantly
shrugged his tired shoulders. They'd had a long day on the
site, three guys hadn't showed up, so he and Jack had
double the work load. They didn't want to go to Bubba's
Bar tonight; knowing if they did, they'd drink a few and not
want to get up at four a.m. to be back to work; so they
figured, why not a movie. It took Shane a few seconds
before he was even able to reach for the door handle and
get out the tall truck. Sallie Ann was on him like a cheap
suit. Jack elbowed him in the arm.

"You coming, or you gonna stare at Sallie flirtin'?"

Shane eased down from the cab and tried to smooth his
wrinkled flannel shirt. His jean jacket was worn and dusty,
but oh well. Thinking again, he yanked it off, threw it back

in the truck, and slammed the heavy door. He rolled up the sleeves of his shirt to let his strong forearms show. Tucking his thumbs in his jean pockets, he glanced down one last time, wincing at his work jeans and steel toe boots.

"You done missy? Or do you need to apply some lipstick too?" Jack stumbled back, laughing hard at his own joke, but Shane ignored him. From where he stood, he could see that the guy was not into Sallie Ann, not even a little bit. His eyes gave it away. He looked more than a little confused, maybe a tad afraid. Well who wouldn't be if a young woman just came out of nowhere and practically molested you on a public sidewalk?

"You best go on over there, I can see you're dyin' to."

"I swear that girl gonna be in a bad way, she keeps that up. Her daddy'd tear her a new hide if he got wind of her behavior."

Jack shook his head, walking beside him. "Yeah, she's quick and slick."

"Slicker than a harpooned hippo in a banana tree."

"Amen to that."

"Go on and get the tickets, I'll be right in."

"Got it."

Shane was shooing Sallie Ann away when the most intense dark eyes he'd ever seen caught his own brown ones and held him there like a hostage. It was startling and fascinating at the same time.

"So you can call or just come by the site in the morning. We're at the corner of Montgomery and North Wilson. My assistant, Jessie, should be at the desk; she can give you the application."

"Shane Jr., we watching the movie or shooting the breeze?" Jack yelled.

He stopped himself from yelling at Jack to fuck off, wanting to appear cool in front of this silent, mysterious man. "Yeah. Coming." He turned his attention back to Llew and stuck his hand out again. A second handshake was warranted when you first meet someone, so he hoped it didn't appear to be what it truly was... his desire to feel that big, heavy hand in his again.

"Likewise. Thanks again," Llew said in an octave so deep, Shane could feel it in his chest. He held up Shane's business card as he said it, and spun on his heel to leave.

Shane watched him walk away. Damn. That was a big man. Shane bet the big man could handle his own in and out of the bedroom. He'd always loved the strong, silent type. So many men these days talked and griped almost as much as the ladies. It'd be nice to spend time with someone who enjoyed calm and quiet as much as he did.

"Dude. Come the hell on!" Jack snapped again, forcing Shane to cut his ogling off before Llew turned the corner out of sight.

See what I mean.

"Jessie, did anyone come by today applying for a job?" Shane asked, bursting through the trailer door. He had one ear trained on her response while the other was tilted towards his hand-held radio, listening to his foreman's directions to where he'd stashed the architect's blueprints.

"Yes. Three people actually. One man and two women. I know you were hoping for more, but give it some time.

We've only had the ad up for a couple days." Jessie swiveled around in her chair and dug out three manila files from one of her many file cabinets. The woman was a stickler about leaving items in their assigned place. She was meticulous, and her organization skills bordered on OCD. No one dared mess with her side of the trailer. Shane's desk; however, had a nonexistent system. His motto was to ask someone else where something was.

"What was the guy's name who applied?" Shane tried to sound nonchalant as he pushed aside numerous papers on his drafting table.

"Um. Llewellyn Garden… no… Gardner," Jessie said, flipping through the application. "I flagged this one."

"Hire him," Shane said, hurrying back to the door, trying to hide his excitement at the possibility of seeing Llewellyn in worn jeans riding low from the weight of a tool belt hanging on his strong hips.

"Shane Jr. there's something you should know about that applicant. I had him flagged for no hire. I mean, he has good experience and references checked out but—"

"Sounds good. Call him today before he accepts a job someplace else," Shane said, cutting off whatever else his office manager was going to say. He was half out the door, his arms weighed down with rolls of paper. Jack was radioing him; barking about the hold up on the blue prints. "I gotta go Jess. Just call him, now."

"Shane, there's something you don't know about Mr. Gard—"

Shane let the trailer door slam behind him. Jessie could go on and on about the smallest things sometimes. Not everyone was so attentive to detail. Llewellyn probably had bad handwriting and Jessie deemed him as a no hire. As long as the man worked hard and showed up every day, Shane could use him.

"What the hell took you so long?"

"Damn, Jack. I was gone fifteen minutes." Shane dropped the rolls down on the workbench, and his foreman quickly began to unroll them and pin down the edges. "I was talking to Jessie about our new hire."

"Oh yeah. You got guys already?" One of the crew leaders asked.

They were all standing around waiting on the specs of the project they were getting ready to begin. Shane was going to need two new crews on the new project and one to finish the current one. This would be a two-year project on the outskirts of town, and he was going to oversee it personally. A three building office park, and each state-of-the-art structure would be four stories high. This was a major victory for the company. He'd bid on it and won out over seven other construction companies. His father had beamed with pride, and boasted about Shane's brilliance all over town. Now he had to make sure the job was done right.

CHAPTER SIXTEEN

Llew was on his one hundred and thirtieth push up when his cell phone rang. He glanced at the screen, smiling a little when he saw his brother's number. He stood up and took a couple of cleansing breaths before hit the speaker phone, not wanting his sweaty face to drip on the screen. "What's up, bro?"

"Hey Llew. Nuttin much, man. How come you didn't call me? You didn't take the truck either." Leslie's voice was tinged with disappointment.

"It's all good. I found a place as soon as I got here." Llew hurriedly tried to put his brother at ease. He knew Leslie would be worried about him, but Llew had to find his own way, a way that didn't involve hurting his brother in the process.

"Really. Are you at a hotel, or what?"

"Naw. I helped this nice lady with her bags when she was coming out of the market, and as I walked her home she told me she had a renovated room for rent. She's great, Leslie. The room is really big and comfortable. The rent is fair." He hesitated slightly. "She doesn't know um… um." Llew couldn't even finish the sentence.

"Llew that's not any of her business."

"Maybe it is."

"Like hell. 'Are you a registered sex offender?' is not a question I've ever seen on a rental application," Leslie argued.

"I just don't want to feel like I'm hiding anything. I'd rather tell her myself than see her get blindsided in the store by some nosy friend, ya know? I'm almost scared to get any furniture for this place. I might have to haul it right back out of here when she finds out the truth about me." Llew went to his fridge and pulled out a bottle of water and the leftover stew Ms. Pat gave him when he got in last night.

"You paid your rent for this month, yea? Well then she can't just put you out, Llew."

"She'll just give me my money back and send me on my way."

"Damn you're pessimistic."

"Eight years in prison will do that to you." *Damnit.* That just came out. Leslie was suddenly quiet, only a sorrowful sigh came across the line, and Llew hated to make his brother feel sad for him. "That was stupid. I'm sorry, Les."

"You can say how you feel, Llewellyn. You have every right to vent."

"Let's talk about something else," he said, shifting the phone to the other ear while popping the Tupperware bowl into the microwave to heat. "I already got a part-time job stocking merchandise in the general store a couple nights a week and I think I may have found a full-time job at Smith's Construction."

"Damn, dude. You only been there one day." Leslie laughed. "You get that shit from Dad, Llew. He was never one to twiddle his thumbs. He got stuff done, and fast."

Llew smiled at that. He prayed he really could be like his old man. Releasing his own breath, he had a sick feeling his parents were turning over in their graves at the clusterfuck he'd made of his life.

"So what about the full-time gig?"

"That's at Smith's Construction. I put in an application this morning. I was honest about the criminal background stuff, but I'm hoping it'll be overlooked. I mean it's construction, not bank management. I ran into the owner last night, and he seemed kinda... " Llew stroked his goatee thinking about the way Shane Jr. looked at him on the dark street corner and no doubt the way Llew looked back at him. "He was maybe, um... "

"Uh oh. What's all the humming and hawing? Was he hitting on you or something?" Leslie chucked a bit, but stopped suddenly when Llew didn't respond. "Holy shit! Was he hitting on you, Llew, and offered you a job? Oh my god. Are you exchanging sexual favors for work now?"

Leslie's laughter was contagious, and Llew found himself actually laughing, too. It sounded odd to his own ears but it felt real good in his spirit. He used to laugh with his brother all the time, and he hadn't realized how much he missed that. "Fuck you, man. Hell no, I'm not screwing for a job. I think the offer was genuine. He just looked at me a certain way."

"Well, he's either really brave and can fight like John Cena, or he's suicidal. If he was giving a guy your size googly eyes, that can be dangerous. He couldn't possibly

141

know you're gay just by meeting you." Leslie paused. "Unless… you were giving him some rhythm too, Llewellyn." His brother sing-songed Llew's name at the end.

"Okay, this conversation is over," Llew grumbled. "I gotta go shower anyway. I'm working tonight; well just to train, and I want to go to the town meeting before I go in."

"Town meeting. Oh god. Not those things. Why are you going to that? It's just a forum for the older folk to gripe and bitch about any and everything."

Llew pulled down one of his two towels hanging in the closet and draped it over his shoulder. "I might can find out some information, get a feel for the people, ya know. Can't hurt."

"Cool. Call me tomorrow. Oh, and I'll come by this weekend with the truck and bring you your bed and some extra furniture I got around the house."

"Yeah. That sounds good."

"A'ight bro."

Llew got in the shower without bothering to turn on the light in the bathroom, opting instead to leave the door open. He'd do everything he could to help conserve in Ms. Pat's home. Maybe she'd overlook any negative comments about him if he made himself a good tenant. He tilted his head forward and let the hot water beat on the tension-filled spots in his neck. He had it on as hot as he could stand it. Despite the horrifically under-sized shower stall, the water pressure was fantastic. It was almost like a massage. He groaned at the wonderful feeling, the sound emerging from his throat sounding almost provocative. It made him think of pretty brown eyes, and a strong, square jaw with full, sexy lips. Lips that were light pink and soft looking. Llew couldn't help but fantasize that kissing Shane would be like kissing cotton candy. He licked his own lips, desperately missing the feeling of a man. Eight fucking years. He stomach fluttered at the idea of being close and intimate with Shane Jr. The man's exterior was the picture-perfect image of a smooth operator, but Llew knew there was a bobcat clawing inside that gorgeous man. An animal that needed taming. Just that fast Llew's dominant side reared its anxious head.

Oh jesus. Llew could picture it. Could see their strong bodies pressed together, muscles flexing against each other. Shane Jr. wasn't diesel but he was certainly manual labor built. He no doubt had velvety-smooth, ivory skin covering that armor. *Damn.* Llew groaned again, running his hand down the ridges on his stomach. He could taste him… *oh my god…* Shane would taste like the sweetest honey. An addictive taste.

Llew could feel the pulsating in his groin as he thought about Shane, but as he pulled and stroked the flaccid appendage, nothing happened. He was horny, beyond horny, but there was no life down there. He poured some conditioner in his palm and squeezed the head of his cock, focusing on the most sensitive part of him. He cupped his balls and massaged them, every couple seconds giving them a firm tug like he used to love to do. Nothing.

"Fuck. Come on, damnit." Llew grunted harshly. He rested his forehead on the cool tile, while he continued the tug and stroke combination. He pictured Shane's beautiful face, pictured his sexy smile and cool demeanor. The feeling was there, the urge to take him and make him his, but in the back of his mind was that word... *rapist*. Shane would never want a rapist.

He gave up. His chest heaved with the exertion, with exhaustion, with disappointment. Llew balled up his fists and just stopped himself from slamming them repeatedly into the tiles. The muscles in his arms flexed as he stared down at his cock. Would he never make love again?

"Ms. Pat. I'm going in to town for the meeting in about an hour. I got time to fix the handle on your bathroom door if you want," Llew said, from the other side of the island in Ms. Pat's kitchen.

"Oh that'd be great, Llewellyn. Thank you, honey. I swear if Jimmy Jr. breaks another thing in this here house, I'ma' start a tab for his daddy." She chuckled, pulling off her apron. "I guess I best get cleaned up myself. You walking into town or do you want me to drive us? I'm going too."

"Sure. I'll pull some weeds in your garden while I wait."

"Llewellyn you're a godsend." She put the cake lid on the pound cake she'd just finished and scurried out of the room.

It only took Llew ten minutes to finish replacing the doorknob. He put the large toolbox back in the garage; grabbed a pair of garden gloves and a lawn bag, and went to work pulling some of the overgrown ground cover. He wasn't just doing this to try to suck up, either. He really did like Ms. Pat. She reminded him of his mom's sister who

144

passed a year after his parents. She was kind and sweet, just like her, and always had something baking. She believed baked goods were like balm to the wounded soul. He hoped Ms. Pat saw the good that was in him. Llew had just tied the bag up and set it on the curb for the end of the week's garbage pickup when his landlady came out the front door. Llew quickly offered his arm, and walked her down the stairs and to her car.

"I tell you, hon. I'm not looking forward to this here meeting. I've heard the gossips got something big cooking." She huffed, sliding into the driver's seat. Llew closed her door and went around to the passenger side. He heaved a weary breath and decided it was probably best to tell her now, since the gossip being cooked up was no doubt about him. "I'm only going because I want to know if they approved our petition to rebuild the town park. I don't have anywhere to take Jimmy Jr. when the summer rolls back around."

"Ms. Pat."

"We got over a hundred and fifty signatures. That should be more than enough, don'tcha think, Llewellyn?" She prattled on while she drove them into town, completely oblivious to his inner chaos. He only had a few minutes, so Llew needed to man up fast.

Llew cleared his throat. His deep voice raspy in the confined space. "Ms. Pat I need to tell you something before the meeting."

"Sure honey," she said, not bothering to look at him.

"Um. I um." Llew felt his breathing pick up and his nerves take over. *Shit. Calm down.* "I wanted to tell—"

"Goodness, honey. What's wrong? You're turning all red." She patted his hand while she steered the big Town Car with her other hand. "I know you're kinda shy. Is it you don't want to go to the meeting? Because you don't have ta."

Llew brought a shaking hand up to his mouth, coughing a little at the bile rising in the back of his throat. He was realizing that he really cared what Ms. Pat thought of him. It made him sick to think that this sweet woman would think him a disgusting pedophile. "N-no ma'am, that's not it. I, um. Y-you didn't ask at the time when you offered me the room, so I didn't think about it — " He paused. He wouldn't lie. He blinked back the emotion welling up in his eyes. "I didn't want to tell you because it's not who I am, but I um… I was in prison for a while before I came to Henderson to start over. The people in my hometown were… they were… they didn't want me back there. So I had to leave. I had to leave my brother so his business wouldn't suffer."

Ms. Pat had parked in one of the parking spaces in front of the Henderson Recreation Building. She turned off the car and turned her body to face him. "Oh honey. Is that all? Is that what's got you so shaken up?" She reached over and cupped Llew's chin, turning him to face her. "Well, darlin' I did a year in a jail when I was twenty-two."

Llew's eyes widened and it made Ms. Pat tilt her back laughing heartily. "It was a college demonstration that went wrong and I ended up assaulting a police officer." She shook her head, looking off wistfully, wearing a smile that looked like she enjoyed reflecting back on those days. "I was so young and full of spirit back then."

146

"I did a little more than a year, Ms. Pat."

She patted Llew's hand again. "We all get into sticky wickets in life, Llewellyn. The trials the good Lord has put you through have only made you into the man you are today. And I know you're a good man. I can see it in everything you do and say. Taking time out of your young day to help a lady carry her bags. Now you may catch some mess from some of these old fogies in this town, but you won't from me, ya hear?"

"Yes, mam," Llew whispered, his heart clenching at the genuine friendship Ms. Pat exhibited toward him. He actually felt things might be alright... but he couldn't have been more wrong.

CHAPTER SEVENTEEN

Shane sat next to Jack in the town's main rec room, where they held bingo twice a week, waiting on the town meeting to start. He rolled his eyes as he watched some of the people walk in as if they owned the world. Just because they had their last name on a pew in the church, or because their last name matched one of the founders of Henderson, they believed that they owned a piece of America. It really made Shane sick.

"Stop looking like that." Jack popped him with the small program listing the meeting order, admonishing him. "What's got up in your craw these last couple days?"

"Nuttin man. Jim Sr. just came in with his stuck-up wife."

"Susan's not stuck-up, maybe just a tad frigid."

"Please. You couldn't pull a quarter outta her ass with a tractor."

Jack busted out laughing, earning a swat from his mother on the other side of him.

"Ow, Ma. It wasn't me, it was Shane."

"Boy, you been using that same excuse since ya'll was boys in the school yard. Now hush up, the mayor's coming in," she said, then turned back to her best friend on her other side.

"Do you know Jim Sr. is still giving me shit about doing the construction on his momma's room?" Shane hissed close to Jack's ear. He saw Jim Sr. sit closer to the front, but not before giving him a dirty look.

"You finished that room over her garage already. You practically did that whole thing on your own."

"Yeah, well. He damn sure wasn't doing it. She was tired of his excuses about how busy he was, or how all his men were on other jobs. So, I did it for her."

"Nothing wrong with that, man. Forget about him, okay? I doubt that's his problem anyway. He's probably more concerned that you keep beating him out on every job you two bid on. He's stuck doing small residential jobs, and now you got that big office park gig. He's no doubt feeling the pinch. Cut him some slack."

"Maybe you're ri—" Shane stopped mid-sentence when he saw Ms. Pat walking in on Llew's arm. There was no way in hell he'd forgotten about him. He couldn't wait for the big, beautiful man to start working for him so he could see him every day, maybe even come up with a reason for him to have to come to his office regularly. He watched Llew gingerly sit Ms. Pat down in her seat, and Shane smiled as Ms. Pat held her head high while the other women gawked at her fine escort. Llewellyn retreated to the back of the room and leaned against the wall by the door. Many eyes were on the new face in town, but Shane watched for a whole other reason. He wanted Llewellyn Gardner.

Jack looked back at him and then followed Shane's line of sight. "Damn, dude. Put your tongue back in your mouth. You're about as bad as these other hens."

Shane ignored his friend, keeping his focus on the man's towering presence. Llew couldn't help but command attention. His tousled, unkempt hair and dark beard gave him a dangerous appearance. But it was that huge, muscular body that made whoever looked at him think nasty thoughts. A few of the high school girls were throwing flirty looks his way and giggling amongst each other, but Llew paid no attention. He was looking over the program, oblivious to the effect he had on Shane... hell, on the whole damn room.

The mayor cleared his throat at the podium and all heads turned and focused on him but Shane. As soon as Llew looked up, Shane was looking him dead in his expressive eyes. He saw Llew's chest expand and fall with his gasp. Shane gave him a small smile but Llew's face was completely impassive. It was those dark eyes that didn't lie. Llew was thinking a few impure thoughts himself. Damn if it didn't make Shane's cock throb in his faded jeans. He felt a sharp elbow in his arm jerking his attention back to his friend.

"What?" Shane hissed.

Jack glared at him. "You're making fucking noises. Stop watching him. Turn around and pay attention, they're getting ready to discuss the office park."

Shane looked up at the podium and saw one of the city council members for the zoning committee was up at the front.

"We're proud to announce that Smith's Construction will begin work on the new office park next week." There was some clapping around the room, and Shane got a couple claps on the back from people sitting close by. "This building will house several medical offices, legal offices and various other office spaces for lease. There will be a few eateries on the bottom levels, as well."

"Like what?" Jim Sr. interrupted.

"Whoever leases the space," Councilman Thomas responded quickly, then moved on. "Smith Jr. asked that if possible, townsfolk avoid taking Sykes Ave; using Baldwin as an alternative to avoid traffic jams while construction is under way. That's for your safety and that of his crew. If you have any questions, Smith Jr. and his foreman are here to answer them.

Shane and Jack both stood and waited to see if there would be any questions. One of Jim Sr.'s guys stood on the other side of the room and faced them.

"You have a question, James?" Jack asked.

"Are you guys hiring some temporary crew for the new job?" the slender man asked. He looked like he wanted the floor to swallow him up right where he stood. Asking that question while his current boss was only a few seats away had to be nerve-wracking, but James had a family to take care of and with Jim Sr.'s workload decreasing, he understood where the man was coming from.

"I'll be damned," Shane whispered for only Jack to hear. "Tell him come on by."

"We are James. We could use good, experienced men like yourself," Jack said in his strong "foreman voice." "Come on by the office. We've posted an ad in the paper for Sunday's listing, but you can all pass the word around." They stood for a few more seconds, but when no one else spoke, they sat down, and Councilman Thomas took over the mic.

"Okay folks. Remember the construction zoning and the detour. This concludes the—"

"Well how long are we supposed to use the detour? Some of us have work out of town, and taking Baldwin will take us five minutes out of our way." Jim Sr. stood with one hand angrily clutching his ball cap.

Councilman Thomas glared right back at him. "Well, hopefully not too long. Knowing Smith Jr., I'm sure the construction will be done quickly and efficiently." Thomas smirked at a seething Jim Sr., and hit the wood with his gavel.

"This concludes the business of the planning and zoning committee." Thomas took his seat in one of the chairs behind the podium. Jack smirked at Shane, surely catching the dig at Jim Sr. and his inability to ever finish a job on time.

Representatives of different departments of city hall took their turns at the podium. Some addressed mundane issues that had Shane playing a few rounds of Diner Dash on his cell phone, and some dealt with more interesting topics, like the city's annual spring jamboree. The high school kids were there to ask if they could put together a committee for the entertainment this year, which was quickly voted on and approved, so long as the high school principal agreed to oversee it.

The mayor finally took to the podium to bring the hour-long meeting to a close. Just when he was about to dismiss them, Mrs. Potts; the sheriff's wife stood and interrupted his closing remarks.

"Mayor Johnson, I'm sure you're not going to dismiss these good townspeople without alerting them to the new threat that has come to Henderson."

The mayor turned to her, his bald spot glistening with sweat as he pulled at his already loose necktie. "I'm not aware of any threat, Mrs. Potts."

"So your office has not been notified of the newly registered sex offender right here in your own county?"

The room exploded into gasps and harshly whispered chatter. Women clutched at their throats while the men turned and grumbled to whoever was closest to them. One of the seniors of the community stood up, his wife pulling at his jacket. "What the heck is going on, Mayor Johnson?"

"Everyone please settle down. There is no threat in Henderson. I assure you." The mayor held his hands up in a placating manner, trying to gain back control of the room.

"Well is there a sex offender here or not?" the man asked with more authority in his voice.

The mayor looked like he was ready to run, but luckily Sheriff Potts stood, and approached the podium to take over. The mayor could have kissed him for cutting him off the hook.

"Everyone quiet down so I can speak." The sheriff's deep voice cut off the ruckus and everyone quieted down. His hand was in the air waiting for complete silence. Sheriff Potts had gone to school with Shane's father. He knew the man was honest and fair, so Shane was eager to hear what he had to say.

Jack turned to Shane, his eyes revealing that he didn't like where this was going. Shane looked back at him similarly. He turned to look for Llew's reaction, and what he saw had his gut seizing. Llew looked like he'd just witnessed an exorcism. His eyes were wide and filled with fear. Sweat was beading up on his smooth forehead and a trickle had leaked down the side of his face into his collar.

"There is a registered sex offender in Henderson. I've been in contact with the probation officer for this individual and according to their office this person has been in full cooperation with to the conditions of release," the sheriff said, calmly.

"Release!" the old man yelled. "As in prison?!"

"Calm down! I have no reason to believe this individual is a threat to the community." The sheriff raised his voice and eyed the room, letting them know he was in control.

"I'd like to start a petition that this person not be able to take up residence here," the old man added before the sheriff could continue. Many people began to yell out their agreement.

Shane watched Llewellyn with a sympathetic heart, because he knew without a doubt that he was the offender they were arguing about. Llewellyn's shaky fist went up to his mouth as he watched the people of the town rage on about him. Shane thought for a minute that he was going to throw up. His shoulders slumped and his eyes searched the room frantically, as if waiting for someone to point him out.

"Mr. Rockford, take your seat! No such petition will be voted on because it's illegal. This person is allowed to reside wherever he chooses, as long as he obeys the law and complies with his probation. And so far he has." The sheriff noted.

"Well who is it?" the senior demanded, with a chorus of "Yeah"s coming in response to his question.

Llew's whole face, spirit; his entire soul crumbled right before Shane's eyes. *Oh no.*

"I'm not permitted to tell you that. The information is public record; you are welcome to look it up yourselves. But I ask that if you do, you don't contact this person. He has rights, and I will not accept the harassment of anyone in this county. I hope I'm making myself clear." Several people had pulled out their cell phones as if they couldn't possibly wait another second to find out who this deviant was.

Shane saw Llew turn and bolt out the door. The room was in such upheaval that no one had noticed but him and Jack.

"I know that look. Don't do it, Shane."

Shane was already up and out of his seat, his coat in one hand as he jogged to the door. He scanned the parking lot but he didn't see anyone. Llew could only have gone one way. He jogged up the sidewalk back towards the center of town. As soon as he turned the corner, he saw Llew's broad back turn down the narrow alley in between the library and Shirley's Cookin' Kitchen. He hurried to catch up, wondering where he could possibly be going since the alley was a dead end. Shane slowed his steps when he passed one of the dumpsters back there. He heard groaning and the sound of gagging, followed by dry heaving. *Jesus.* He was almost to the end of the dark alley, and he could see Llew bent over clutching his stomach. His back rose and fell as his stomach uselessly tried to rid itself of its contents. It held nothing but anguish now. He didn't think Llew knew he was there yet, and he felt like he was spying on a personal moment. Llew stood up straighter and rested both hands on the brick in front of him while he tried to catch his breath.

"Llewellyn." Shane tried to keep his voice soft, but it still scared the big man. He whirled around, his sad eyes nervously scanning the alley.

"What are you—" Llew raised one hand up, and backed further into the corner. "You can't... just stay... I'm not gonna hurt you."

"I know, Llewellyn. *I* followed *you* though." Shane stressed the "I" part as he walked closer. Llew looked like his legs were gonna give out, and it made Shane want to wrap his arms around him, but he stayed put.

"Let me guess. You're here to tell me I didn't get the job." He chuckled humorlessly. "I figured as much. They sent you to get rid of me, huh? Well do what you came to do. I won't fight you or hurt you." Llew turned back towards the wall, his entire body shaking as he fought to control himself. "I've never hurt anyone in my life," he whispered painfully.

Shane wasn't sure why yet, but he believed Llew. He truly did.

Shane timidly put his hand on the man's broad shoulder and gently turned his body to face him. He needed Llew to see his sincerity. "No, Llewellyn. I'm not here to get rid of you. I came to walk you home. Make sure you get there okay. You looked really upset, and um... I didn't want you to think that everyone in this town thought alike."

"You know the sheriff was talking about me right?" Llew's voice was so deep and gruff, probably due in part to the nervousness that had overtaken him, but most of it was just the man's timbre. It made Shane pause.

Shane had to clear his own throat. "Yes, Llewellyn."

Finally, Llew looked in his eyes. "You can call me Llew."

"Is that what everyone else calls you?" Shane smiled.

"Yes."

"Well I have to do something that sets me apart from the rest." Shane shrugged. "So, where you staying, Llewell?"

He thought he saw a faint smile on Llew's face, but the alley was dark. He hoped he could get Llewellyn to trust him; he was going to need a friend.

"I'm staying at Ms. Pat's. I rent a room there. At least I did," Llew said sadly.

"Come on, let's go." Shane nodded his head towards the entrance of the alley, and Llew fell in step with him. He loved how tall Llew was beside him. Shane was just a little over six feet but Llew had to be six four or six five. He could climb this man like the strong oak tree that he was. "So, you like the room?"

"Um. Yeah. It's real nice. Why?" Llew looked down at him, and Shane's stomach did that fluttering thing that happened whenever that intense gaze was on him.

"Well, I built it so I was just wondering," Shane said, teasingly.

"You do good work, Shane."

Shane wanted to stop right where they were and breakdance on the sidewalk. He loved the way his name sounded in that deep tone. He could listen to Llew talk all day and night… especially at night. "Thank you," he whispered.

They turned down Ms. Pat's street, surprised it only took them a half-hour to walk to that side of town. Shane wished it could've been longer. They were probably both glad that no one was out and about yet. Most everyone was probably still milling around the rec center arguing their points to whoever would listen. He knew inside that Llew was going to have a storm coming his way, and he hoped he was strong enough to withstand it. Maybe with the right man by his side, they could weather the storm together.

They were only a block away and they'd simply enjoyed walking shoulder to shoulder on the narrow sidewalk. The silence wasn't strained, it was peaceful and it allowed him to think about how he felt being in Llew's strong company. He felt safe with him.

CHAPTER EIGHTEEN

Shane called him Llewell because he wanted to be different from everyone else. Well he most certainly was. Llew thought he was home free at the town meeting. All the business had been wrapped up and the mayor was concluding; but of course, things were never easy for him. The sheriff's wife blew his presence wide open. By tonight everyone and their momma would know who he was and what he'd been accused of... including Shane. He wanted to believe Shane was different, but there was still some critical information Shane was missing: the exact nature of Llew's crime. The title of "sex offender" covered a broad spectrum of crimes. Of course, there were the more obvious crimes; like rape and sexual assault, but it also included kidnapping, peeping toms, perpetrators of incest, indecent exposure, hell, even public urination in some states.

Llew was wondering if he should just tell Shane, it couldn't hurt any worse than it already did. He was pretty sure Shane wasn't going to hire him, but he may have one friend in this town if he played his cards right. They were just a couple doors down from Ms. Pat's house when he saw her Town Car in the driveway along with a large F-350 that had ladders secured to the top of it.

"Um, Shane. You may not be interested in what I have to say, you may not care why I was in prison, but I want to be honest with you. I know people think every convict has an excuse for his crime, but like my father always told me, 'Excuses are like backsides. Everyone's got one and they all stink.' So I'm not looking to excuse my —"

Llew had to stop before he even got started with his explanation because Shane was laughing so hard.

"That wasn't meant to be funny," Llew said, staring at the handsome man.

"I'm sorry. I'm just... I'd never heard that before." Shane wiped the corner of his eyes. "Sounds like something my dad would say."

"Momma, I don't care that you think he's a nice guy, he's not staying here!" A loud male voice boomed through Ms. Pat's front screen door. "You think I'm gonna let a sex offender live with my elderly mother?"

Llew heard some dishes clanging and then Ms. Pat's usually soft voice was firm and loud. "I'll show you elderly if I go upside your head with this here frying pan."

"Momma this is crazy. I can't believe you are actually considering letting him stay here. He's a rapist! He actually took someone against their will! Forced them to have sex with him!"

Llew's knees gave out and he had to catch himself on the porch rail. He sat down on the top step and buried his head in his hands. He dragged his hands through his hair, squeezing his eyes shut against the pain. Pain in his head, his chest and in his heart. He'd give anything to have his big brother here right now. He pulled out his cell phone but his hands were shaking so bad he had to dial the number three times before he got it right. Ms. Pat was still arguing with her son while he listened helplessly. He put the receiver to his ear and listened to it ring several times before his brother's voice said he was busy and to leave a message. "L-Leslie can you call me, p-please. I need to talk to you, bro." Llew hung up and clutched the phone to his chest like it was a lifeline.

"Llewell."

Llew jumped at the sound of Shane's voice. He was still there, squatting next to him, his large hand on his shoulder. He looked into the beautiful brown eyes, wishing that he could take back everything about tonight. Llew just shook his head, his eyes watery and burning. "I swear on everything I know. On my parents' graves, Shane." He pleaded for the beautiful man to believe him. "I didn't rape my boyfriend. We were young and he freaked when his dad came in. I thought for so long that he'd take it back but he never — " Llew tried to control himself, tried to stop the shaking, the tears that flowed down his cheeks. Probably because he'd held those tears in for so long. Scared to cry in prison, now he couldn't stop them. "I loved him. I loved him so much, and he left me in there. Left me in — "

Llew gasped when he was pulled into a tight hug. Shane clung to him and let Llew have his moment. He squeezed Shane back, seizing the fabric of the thick jean jacket in his grip. "Shhh. Don't say anything else, Llewell. It's okay."

He felt Shane's hands rubbing up and down his back, the most comforting gesture he'd received in years. Shane's hot breath was on his neck, and it calmed him, warmed Llew deep inside. Shane murmured softly in his ear in that voice that sounded like an angel's. For just a few minutes, it felt like everything would really be okay. Until Llew heard the sirens, and saw the bright blue and red lights of

the sheriff's cruiser. Llew reluctantly pulled back from
Shane, who actually looked disappointed. He stood and
waited for the inevitable; he was about to be escorted from
the premises. Hell, maybe even slapped with a restraining
order. Even though he'd done nothing wrong, that'd never
stopped the law from screwing him.

"What is going on out here?" Ms. Pat's voice reached
them before she got to the screen door.

"Oh, Llewellyn, there you are. Honey, are you okay? I
was worried sick." She came through the door and reached
up to hug him around his neck. "Why'd you take off like
that, and Smith Jr., what are you doing here?"

"Momma, get away from him."

Llew looked up and saw a broad man with graying hair
at his temples and eyes just like Ms. Pat's pull her back
away from him. The man tucked her behind him as if she
were in danger. Although he was a foot shorter and
significantly smaller than Llew, he had no qualms about
getting up in his face. "You stay the hell away from my
mother, you... you... deviant."

"Oh my lord. Jim Sr., you stop this foolishness right
this instant. What is Sheriff Potts doing here?" she said,
twisting out of her son's grasp.

"I called him. I want this man out of here."

"Well that's not for you to say. This here is my house,
and he's paid his rent!" she yelled.

"Here." The man pulled out his thick black wallet and
unfolded several bills, throwing them at Llew's chest. He
watched them fall to the ground, his head hanging heavy
with self-hatred. He wouldn't dare confront this guy. He
couldn't and wouldn't violate his probation by getting into

any altercations. He'd keep his mouth closed like he was used to doing. "Rape has the highest rate of recidivism… a very difficult habit to break isn't that right, Luigellan?"

"Oh my god. Llewellyn, I'm so sorry. Jim you stop it. Stop it, right now!" Ms. Pat wrung her hands in her sweater. She suddenly looked older than her actual years, and Llew didn't want to be the source of her stress. Clearly, this was too much for her to handle.

He backed up from her seething son. "I'll just get my things," he said softly, turning to go around the side of the house where the stairs led to his once room. He noticed Shane's face was bright red and angry, and his body was strung tight. He didn't want him to get into any trouble either, especially not over him.

"Thank you for the walk, Shane. I appreciate it," Llew said shakily. "Can you point me towards the nearest hotel, please?" This night was a catastrophe. He knew now he'd never be able to get his life together, not unless he went to a big city like New York or Miami. A place where there were thousands of sex offenders and no one could even keep up with the registration. But it was going to take a while for him to get approval from his PO for another transfer. Llew loved everything about quaint small towns, but they couldn't be for him any longer. He had to live in a place where he'd be lost in the crowd, so no one would ever notice him. He thought of being so far away from Leslie, too, and it only made the pain crippling, so he stamped it down for now. He'd deal with one disappointment at a time.

"Your life after prison. It ain't gonna be easy Llew, but that don't mean you can't make it." He tried to remember

everything his counselor ever said to him, tried to hold onto those words for times like this.

"No. No Llewellyn, you're not leaving." Ms. Pat shuffled past her son. "Just go on up to your room, honey. I'll handle this mess, then you can come down for dinner and we'll talk, okay. Okay, Llewellyn?" She gently patted his cheek, and he managed to give her a slight nod, and what may have passed for a smile. With her hands on her hips, she turned and added, "Smith Jr., you go on up with him. I don't need you and Jim getting into it right now."

They both rounded the corner of the house just as the sheriff was walking up the walk to the porch to talk to Ms. Pat. Llew hoped she could handle it, but he wasn't optimistic… not yet. The sheriff might just talk her into giving him back his rent and sending him on his way. Most likely his probation officer had shared the details of his crimes with local law enforcement.

He took his key out, and had to try a couple times to get it in the lock. Shane's presence behind him was only slightly reassuring, but he was kind of waiting on him to drop a bomb on him, too. Llew went inside and flicked the light switch on the wall, illuminating his empty room. Well at least he didn't have any furniture to transport. He went to the closet, pulled his duffle bag from the top shelf, and started yanking down the few items of clothing he had hanging up, throwing them inside.

"Llewellyn, what are you doing? You heard Ms. Pat. You don't have to go. Jim don't run this house, she does. I know Ms. Pat, she's strong, and a great judge of character. If she's comfortable with you staying here, then it won't be long before everyone else gets comfortable, too. She's a big influence around here. Her father helped build this town. She's also my mom's best friend and my godmother, which is why me and Jim don't get along so well. I always picked up his slack when he fell short in the son department. All he likes to do is bitch and throw his name around, but he's all bark and no bite." Shane tugged on Llew's arm, stopping his packing. "Come here."

Llew sighed and stood back up. He brought both hands up and hooked them on the top of the doorframe, looking down at Shane. Something in Shane's eyes made him want to do anything for him, anything that would keep him looking at him like that. He watched as he came closer and closer until Shane's head was tilted up to look at him.

"Don't go okay?" he whispered, standing close enough that his breath ghosted over Llew's chin when he spoke. "Stay, please."

"Why?" Llew asked, his voice dark and full of hurt.

Shane shook his head and ran his hand through his hair. "I don't know yet. But... just don't go, alright. I need to get over to my parents' place for dinner, I'm already late. But, um. I'll see you at work tomorrow, seven sharp." Shane give a him a cute wink. "Don't be late either, your boss is a real ballbuster."

Llew ducked his head and smiled.

Shane backed up and snorted a startled breath. "Wow. You look so different when you smile." He pinched the bridge of his nose and shook his head like he was searching for the right words. "Not better... just different."

Llew watched him go, his spirits a little lighter since he hadn't lost his chance at the job he needed so much. He pushed his bag back in the closet, but didn't unpack. He went to the kitchen and got a bottle of water for his dry mouth. Looking around the room, he thought it looked so much better with Shane in it. He dropped down to the floor, glancing at his watch. He had an hour and half before he was supposed to be at the general store for his training. He doubted he was still employed, but he'd show up, nonetheless. When he contemplated his life now, he thought about Shane.

CHAPTER NINETEEN

Llew tucked his hands in his pockets while he walked the short distance back into town to the general store. It was late, and he was glad that most people in small-town USA didn't venture out past nine o'clock. He didn't want anything ruining his mood right now. Ms. Pat had been so sweet to him after the sheriff and her rat-bastard of a son finally left. The sheriff reasoned there was nothing he could do if Ms. Pat wanted him to stay. Jim finally left when the sheriff said his yelling was bordering on disturbing the peace.

He quietly ate his baked spaghetti and sweet potato pie with her while she rambled on about him not being ashamed of himself or letting people railroad him out of town. But the most important part, and the bit he'd keep tucked down in his soul for when he did meet adversity, came as he was leaving. He'd remember her saying the words to him before she went to her room for the night. "I really am fine with you being here Llewellyn. I'm safe here. Because when I look at you, son; I don't see no raping in your eyes." It took everything for Llew not to break down again. He kissed her lightly on her cheek, just like he used to do his mom and saw her to the stairs before he left for work.

He walked up to the automatic doors of the supply store and tapped softly on the glass. The store closed at nine p.m. and since it was ten, he had to wait for someone to let him in. He waited a few more seconds and knocked a little harder. A woman in an orange smock with her jet-black, pixie hair worn in a doll-like style was smiling on her way to the door, until she saw him. Her eyes widened and her hand flew to her mouth like she was looking at the devil himself. Llew shoved his hands deeper into his pockets and took a couple steps back from the door.

"Good evening. I'm supposed to start training today for the stocking job. Um, Mr. Graham hired me yesterday."

It was obvious she heard him through the thick glass door, but she still hadn't moved. Llewellyn lifted his head skyward, choosing not to bother with a small prayer this time. He wasn't sure god listened to him, anymore.

"Can you tell him I came by?" he turned to leave, but hadn't gotten very far when he heard his name called.

"Mr. Gardner I won't be needing you tonight," Mr. Graham said, through a cracked-open door.

"Did you want me to come back tomorrow?" Llew wasn't sure why he asked that, he knew damn well he was no longer needed.

"The position's been filled. I didn't realized my assistant had hired someone else." Mr. Graham didn't wait for Llew to respond, he simply closed the door and aimed his back to him. The lock clicking securely into place pinched his spirit, but it wouldn't break him. He headed back toward home, but decided to take the long way, needing the air to clear his head.

"Why the hell are we over here, man? If we get caught in an unauthorized area, we're both going to the hole."

"Chill out, Llew. I got some business to handle."

170

"Ace. I ain't with this." Llew looked around the corner, checking the blind spots while they stood in front of Big Waldo's office – that was the name for any high ranked commander. Captain Jessup was head of all the guards in the entire prison compound. He was a hard-ass and any time he was on the unit, he came either with five to ten of the guards, or with the Feds. The inmates made a loud siren sound when he moved through the compound. It meant someone was about to be apprehended, or their cell tossed; one or the other, but neither was good. Llew couldn't see anything through the small glass window to Jessup's office, since it was pitch dark. He dreaded the thought that Ace was going to try to break into it. Even if Llew was just the lookout, he was going down big time if they got caught. *"We're missing chow, Ace. Let's go."*

"Have I ever let you down, Llew?" Ace asked in his careless tone. He leaned against the rough brick with one Timberland boot propped against the wall. He had on his dark jeans and a starched white t-shirt showing through an open khaki button-up shirt. If a person saw Ace in the street right now, he'd blend right in. His hair was shaved in a tight buzz cut that looked soft to the touch. His blue eyes shone with mischief and Llew had to fight the urge to turn and walk away.

"No. I'm not saying that. I just don't feel right about this. What exactly are we doing?" Llew talked while he walked from one end of the hall to the other, checking the corners for anyone approaching. That was his job. To watch Ace's back at all times, and he was damn good at it. Ace never required him to do anything sexual, dangerous, or illegal. He kept Llew especially close to him and didn't

171

let him interact with too many of the other inmates. Llew was still considered a child molester, so he would be in danger if he were left alone.

"Shit. Red light, Ace." Llew sprinted back to where Ace was standing, and grabbed his arm, trying to yank him around the corner.

"Llew. Damn man, calm down. It's time you knew," Ace said, straightening his shirt back up.

"I know Captain Jessup is getting ready to turn that corner," Llew hissed.

"Yeah, and he's late too."

"What?" Llew said, dumbfounded.

Jessup strolled up the hall with all the power and prestige that he possessed, his thick chest stretching the front of his dark blue suit, his dress shoes making a loud tapping sound on the dingy linoleum floor. Llew took in the man's intimidating appearance. His jet-black hair was slicked back with god knows how much product. His green eyes glowered at them under the florescent lighting as he strolled right up to Ace and gripped the back of his neck, pulling him into a hard and hungry kiss.

Llew's mouth dropped open as he watched Captain Jessup devour his leader… his friend.

Jessup came up for air, his eyes glazed over as he nipped and licked at Ace's mouth. "Baby. Come on let's eat, we're starving," Ace said to Jessup between nips.

After a few seconds more, Jessup finally looked in Llew's direction. "How you doing, Gardner? Mike told me he was bringing you over today, I brought you Mexican. You like quesadillas?"

Ace walked in the medium-sized office right behind Jessup, propped his hip up on the desk, as Jessup dropped down in his chair, and started unloading the bag of food that quickly flooded the office with a delicious aroma.

"Did you bring that red sauce I like?"

"Of course, and I got those tortilla chips too." Jessup leaned in for another long kiss before adding, "How was your class today?"

Llew stared at Big Waldo as if he'd never seen him before. Looking at him like this... he hadn't. Had never seen him calm, likable and charming, domestic even. When he looked at Ace, he sported a smile that a man only wore when he was in love. But that was fuckin' unreal. He'd heard of guards receiving sexual favors, sneaking things to the inmates for money, but never at this level. Not with a prison official. Ace and Big Waldo were in love. Now it all made sense. This was why Ace could move around freely; do and arrange the things he did.

"So, Gardner." Jessup turned to him and noticed Llew hadn't touched his food. "Eat up. What? You not hungry?"

"He's probably still a little shocked, babe. He didn't know." Ace winked at him.

"Well shit. I guess he is. Its fine Gardner, go on and eat before it gets cold."

As Llew ate like a soldier in boot camp who had only ten minutes for chow, Jessup informed him that his work transfer was being granted. Llew had just turned it in two hours ago. It took weeks for an inmate to change jobs. He wanted to leave the laundry room and work in the library attached to the woodworking classrooms. That way he'd be allowed to go in there and build when he wasn't busy in the library.

"Thank you," Llew said around a mouthful of steak and shrimp quesadilla. He couldn't believe any of this was happening. Jessup turned on the television in his office and they watched an NBA playoff game while they ate. Jessup and Ace talked like they did this every night, like Jessup had just come home from work and was having dinner with his partner. Ace asked him how things were going on his home renovations and if he remembered his appointment with his allergist today. Fuckin' surreal. Once they finished the game, it was getting close to the time they needed to get back to their wing.

Ace stood and walked Llew to the door. "Wait for me at the end of the hall. We need some alone time."

Llew nodded and turned to leave.

"Gardner, you let Mike know if you need to see me. My man trusts you, so you're alright with me."

With another head nod, Llew took up his post at the corner like he was told. He rubbed his stomach, grinning at the awesome meal he'd just had, and how everyone else just ate burnt grilled-cheese sandwiches on bread thicker than your hand and watery tomato soup. It was a given he was to keep his mouth shut about what he'd witnessed, and he was more than fine with that, because having Big Waldo on his side just might make this place halfway tolerable until his release.

CHAPTER TWENTY

Llew pulled on his hand-me-down steel toe boots, tying them tight around his ankles. It was five minutes after six. He'd already been up for a two hours. He done crunches and pushups for an hour, and jogged the second. After a long, hot shower and a useless attempt at getting his cock to work, he was almost ready for his new job. With his tool belt at his feet, he stared out the window as daylight broke through the morning dusk. The knock at the door that led into Ms. Pat's house had him frowning in that direction. *What's she doing at my door this hour?* He opened the door and Ms. Pat had a wrapped sandwich in one hand and a large brown paper bag in the other. But it was the smile that was the most welcome.

"Morning Llewellyn. Smith Jr. told me on his way out last night that you were starting on his crew this morning. So I thought you could use a bacon and egg sandwich; something to stick to your bones until lunch. Annnnnd," she sang, holding up the brown bag. "I put you two meatloaf sandwiches in here, some fruit, and of course a piece of pie."

Llew gave her a large, genuine smile and reached out for the sandwiches first. "Ms. Pat, you didn't need to do that. This is too much."

"Oh, nonsense. Gave me something to do with my morning," she said, looking around his still empty room.

"Do you need help with getting some furniture, Llew? Betsy owns the consignment store on Andrews. I could ask her what she's got over there. Did... did you sleep on the floor, Llewellyn?"

"It's okay. My brother is coming this weekend with my bed and some other furniture. I'm fine sleeping on the floor for now," Llew said, before taking a large bite of the steaming sandwich. Damn it was delicious. The bacon was crisp and the egg scrambled just right, with cheese on top. *Thank you lord for this wonderful lady. I don't deserve her kindness.*

"Oh, good. That's a relief. Is he coming Saturday or Sunday?"

"Saturday afternoon."

"That'd be fine. I'll make a dinner fit for kings. Doing all that hauling, I'm sure you boys will have worked up a hearty appetite." She laughed, walking back towards the door rambling about going to the market for "Potatoes, stock for my dumplins and hmm, maybe—" She stopped suddenly, twirling like she'd just thought of something. "I think I have a pretty decent-sized air mattress in the attic. You can go check when you get home. I have bingo tonight and I'll spread the word on the good handiwork you've been doing in my home here, see if anyone needs some stuff done."

Instead of arguing that no one would dare let him in their home; or that'd he had no use for an airbed, he just nodded his head, making her as pleased as punch. He had no clue how that woman kept all those things sorted in her head.

"I best get back downstairs. Little Jimmy be here soon. Have a good day, Llewellyn. And you tell Smith Jr. he'd better not work you too hard, or he'll be grounded from my cakes for a month."

"Yes, ma'am." Llew let loose a light chuckle, and closed and locked his door behind her. He needed to go if he was going to be on time. He threw his tool belt in his backpack and left through his side door. When he got to the metal gate, Ms. Pat's son was getting out of his truck in the driveway; his little boy leaping out of the back, and bounding up to Llew.

"Hey, Mr. Llew." His little face wore a milk mustache and a look of innocence that only kids possessed.

"Morning, pal." Llew kept his eyes off Jim Sr., hurrying to get through the gate before he approached. He turned down the sidewalk, not looking back.

It took Llew twenty minutes to walk to the job site. Tomorrow he'd leave a little earlier. He wasn't scheduled to work until seven, but it looked good if he was there by six-thirty. There were men all over the place. Some leaning against the trucks, others standing around. But no one was working. Several heads turned in his direction, but Llew kept his head high, just like Ms. Pat told him to. The owner had hired him; he'd have to prove himself to these guys. Just like on any crew, the bosses did the hiring and firing, not the laborers.

Llew wasn't sure which way to turn; so he headed towards the trailer, just in case he had some paperwork to complete first. Before he could reach the first step, the man that was with Shane at the movies opened the door. His eyes widened before he schooled his expression. With his large hand stuck out in Llew's direction, he gave a curt nod. "I'm Jack Truman, foreman. Glad to have you aboard, Llew." Llew shook his hand, matching Jack's strength with his own. "I'm gonna get these fools assigned, then I'll be back in. Jessie has some paperwork for you first though, so go on inside."

Jack leaped down the stairs and walked towards the guys, barking at them to shut up and get over to where he stood. They grumbled and talked trash, making Jack throw his head back and laugh at the ribbing thrown his way. It looked like the man ran a tight ship but he wasn't a bastard of a boss.

Llew ducked into the trailer, looking around at the three desks positioned at the far end. There were drafting boards on one side and a row of file cabinets stood opposite them. A woman stood in front of one the cabinets with her back to him; her shiny black combat boots laced up over her black tights. Her trendy turquoise and gray sweater-dress tapered in at her small waist and stopped mid-thigh. With sandy brown hair pulled up into a high bun, and curly tendrils strewn about, she looked nothing like a contractor's assistant, more like a buyer for Forever 21.

"Excuse me, Jessie?"

Llew's voice must've been too deep inside the small space, because Jessie jumped high enough to almost hit the celling; and the files flew out of her hands, scattering across the floor. She clutched her hand to her heart, gasping. "Oh god. You scared me. You're - You're Llewellyn, right?"

"Yes. I filled out an application the other day. Shane. I mean, Mr. Smith told me to come in this morning." Llew stammered. He backed up as far as he could, because Jessie wasn't looking as friendly as she did when he was here filling out his application. Before, the woman couldn't have been more helpful. Now she watched him with narrowed eyes, most likely making sure Llew kept his distance. He needed to get out of this trailer with her in here alone. His counselor told him to be mindful of the situations he put himself in. These men didn't know him, all they knew was what was on paper and what gossip was milling around town.

"I got your papers ready, they're over there on the table." She pointed to the oblong table in the corner, on the far opposite side of the trailer.

Llew adjusted his backpack and picked up the papers. "I'll just fill them out outside."

"Okay," she said, quickly.

When he reached for the door, it opened before he grabbed the knob, and Shane stood there smiling at him as if he'd been waiting to see him. Oh, how he hoped that were true. "Hi. Llewell. I'm glad you made it. You got all your papers done?"

"I was just heading outside to fill them out."

Shane's head jerked back in surprise; a slight frown creasing his brow as he peaked around Llew's broad shoulder to look at his assistant. "That's silly, they might fly away. You can sit right here and fill them out." Shane's boots were loud as he walked across the floor. He pulled off his black skullcap and ran his hand through his wayward hair. His jeans were well worn and fit him just right. He had on a navy blue flannel shirt under a puffy black vest. But it was the low-riding tool belt that had

Llew's heart pumping harder in his chest. Nothing sexier than a well-built man in a tool belt. He stopped staring, and sat down to complete the tax forms.

"Jess, can you get us a couple cups of coffee, please?"

"Sure." She hurried into the other room, and Llew felt Shane's hand on his shoulder before he bent down, putting his cheek way to close to his.

"You okay, Llewell?" He whispered, very close to his ear.

Llew had to clear his throat before he could answer. "I'm good." He kept his eyes downcast, focusing on his forms, because if he turned his head, his lips would've brushed Shane's cheek.

"You'll be with me on the new site. Is that alright with you?"

"You're the boss."

Shane huffed an indignant sound before adding, "Not always."

Before Llew had time to figure out what Shane meant by that, Jessie was setting a cup of coffee in front of him.

Shane had watched Llewellyn the entire morning, except for when he had to leave the site to meet with the architect. From the moment he'd walked into his trailer and seen Llew standing there in faded jeans and a long-sleeved long john shirt under his thick camel Carhartt, he hadn't been able to keep his eyes off him. He was so gorgeous. Those expressive eyes told Shane that Llew wanted him too, but was scared to death. When he'd bent down next to

Llew's ear, he'd caught a whiff of his deodorant and it made him want to bury his face in his underarm.

Right now, it looked like his foreman had moved Llew from traffic control to unloading and distributing materials, he was currently erecting concrete forms for the scaffolding. Jack must've gotten more information on Llew's work experience, because that job required a certain level of knowledge and skill to do right. It also required him to work closely with the other guys. Shane noticed that his crew wasn't communicating with Llew and it'd caused a couple of problems. It was Jack's business to handle those issues and Shane didn't override his foreman's authority.

"Tony! Joe! Get your asses down here!" Jack yelled, moving around the half-built scaffold. "What is the deal with you two? Didn't you hear Llew say to hold on to that two by four before you released it? Are you trying to kill someone?" Jack barked at his guys.

Shane cringed when he saw the board in question clip Llew on the side of his hard hat. If he hadn't acted quickly, the board would have knocked him out, hard hat or not. Llew was standing off to the side, his hand squeezing and releasing the back of his neck as if he were trying to calm himself. Shane wouldn't intervene, but god knows he wanted to go over there and tell those guys they could pick up their last checks at the end of the week. When Llew turned back around, he met Shane's eyes. *Damnit.* He knew the man was strong, but the treatment he was receiving at the hands of the crew was bordering on ridiculous. How could Llew possibly work on a site where he couldn't trust the men to have his back? That's how injuries and casualties happened on job sites.

"He should speak up then. Not that anyone cares what he's saying, but I didn't hear him, Jack!" Tony yelled.

"Well maybe you should carry your ass home until you can hear. Go on! Get the hell off my site!" Jack barked, throwing his hand over his shoulder.

"What the hell? Are you serious?"

"Do I look serious?" Jack stepped closer to make his point.

Tony threw his hard hat to the ground, stomping off towards where they'd parked their vehicles. He knew better than to go to Shane. During all the years Jack had been Shane's foreman, he'd never reversed one of the man's decisions.

"I need this scaffold done today. Let's go! Daylight's burning." After they saw what happened to Tony, everyone quickly got back to work. This time working as a crew, like they were supposed to. By lunchtime, things were running smoothly.

Jack grabbed his lunch pail out of his truck and met Shane in the trailer. Jack started to talk before Shane could utter a word. "I know what you're about to say, so save it. Llew's gonna have to find his own footing. I can't send home every guy that gives him shit, but I think I made the point this morning, they know now that bullshit won't be tolerated on my site."

"I'm not disputing you did the right thing. I just—" Shane yanked his hat off, slamming it down on his desk. Jack took one of the chairs and pulled it up to the other side, and began pulling sandwiches out of his box. "What the hell was I thinking? They're gonna try to kill him. I can't let that happen."

"Calm down, Scarlett. Let the man be a man. Personally, I don't know what the hell it is with you and lost souls, but if you want to save Llew's, let him win the guys over on his own. You can't force it because you're the boss; that would only end up making him resent you for emasculating him."

Shane cocked an eyebrow at his best friend. "Are you fuckin' Dr. Phil now? What makes you an expert?" he asked, turning back to watch out the window as the guys situated themselves around the site for lunch. Most guys brought theirs from home to save on time and money, but a few preferred to go off-site for a hot meal.

While he watched his crew, Jack went on about the OSHA rep he'd met with after work the day before. "We gotta get the guys to Wilson in a couple days for their next training seminar and test, or we'll have to postpone starting the new building for a couple of weeks until we can get a rep to come to Henderson."

"Goddamnit! Why the hell do we have to go through this now? All my forklift operators have OSHA certifications," Shane barked. "We can't postpone. Especially for two fuckin' weeks!"

"True. But you have a shitload of new employees who are around forklifts all day, and they don't have OSHA certs… so stop whining and suck it up. I already have Jessie checking on hotels for a night. We'll go down Friday afternoon after work; stay overnight, and be up the next morning for the class at seven. We don't want to risk any of the guys not being able to make it down Saturday morning, or being late for the class and having to wait to do it in a couple weeks."

"Yeah, I guess. Just handle it, Jack."

"I always do," Jack said, with a mouthful of bologna and cheese.

A few of the guys were sitting on large stacks of concrete, and Shane perked up when he saw Llew sit down on one of the stacks and open up a brown bag. It looked like everyone was quiet and focused on eating; but something must've been said, because Llew's head snapped up quickly, his hard eyes locked on Shane's signal operator.

"Great. What now?" Shane groaned.

"What is it?" Jack said, getting up to look out the other window.

They both sighed at the same time when Llew stood to his full height, his fists clenched at his sides. Shane saw his chest deflate and then he picked up his brown bag and stormed off in the direction of the wooded park that ran along the edge of the job site property.

"Damn." Shane sighed.

"You had to expect this." Jack clapped him once on the back before going back to his lunch, but Shane's stomach was in knots. There was no way he could eat right now, when someone he truly believed was a good person was being grossly abused. Yes, he'd expected a little ribbing and hazing of the new guy but not to this level. Llew's eyes had shown surprise, disgust, and then rage before he'd walked away. Suddenly, Shane feared that Llew might have left for good. He grabbed his jacket, but Jack yanked it out of his hand when he went to move past him.

"Don't you even think about it, Smith Jr. Let 'em be for a while. He ain't going nowhere."

Shane swung at the air before plopping down, defeated behind his desk.

Fuck!

CHAPTER TWENTY-ONE

Even though they were on the same site, Llew hadn't talked to Shane at all that day. He'd seen him reviewing blue prints and working on the cement mixer, but that was it. Most of the time, he was in the trailer. It was probably for the best anyway, because he had a hard time not looking at Shane like he was a dying man's last meal. It'd also give the crew something else to rag on him about. Trying to advance on the job by get into the boss' pants.

Llew knew straightaway that most of the crew had heard about the town meeting yesterday. The ones that didn't know when they got to work that morning knew about him by lunchtime. When he sat with them at lunch, one of the crew leaders hadn't even let Llew take his first bite before he zeroed in on him.

"So you're the sex offender, huh? My wife looked up your case. You're from Emporia, right? Llewellyn Gardner. Top ranked football player."

Llew didn't bother responding to these questions, the man wasn't looking for answers, anyway. He just stared at the lanky man with ears way too big for his abnormally small head. Everyone else listened, but no one chimed in. Only this asshole wanted to test him. Llew felt the vein in his neck throb as anger swirled through him like a tornado. All he had to do was go over there, and take the asshole's large, metal Thermos and bash it over his head as many

187

times as it took to fracture his skull. Then he could go back to his lunch, daring anyone else to say a word. For the first time since he was released, he missed Ace. Ace would've put an end to this shit real quick, and not in as nice a way as Llew was thinking, because a fractured skull wouldn't have been enough to satisfy Ace's rage.

"So what's it like to just take someone against their will, Llewellyn Gardner? Huh? A big guy like you get off on that shit?" The man snarled.

Llew stood up fast, making a few of the guys flinch upon seeing his towering height up close and personal. He stared down the asshole trying to remember anything positive anyone had said to him, and replaying it in his mind to keep him from strangling the guy.

"They gonna test you, son. Be strong. Stronger than them. Show them the strength of being able to walk away. Don't let 'em take your freedom again."

Llew exhaled and gradually loosened his fists. How many counseling sessions was he going to have to conjure up? At the rate he was being tested, he was going to run out of words of wisdom. He slowly turned and picked up his bag lunch, deciding he'd find somewhere else to eat.

"Yeah, that's it. Walk away, because I got your probation officer on speed dial and so does my wife. You best stay away from my neck of the woods, boy."

Boy. Llew clenched his jaw tight. He chanted internally instead of remembering Doc's words. *Don't look back. Keep walking. Keep walking.*

He'd thought the fucker was done with him but Llew wasn't quite out of hearing range when he heard the bastard fire his kill shot. "Well I guess my wife doesn't have to worry, since Llew here prefers to rape little boys. You guys be sure to watch your sons." The curses and insults faded as he got farther away.

Llew found a large oak in the wooded area and squatted down behind it; one hand braced on the large trunk, while he dug in his pocket for his cell phone. His fucking hands were out of his control again. He should've thought about putting some of his important numbers on speed dial or that voice recognition thing Leslie told him about.

"Shit, shit." Llew shakily hit the end button and tried again. He finally got all ten numbers right and hit send. He dropped down to his knees and put his back against the tree. The numbers blurred when he looked at his watch, and he blinked to try to get them back into focus. Hell. He only had thirty-five minutes left of his lunch hour. Maybe he shouldn't go back. But how would he pay Ms. Pat's rent? His bank account wouldn't hold up without a regular paycheck coming in. Llew tried to take a few deep breaths, but they weren't coming. His body ignored his commands to remain still.

"St. Bride's Correctional Facility, what department?" the bland female voice asked.

"T-treatment P-planning." Llew coughed at the ache in his throat, the tightness in his chest. He couldn't fucking breathe. It felt like forever but it was actually just a couple seconds later when another female voice came on the line.

"Treatment Planning."

"Yeah uh, this is inmate 5024 — " Llew stopped immediately. What the fuck was he saying? "S-sorry. I mean this is Llew Gardner. Is Dr. Jackson in today?"

189

"Sure. Hold one moment."

Llew spit next to him, his mouth tasted like someone had pissed in it. He searched in his brown bag for the bottle of water, and ended up spilling most of it by the time he got the top off and the bottle up to his mouth. *I can't fuckin' do this. I can't. I gotta move.* He thought about leaving Shane and Ms. Pat; the only two people who had shown him an ounce of real kindness, and it made his stomach cramp into a painful ball.

"Llew. How are you, son?" Dr. Jackson said, cheerfully. "I was going to call your brother's house this weekend and see about you."

Silence.

"Llew? Llewellyn."

Silence.

"Talk to me, Llew. What's going on?"

Llew gulped but choked on the air he tried to take in.

"Breathe, Llew. What's happening? Where are you? Do you need me to send someone?"

"No." Llew gasped. "No. I'm at work, Doc. He, um. One of the s-supervisors." Llew hacked and choked again. "He called me a... a... he said I raped little b-boys and everyone should watch their s-sons."

"Jesus Christ. Okay, Llewellyn; listen to me. Let's breathe first." Dr. Jackson dropped his voice to that easy, calming tone he used whenever Llew had his panic attacks. "We talked about this, Llew. Deep breath in." Llew remembered these exercises, and he let everything fade away but the voice on the other end of the line. He inhaled. "Listen to my voice. Imagine you're here with me for a minute. Exhale. What's happening to you now is but a

190

moment in your life. Inhale. You survived eight years in here by doing it one moment at a time. Exhale. Those men you work with don't know you, Llew. All they've seen is a court transcript or a fabricated newspaper article. Inhale. There'll be an opportunity for you to prove yourself, but it won't happen overnight. Exhale."

Llew followed that pattern for the next couple minutes while Dr. Jackson told him an mindless story about how he missed his wife's parents' anniversary dinner because he was working on a case, and he's been sleeping on the couch for a week. Dr. Jackson had told Llew every piece of advice he knew to give. Now he'd do breathing exercises with him and tell him stories to take his mind off his current situation.

"Llew, I heard you're in Henderson now."

He was finally breathing normally and was able to respond. "Yes."

"I know a therapist out there that specializes in post-release clients. Her office is only about forty-five minutes from there."

"I don't need any more therapy, man," Llew grumbled.

"Oh, yes, you damn well do. Now give me your number. I'm gonna tell her to call you." Dr. Jackson's demand brooked no argument. This was why he was in the position he was in. He could handle his patients like no one's business. He didn't let anyone bullshit him or tell him how to do his job. But he cared so damned much, so much that he'd get in the dog house with his wife if it meant helping someone who felt like they had no choice but to take their own life if they had to spend another day in prison.

191

Llew checked his watch. He had to go back now. "Hey, uh. Thanks, Doc."

Dr. Jackson barked a short laugh. "Anytime, Llew. I'll be in touch, but you have my cell now. Use it. Anytime, day or night. Use *it* first, before you do anything else." Llew knew what he meant. Use the number before he ripped someone's lips off and shoved them up their ass.

"Bye, Doc."

Llew walked away from his seclusion. He didn't hear anything but Doc's voice when he'd been out there in the woods, but as he drew closer he heard the tractors and the powerful engines of the dump trucks. If anyone was still talking about or to him he couldn't hear it, thank god. He walked up to Jack and tapped him on the shoulder.

"Llew. Something on your mind?"

"No. Well. I was thinking I could direct traffic for you the rest of the day." Llew was way overqualified to just wave people through the site and judging by the disappointed look on Jack's face, he knew it too. Just when Llew thought Jack was gonna dismiss him to do the menial task, he straightened up and narrowed his eyes before hissing out a stern, "No."

"I need you on scaffolding." Jack nodded his head back in the direction of the crew. Llew hesitated, noticing more than a few scowls and disgusted faces on the men. He felt like Jack was sending him out on the plank with a two-ton weight chained to his ankle. "Get back on the horse, Llew. Go on."

He ignored the men and their snarling and got back to work. He did hammer a little harder than he needed to, but Jack didn't comment. The afternoon went without further

incident and Llew couldn't have been more relieved when
Jack announced it was quitting time. Typically, he'd like to
be the first to arrive and the last to leave, but not now. He
shoved his tool belt in his backpack and powerwalked to
the road entrance. Men drove past him in their trucks, not
one offering him a ride. He kept his eyes forward as he
walked into town. He'd seen a bookstore when he went to
the town meeting yesterday, and since he didn't have a
television yet, he needed something to pass the long nights
when he got tired of working with his building software.
He dropped his bag at the entrance and gave the woman at
the counter a quick wave.

He was browsing through the biography section when
he felt eyes on him. Keeping his head bowed as if he was
still reading the book's jacket, he cut his eyes up and saw a
man watching him from around the bookcase. Llew sighed
heavily and picked up another book on modern
architecture, taking them both up to the counter. The young
woman cringed when he set the books on the counter. He
glanced her way but diverted his eyes back down to the
counter. She didn't ring up his books, just stared wide-eyed
at him like he was on exhibit in a zoo.

Llew reached into his back wallet and quickly pulled
out a few bills, but very slowly placed them on the counter
and slid them in her direction. He didn't wait for change.
With his head hung low, he tucked the books under his arm
instead of asking for a bag. This was his life now.

Since he hadn't had lunch, he was practically starving,
having worked all day with just a bacon sandwich and
water. Now it was almost six-thirty. Ms. Pat was at bingo
and he wouldn't dare go in her kitchen without her being

there. He slowed his steps as he approached the Country Kitchen. It was done up like a Cracker Barrel, but smaller. Everything old western; rusty tire wheels, ropes, and saddles turned into decorations. Llew peeked through the window and saw a few older couples siting at tables but it wasn't crowded. He'd order his meal to go and be on his way. Hopefully, they wouldn't refuse him service.

"Can I help you, shuga?" the woman asked him with a huge smile. Llew looked behind him to see if she was talking to someone else. She shook her head at him and laughed harder. "You must be that boy Pat was in here talkin' 'bout this mornin.' She said you's a shy one. Also say you do good handiwork and I told her I was gon' call her this evening and see if you could take a look at my two booths over there. Both the benches need bolting down and the table leg is split on that other one, most likely needs replacing."

Llew tried to keep up with her fast-talking country grammar as he turned and looked where she pointed.

"Yes ma'am I can fix them," he said quietly.

"Good, then. When can you come back?"

"I can just go get my toolbox and come right back." Llew picked up his backpack, and made to leave.

"Well, hold on. I assume you came in to eat."

"Yes. I can take it to go."

"Oh shuga', I don't do 'to go' orders. I like to hear the moans when someone eats my food." She laughed loud enough to turn heads. "So what'll you have this evening? Everything here is good. I'm Shirley, by the way."

Llew blinked as she rambled on about who knew what. He looked up at the chalkboard, saw the daily special was the fried chicken and mashed potatoes dinner, so he went with two orders.

"You boys and dem appetites." She shook her head, scribbling down his order on a notepad. When he tried to pay she waved his hand away and shooed him to go wait at a table. Llew mustered a slight smile and sat at the table off to the side waiting for his meal. His stomach rumbled while the pleasant smell of fried meat wafted into the dining room. He'd sure needed that small act of kindness from Shirley right about then. He guessed Shane was right after all. Ms. Pat did have some influence in this town. He'd just have to be patient.

Llew scrubbed at his eyes. Work had been hard but satisfying; it made him feel like a man now that he was earning a decent wage. He pulled out his modern architecture book and flipped through the pictures of some of the more fascinating buildings in the twenty-first century. He felt his cell phone buzz in his pocket and saw a text message from his brother.

Hey bro, you alright??? You sounded bummed... I'll call you as soon as I get home.
miss you man

Llew tucked his phone back in just as four guys from the work site came in still wearing their work clothes. Instead of ducking his head, he met each one of their glares as they walked by him on their way to the counter.

Shirley brought his food out to him on brown plastic tray and set it in front of him. "You need anything else?"

"No ma'am, thank you. Looks good."

195

"I know." She laughed. "But tastes even better."

Llew set his book aside, and picked up his fork.

"Maybe Joe spit in it, it'll serve him right." Llew heard one of the guys mumble at the counter. Llew's fork was only half way to his mouth when he heard the disgusting comment, but he wouldn't let it phase him. He ate his food. If someone spit in it, then it was the best damn spit he'd ever eaten. With only a few mashed potatoes left on his last plate, he looked up and saw Shane and Jack walking in. The smile Shane gave him was like nothing he'd ever seen. Pure and sincere. He thought he saw him give a slight wink, too, but it was gone so fast Llew couldn't be sure. He watched Shane tap Jack on his arm and nod his head in Llew's direction before breaking off from him.

"Hey, Llewell," Shane said in the most wonderful sounding voice. He spoke to Llew like no one else. Looked at him like no one else did. He couldn't understand how a man's voice could be soft and deep at the same time, but Shane's was.

"Wow. Now he's suckin' up to the boss man." One of his coworkers grumbled on his way past with his tray.

"Ignore them." Shane shrugged. He slid Llew's new architecture book in front of him and glanced through a few pages. "You know you don't have to know architecture to work for me, Llew."

You think I'm just some stupid criminal. Building and design is everything for me… was everything.

Llew watched his boss for a few more seconds, then placed his used napkins on his tray. "I'll see you tomorrow, Shane."

"Wait, Llew don't go. I was just — " Shane looked over at his guys and shot them a look that made all of them turn and look the other way.

Llew got up and emptied his tray. Shane was nice, but he thought just like everyone else. Either he was to be avoided like the plague, or he was helpless and needed saving. Shane couldn't come to his defense or shield him from every attitude he encountered in this town, the man had a day job. He went to the counter, told Shirley he'd be back in thirty minutes, and strode out the door, careful not to throw Shirley's door so hard that he had to fix that, too. He had only made it a half-block when he heard Shane's beautiful voice calling him.

Shane watched Llew leave, wondering what the hell went wrong. Llew looked at him like he'd insulted him, but he was just trying to make things easier for him, lord knows everyone else was making it harder.

Jack came up to him and clapped him on the shoulder. "Struck out again, huh?"

His friend wasn't teasing him. He knew that he felt something for Llew. If he couldn't be his lover, he at least wanted to be more than simply his employer.

"I guess so." Shane huffed. "Come on let's eat."

They placed their order and sat down at their table to wait. "Smith Jr., are you the only person that hasn't read any of the articles on Llew?"

"I was respecting his privacy," Shane grumbled. "Unlike some people."

"It's public record. There were several news articles about—"

"Look." He turned hard on his friend. "I don't give a fuck what those articles said."

"Well maybe you should. Then you wouldn't have put your big foot in your mouth just now."

Shane frowned waiting on Jack to elaborate.

"All that shit went down his senior year of high school. He was a huge deal at his school. He played football and had scholarships up the wazoo, but he also had an architecture scholarship to Virginia Tech, since he'd won the ASCA Student Design Competition in his district three years in a row. The house he designed is still on the—"

"Fuck me," Shane hissed, bolting up out of his seat and through the door. He had insulted Llew. He had no clue what he'd been thinking. *Damnit.*

Shane ran the best he could in his large work boots. When he crossed over Jackson Street he yelled Llew's name. He thought he might not stop, but he saw him turn and lean his large frame against the wall of the movie theater to wait for Shane to catch up.

Shane was huffing when he got to him. "Damn, you walk fast. I just wanted to see if I could walk with you."

Llew just stared back at him.

"Jesus, Llewell. Please don't look at me like that."

Eyes darker than a night sky in Texas, Llew looked at him like he could devour him, and Shane had no doubt that he could. The hunger there was diluted by regret and disappointment.

"Llewell."

"You think I'm stupid, Shane. You probably think I gotta get a damn book to know how to operate an excavator."

"What?" Shane gripped the back of his neck. This was not going the way he wanted it to. "First of all, I don't even know how to operate the goddamn excavator; I don't prepare the ground... I build on it. Second, I don't think you're stupid, I just don't know enough about you, because you won't fuckin' talk to me, Llewell. I swear, I don't think you're stupid."

Shane watched him, waiting on Llew to tell him to go to hell, but all he got was that penetrating glare. Shane sighed. "Yeah, uh. I'll see you tomorrow." He'd only taken a few steps when Llew called out to him.

"I thought you were gonna walk with me."

He'd take the slight quirk of Llew's mouth. That was a great start. He nodded and said, "Sure. I'll walk with you."

He waited until they were through town before Shane decided he'd try to get to know Llew by maybe giving him a reason to talk to him. "I didn't know about your architecture education. I didn't want to read the articles or research you. I'd prefer to hear your story when you want me to."

"So how do you know now?" Llew's deep voice made Shane's stomach flip.

"Jack told me just now when he said I'd put my foot in my mouth. He told me about your Collegiate School of Architecture awards. That's... that's impressive, Llew; especially for a high school student." Shane watched Llew's tanned cheeks turn a sexy pink shade as he turned his head in the other direction. *Looks like someone blushes at compliments.* "Maybe you can show me some of your designs sometime. I was never the best at that part. I'm a builder; I'll leave the hard stuff to the architects."

The neighborhood was quiet, as they got closer to Ms. Pat's house. The narrow street was lined with large trees that sat in front of brick family homes. Many of the homes that his grandfather had built, many that had been remodeled by his father. Shane needed to hear Llew talk, had to think of something that didn't require his typical head nod as a response.

"So do you like the work? Construction isn't for everyone."

"I like it."

No. I need more than that. "I'm sure you do. Now that Jack knows how good you are, there's no telling what he'll have you doing."

Llew continued to walk next to him with his hands deep in his pockets. Shane's shoulder was at Llew's bicep and it made his mouth water the way it strained under the thick wool jacket. Thank goodness the days were warming up fast with the approach of spring, because he desperately wanted to see Llew sweating in a tank top as he swung his hammer to build for him.

"So what else are you good at?" Shane purred, the innuendo dripping from his tone.

Llew smiled, and Shane didn't think he'd ever get tired of seeing it. It happened so rarely, and he was secretly pleased that he was the only one who made him do it.

Llew took a deep breath. "Well. I can dissect the hell out of even the most complicated blueprint."

Shane gripped Llew's elbow; spinning him to face him, a look of complete shock on his face. "Really."

Llew nodded. "Yes, really. I've studied them since middle school."

Shane wasn't sure if he should mention it or not but what the hell. "Even in prison."

Llew's eyes darkened but he didn't turn away. "Especially in prison."

"How'd you get them?"

Llew smirked. "I had a friend that helped with that."

"That's good," Shane whispered, moving in closer to Llew's body. His huge chest called to him, made him want to bury his face in between those thick pecs. "Maybe you can help me out if I ever have trouble dissecting some." *Perfect reason to call you into my office.* Damn if this wasn't unprofessional, but fuck it. Shane slowly reached his hand up and ran it through the thick strands of Llew's dark hair.

"How's your head?" Llew flinched when Shane's finger lightly brushed over the knot that had formed where he was clipped by the large piece of falling wood. Llew's hands were down by his sides, still refusing to touch him. That was okay for now. Baby steps. "I'm sorry that happened to you."

They stood there staring at each other, the tension building high enough to cause a tsunami. Shane continued to rub the back of Llew's head, tilting it down so he could see his eyes better. He made sure there wasn't an ounce of space left between them as he molded himself to Llew's body. His overly muscular, well-defined body. Llew bowed his head until his forehead ended up touching Shane's.

Warm puffs of breath raised goose bumps all over Shane's cool skin. Although he was as close to Llew as he could get, there was still two large jackets and a couple layers of clothing keeping him from feeling what he wanted… from feeling flesh. Shane slid his other hand up Llew's chest and around the back of his neck. He wanted to feel if those firm-looking lips were actually soft. "You can touch me, Llewell."

It took a few seconds but Llew slowly raised his arms, settling his large hands on Shane's waist. If he wasn't so amazingly turned on right now he would've been embarrassed at the satisfied groan that left him. Running his hand down Llew's cheek, ghosting over his eyes, Llew squeezed them shut, his hands simultaneously squeezing his waist.

"Yes," Shane moaned. It was as if the world had closed in around them. There wasn't a sound on the dark street. The trees afforded them only a little privacy.

"We shouldn't be out here like this," Llew rasped. His voice had gone even deeper and rougher than usual.

"Oh god. Your voice is too much for me to let go." Shane tightened his grip on Llew's neck. "You're gonna have to pull my hands off of you."

There it was again. That hint of a smile and if Shane's own face wasn't as close as it was, he'd probably see that pretty shade of pink on Llew's cheeks again. Llew reached up, unclasped Shane's hands from behind his neck, and brought them down in between them. His chin was close to his chest, as if they were praying together. Those goddamn smoky eyes peered at him between silky black lashes as he brought Shane's hands to his mouth and kissed his knuckles gently. No one had ever kissed his hands before, so sweetly and full of passion. Shane's knees weakened and his cock throbbed and pulsed against his jeans like a bass drum in a rock band. He was actually fuckin' swooning. *Holy fuck. Llew's a secret casanova.*

Llew turned them. "Let's go."

Shit. And he was demanding.

He waited not so patiently behind Llew while he unlocked his door. It was dark and cool when they got inside, but Shane had a feeling it wouldn't be cool very much longer. The blinds were raised, providing was just enough light from the lamppost outside to illuminate parts of the room. He saw that Llew still didn't have a lick of furniture. Just a comforter folded up on the floor in the corner and a laptop charging amidst a slew of books. Some novels, but most of them instructional. *No. Definitely not stupid.* He couldn't wait to find out just how smart Llew was... but not right now.

"Looks like you read a lot."

"I don't sleep very well," Llew confessed, leaning tall against the far wall. If Shane didn't know better he'd say Llew was trying to put some distance between them. *Not happening.* He walked over to where Llew stood and pressed against him. It was time for a little honesty, to show that he could be trusted. He'd put himself out there and hope Llew would do the same.

"I like you, Llewell. I know you may think this is a bad idea but—"

"Yes. It is a bad idea. People will turn on you, Shane. Your friends will abandon you and your business will suffer. Just like—"

Shane cupped Llew's course jaw. "Just like what?"

"Just like my brother. He almost went under when I got out and started working for him. People started pulling their contracts left and right. So I… so I left, and it hurt him bad. But I knew it was right. Just like now."

"Jack would never abandon me and he already knows that I like you. As far as my business, people either want to be assholes or they want to use the best and get their buildings constructed, I think more people will go for the latter. I've had ex-cons work for me before… still do. You are not the only one with a record on my crew, Llew."

"No maybe not. But I'm sure I'm the only sex offender." Llew cast his eyes down.

Okay this was wrong. Going into all this was unnecessary. They were talking about his personal life here, which was exactly what it was. Personal. Hooking his hands on Llew's shoulders, he looked him in the eye to ask the only thing that was important right now. "Do you like me, too?"

Those eyes gave away the answer way before Llew did. "Shane. I like you more than you could imagine." Llew's hand was on his chin, tilting him to look at him. "But you deserve so much better than me. You deserve a man that's… that's whole."

"Llewell what are you talking about?" Shane shook his head rapidly. "No. Forget that. Let's just spend a little time together first and get to know each other before either one of us presume what the other needs." Shane paused and began to unzip Llew's coat. "Although, I thought it was pretty obvious what I needed when we were outside."

204

Shane's cock had never lost its erection. He pressed against Llew's hard thigh, smiling up at him. "I think you need this too." He rose up to connect with Llew's mouth and the heat that seared down his spine was like lava through a delta. Llew's mouth closed over his and took control of him. His thick tongue delving deep inside for the truest taste of him. Oh my god. Llew held him tightly to him as if Shane might disappear if he loosened his grip. The way the man kissed him made Shane wonder when the last time someone really kissed Llew was. With a renewed surge of even hotter passion, Shane pushed in harder, squeezing Llew around his neck, bringing him down as close to him as he could.

"Oh my god. Llewell. You feel so damn good." Shane licked and bit at that deliciously stubbled chin. "Wanna feel you."

CHAPTER TWENTY - TWO

There were no words to describe how Shane felt in his arms. Lips that he'd dreamed of felt just as soft as he'd imagined. So beautiful and full of spirit. But Llew's mind was doing a number on him. He tried to let himself just feel. His heart pounded and his body thrummed at being touched again. However, Llew tried to be mindful of the grip he had on Shane's waist, he didn't want to hurt him… or scare him. *Fuck. My head's too fucked up for this.* Shane was so into him but all he could think about was *'What if something goes wrong? What if he gets scared?'*

Llew's eyes closed slowly as Shane's tight body rubbed up and down him like a hot sex fiend. The man wanted him. No doubt in Llew's mind. But he couldn't shake the feeling that he wasn't good enough for Shane. He kissed Shane like it was going to be the last time – because it was. He kissed him with everything he had so he would remember it.

While Llew searched Shane's mouth for every possible flavor he could find, he felt his jacket open and warm; sure hands worked their way up under his shirt and thermal. "Mmmm. You're so warm," Shane moaned. "Jesus, Llewell. Your body is so fuckin' sexy." He licked at the side of Llew's mouth, nuzzling against his beard.

This wasn't fair. He pulled Shane against him, not wanting to let him go. He wanted him to be his. Wanted to make love to him, wanted to dominate him and protect him, like Llew was made to do. But that part of him had been taken away. He was incomplete. Damn if he didn't wish things could be different for him and Shane. Maybe he could just get Shane off, feel him come just once against his skin. Smell his sex, lick him everywhere, and please him.

Llew's muscles flinched under Shane's touch. He groaned so low in his throat, it sounded scary even to him. His body and mind warred with each other.

"God, Llew. Let me have you. Let me have you, now. Fuck, babe. Your body is so beautiful." Shane's hands slid across his stomach and around to his back. "So damn hard. Mmmmm. Shit. Are you hard everywhere, handsome?" Shane purred, grinning up at him.

Llew opened his eyes. He was wondering how long he had to enjoy the moment. But there it was already, reality rearing up and slapping the shit out of him. No. He wasn't hard everywhere. In some place yes. But not where Shane needed him to be.

Before Llew could grab Shane's wrist, his hand was eagerly pressing against the front of his jeans, searching for his hardness, instead finding a lifeless, useless muscle.

Llew jerked out of Shane's hold, twisting awkwardly to the side to get away from him. He only caught a glimpse of the confused look plastered on Shane's face, but it was enough to make him feel like a worthless piece of shit. He was glad it was still dark in his room because he was sure his face was bright red from embarrassment. He hadn't meant to let things go so far. He just wanted a kiss. One kiss. Now he had this young, strong, virile man in his room wondering what the hell kind of gay man wouldn't have a stiff dick when faced with the extremely strong likelihood of having sex.

"Llewell, I'm sorry. I'm not trying to pressure you." Shane fidgeted.

Jesus. This was not something a man could talk about easily; it didn't just roll off the tongue. *I'm impotent.* But he didn't want Shane thinking it was him. He especially didn't want him thinking Llew wasn't attracted to him. He stood in front of his one window, his back to Shane so he didn't have to see his face. See the pity, the disappointment. "I... It's not you, Shane. You're not pressuring me. I want to. *Damnit.*" His voice lowered like what he was about to say was a secret he couldn't bear to say out loud. "I can't get an erection."

Saying that aloud to someone else had Llew's breathing going shallow and his hands starting to shake. Fuck me. He had to get Shane out of there. If he was about to lose his shit, he didn't want the man to see that too. "I need to get back to Shirley's now. She's expecting me."

Llew was still looking out the window when he felt Shane's hands come around his waist, pulling him back into a strong, tough chest. "I'm sorry, Llew."

Fuckin' great. Another person to feel sorry for me.

"Don't be sorry. It is what it is. That's why I said... I'm not good for you."

"We don't have to have se—"

Llew spun fast, cutting Shane off. What the man was about to say was a boldface lie. A man as young as Shane would need sex... lots of it, too. "Don't say it. Don't say what you know ain't true. Don't say bullshit like 'sex don't matter' and 'we can just get to know each other and connect on a more spiritual level'. That's crap and you know it. Now if you don't mind. I gotta get going."

"Llewell, just give me a minute to gather myself here."

"Why?" Llew said between clenched teeth, angrily zipping his coat back up. "There's nothing to gather."

"Yes. Yes there is." Shane looked nervous as if he was truly struggling with his words. "Can I please just ask one question?"

Llew didn't roll his eyes at the obvious, because he knew exactly what Shane's question was so he saved him the trouble. "No. I haven't tried Viagra, Cialis, or any other erectile dysfunction medicine. My problem is psychological… it's all in my fucked up head."

Shane's eyebrows shot up. "Well then I —"

"Save it. I'm not something for you to fix, contractor." Llew opened his door, a symbolic showing that their visit was over.

"Okay, Llewell." Shane stood in the small doorway staring up at him. Damn, he'd give anything to lean in for another one of Shane's sweet kisses, but what was the point… it'd go nowhere. "Work is on hold until we get the OSHA certs done so you're off tomorrow."

"Yeah. Jessie sent me a text."

"Do you need a ride there?"

"I'll manage."

"It's not walking distance, Llewell."

Llew snorted. "Yeah. I can comprehend where Wilson, North Carolina is, Shane."

"I wasn't trying to be smart-mouthed."

"I know," Llew whispered. He and Shane stood staring determinedly for a few seconds.

Shane reached up and stroked the side of his cheek, watching him watch him back. "I don't give up easily, Llewell."

There was nothing Llew could say to that. So he just watched this perplexing man. Shane may never be his lover, but maybe they'd be friends. The thought was fucking depressing. The hottest man he'd seen in years could only be his friend. If Llew stayed in Henderson, he'd watch Shane eventually meet a strong stallion that could fuck him until the break of dawn. They'd fall in love and live happily ever after, while Llew lived over Ms. Pat's garage... alone.

CHAPTER TWENTY - THREE

"Did you make the reservations?" Shane asked Jessie, his voice a little louder and sterner than he'd intended.

"Yes, Smith Jr."

"Did you pay the registration for all the guys?"

"Yes, Smith Jr.," she said, more dryly than the first time.

"Don't sass me girl," Shane snapped at her.

"Oh, my gosh. I'm not. What is wrong with you?"

"Pay him no never mind, Jess. He's mad because Llew keeps shooting him down," Jack said from behind his desk. Only the three of them were on the site, making sure they were ready for the one-day trip to Wilson. They were already losing two days of labor on this; they didn't need any further delays. Yeah, Llew had invaded his dreams last night and cost him an entire night's rest. That didn't mean he was pining.

Shane stood with his hand on his hip, glaring at his best friends. "He's not shooting me down. We're just getting to know each other first. On a more platonic level."

"Code for 'shot you down'." Jack laughed. Jessie joined him and Jack took the opportunity to really heckle his friend. He stood up and made his voice as deep as he could as if imitating Llew's bass-filed drawl, "Smith Jr., I think we should be friends first, because that's the benefit of being gay and dating a man. We would rather get to

213

know each other and talk first, share our feelings, before we jump into bed.'"

Jessie covered her mouth, trying not to laugh harder, and even Shane had a hard time not smiling. Jack was right. Men did like to connect emotionally but they didn't mind learning the physical side of their partner simultaneously. Why wait? *Wait if the other had performance anxiety.* He wouldn't dare let them know about any of that though. He'd have to figure out something.

"Are you sure, Llew's going tomorrow?" Jessie rifled through her paperwork.

"Why?" Shane asked, confused. "He's an employee on the new site. He has to be there."

"He didn't respond to my e-mail or text. Maybe it has to do with last night."

"What about last night?" He and Jack said at the same time.

"Well, I had breakfast at Shirley's this morning and Missy Jean told me that some guys were really jaw-japing at him yesterday while he did some work for Shirley."

Jack waved his hand dismissively in the air. "Llew has to toughen his hide if he's gonna survive. Words ain't never hurt nobody."

"But they sure sting like heck." Jessie conceded.

"Llew's gonna have to learn how to tune out the world."

Shane spun around. "What'd you just say?"

Jack looked quizzically at him. "I said he'd have to tune 'em out."

"You're brilliant." Shane beamed, yanking his coat off the back of his chair. "Thanks for the great idea, buddy. I'll see ya'll tomorrow in Wilson."

He left them standing there with their mouths hanging open. He wanted to check on Llew after making a quick stop at his house. He searched for his gym bag in his coat closet, quickly pulling out what he needed and turning to go back out the door.

As soon as Shane turned the corner onto Ms. Pat's street, he saw a long torso, bent over in low-riding denim jeans and heavy boots, hammering away at the porch stairs that led to the front door. Fuck, Llew was too fine not to pursue. He looked awesome in a tool belt, like a rugged, bearded man who could fill the role for a construction worker porn star.

He pulled up to the curb and when Llew saw it was him he stopped and stood up, tucking his hammer back in his low-hanging tool belt.

Llew couldn't believe Shane had come back. He thought the guy would be repulsed at what he'd revealed to him. But here he was, in his dark denim jeans and blue and white striped t-shirt. Oh god, he was so beautiful, with those light brown eyes and blond wind-swept hair. He was just so energetic and full of life. Llew couldn't figure out for the life of him why Shane kept coming around trying to pull dead weight along with him.

"Hi, Llewell. Ms. Pat finally got someone to redo these steps, huh? She been complaining about them for months now," Shane said, propping one foot up on the first step to the porch, leaning in to rub his hand across the large boards Llew had just finished hammering. "I told her I'd send a guy over to do it, but she insisted on letting that good-for-nuttin son of hers continue to feed her excuses."

When Llew was caught staring, Shane stopped talking and stared right back. Llew was beginning to really like that about him. Shane tipped his head down, tucking his thumbs in his pocket like he battled with what to say next.

"Believe it or not, when you look at me like that, it's hard for me to gather my wits. But I'm gonna say what I came to say."

Silence.

"I thought about you last night," Shane said, quietly. "I thought about you a lot."

Llew had to take a breath before he could respond to the intimacy of Shane's confession. "Don't say stuff like that, Shane."

Ignoring him, Shane kept going. "While in my bed, alone. I thought about your eyes. Your strong touch. Your smell." Shane stepped closer to him and Llew refused to retreat. Shane Smith Jr. didn't intimidate him. Llew was fascinated, actually. He was setting himself up for disappointment if he allowed himself to be fooled into thinking Shane would be satisfied with him. "You don't want me to say stuff like that? You mean the truth? It's all I know, Llewell. I'm not a phony man and I don't play games. I want you, and that's all there is to it. And if you think I'm gonna give up, you're wrong."

"There must be a serious lack of options in this town," Llew said stiffly.

"I wouldn't say that. There's plenty of options here and there's neighboring cities with even more options. But I prefer the option in front of me."

"I'm not an option."

"On the contrary."

Llew couldn't hide his satisfied grin before he went back to hammering another board in place. Shane's next question was whispered into the shell of his ear as he bent over him, making Llew stop his hammering mid-swing.

"You thought about me too, didn't you?"

Llew let the hammer fall from his hands, the loud clanging against the hard wood sounded like an admission of finality. He'd given up, he couldn't fight anymore. He liked Shane, liked him a lot. As a friend, as a boss, as a... goddamnit, a lover.

Maybe Shane could see the war waging inside him, because his smile dropped slightly. When the sun hit him just right, the soft glare radiating from him reminded Llew of the color of sand across the Libyan Desert. Sparkling and radiant.

"Take me to your room."

When Llew didn't move in response the command, Shane kept on.

"I'm not gonna pressure you, babe. I got something for you."

Llew's brow uplifted.

Shane shook his head at him, his lively smile now back in place. He put his hand on Llew's waist, squeezing the sweaty skin beneath his t-shirt. "That's not what I'm talking about, but when you're ready, you're welcome to that anytime."

Llew didn't want to move away from Shane's touch, but he unhooked his tool belt, never taking his eyes off Shane, and walked around the back of the house. Curiosity, if nothing else, had Llew's long legs moving quickly towards his still un-furnished room. He'd be glad when Leslie came in a couple days, this was getting to be embarrassing.

Llew unlocked his door and let the only company he'd had in his new home inside. He didn't bother turning around, just went into the kitchen, and grabbed a couple bottles of water, setting one on the counter for Shane. Again, he was over at the little corner Llew had set up for his books and laptop.

"I know where you can get some book cases."

"Oh, yeah?"

"Yeah. I make them." Shane shrugged nonchalantly, picking up one of Llew's sketchbooks. "In my garage. I got a whole workshop in there. Drafting table, cabinet saw, a stand planer. Everything I need. Even though I.... " Shane stopped talking while he flipped through the pages of Llew's book.

He had an urge to go and ease the book from Shane's fingers, because, of course that nagging feeling you'd get when someone looked at your art and they may think it's not good enough was swirling around in his gut. Llew had been designing buildings and homes for as long as he could hold a crayon. He was also hoping Shane wouldn't touch his laptop, waking it up to reveal the last thing he'd looked at before falling asleep. Finding a half-naked model splayed across the screen that looked as similar to Shane as he could find would probably freak him out.

"Oh, my god," Shane said, flipping each page carefully. "I've never seen anything like this. They're so detailed; and sleek as fuck, man. How did you learn to draw like this?"

Llew didn't have an answer. He didn't want to seem arrogant by saying it came naturally to him, but it did. He had some training in high school, did all the camps, clubs and seminars for youth architects, but most of his craft was fine-tuned in prison. He bet that would look stellar on a resume. Big Waldo kept him up-to-date with the latest textbooks and instructional DVDs. It helped him stay sane all those years being able to continue to learn about what had always been one of the most important parts of him. He knew he could go back to school now. There were state programs and funding available for him, but he knew design like the back of his hand. If life held him back too much longer, he'd get the piece of paper – a bachelor's degree in architecture and design, if it was the only way for him to advance. He felt his blueprints and drafts spoke for themselves.

"Damn. How many stories is this?"

"Seventy-two." Llew didn't have to see what page Shane was looking at to know he was referring to his skyscraper.

Shane chuckled deeply, carefully closing the large book and placing back on the floor. "Wow. I've never seen anything like these. Probably never will. You should be with a big-time firm in New York or somewhere, Llewell. Not wasting time here in my little company."

"Gotta crawl and walk before you can fly," Llew said, casually.

"Quoting Nietzsche." Shane laughed again, approaching him and wiping a smudge of sawdust off Llew's bicep.

"This what you had for me… advice? To tell me I should leave and work for a big firm? I'll keep that advice in mind but I'm pretty sure sex offenders aren't the first hired."

"I know you keep getting lip everywhere you go but you won't get it from me, so drop the attitude." Shane snapped back at him, and Llew was shocked. "Now. If you're done being snarky, I have something else for you."

Llew finished his water, anything to keep the huge smile off his face. "What?"

"This."

"What the hell is that?" Llew said looking at the small, black rectangular device. It looked like a mini cell phone.

"It's an iPod."

"What's that for?"

"To drown out your demons," Shane said, with a sexy grin.

"Yeah, well my demons can swim. Thanks anyway." Llew walked back towards the door, but Shane beat him to it.

"Llewell, just try it." Shane squeezed in front of Llew, putting them chest to chest. He kept eye contact with him while he unraveled the ear buds and slowly brought both hands up, gently grazing the sides of Llew's face as he tucked each one comfortably in his ears. "I got good stuff on here, babe," Shane said, while the device powered up. "Some Stones, Linkin Park, Foo Fighters, Muse, a little R&B, the smooth stuff, jazz… and of course Cher."

Llew jerked his head up, frowning.

Shane threw his head back, a bold laugh escaping his full lips. "Just joking. I was checking to see if you were listening."

Llew laughed too. It felt so good, and Shane was the one who made him do it.

"I love your laugh. It's so rich and deep. "

"I love that you make me laugh," Llew said, against Shane's lips. He brushed his mouth back and forth, teasing the both of them.

A deep purr left Shane and Llew wrapped his arms around him, pulling them tighter together.

"Now, you turn this on and you won't hear anything anyone has to say. All that'll be in your head is good music and the memory of me in your arms." Shane pushed the play button and Llew was greeted by the lyrics of *I'll Be There for You* by Bon Jovi. It was perfect for the moment and Llew wondered if Shane had cued it to this song on purpose. The way he was looking at him right now told Llew that he probably did. He leaned in and let his body react without the hindrance of the constant barrage of negative thoughts, as the heartfelt lyrics flooded his mind, drowning out the hate.

I'll be there for you
These five words I swear to you
When you breathe, I want to be the air for you
I'll be there for you.
I'd live and I'd die for you
I'd steal the sun from the sky for you
Words can't say what love can do
I'll be there for you.

Llew kissed Shane like he was his air and he'd been suffocating for over eight years. The way Shane kissed him back, with fire and power, he wondered if he'd been suffocating, too. How long had he been alone? Llew jerked Shane in tighter, and immediately his brain short-circuited. He didn't want to scare him.

"Hell no. Don't you dare," Shane hissed against Llew's cheek, nudging him forcibly with his forehead. He gripped Llew's face hard, snarling against his mouth. "I'm not some over-privileged little twerp that's afraid someone's gonna find me making out with my man and fuckin' lie about it. Do what comes naturally to you, Llewell. I'm not afraid of you. I need you as much as you need me, baby. Now all *you* need to do is believe it."

Llew's cock jerked in his jeans, making him gasp. He gripped his dick through the rough denim, his eyes fluttering closed when he felt the stiffness there. Not fully erect, but sure as hell not limp either. "Fuck."

Shane paused the music and smiled a shit-eating grin at him. "Don't question it. Don't overthink it. Kiss me. Kiss me like you need to."

Llew bent at his knees, pulled Shane hard against him, and dove into his mouth even more voraciously than before. He didn't hold back, and Shane showed him just how much he appreciated it. Llew's back was clawed through the thin material of his t-shirt, while Shane bit and moaned against his mouth. Tilting his head back when Llew went for his throat, completely baring himself to him. "That's it, babe." Shane groaned, his hands snaking back to the front and down his sides. Llew ground his aching cock against Shane's own and he was so caught up in making Shane feel wanted and appreciated that he didn't realize what it was doing to him… to his body, until Shane got a good hold of his cock and gave it an achingly sweet squeeze.

"Oh god," Llew shouted. His dick was so hard it was fucking painful. Shane had one hand on his length and the other behind his neck. Llew had a million feelings attacking him at once. He was elated, scared, stunned, hell maybe in love with the man making him *feel* for the first time in what felt like forever. He squeezed his eyes shut, praying he didn't start bawling like a baby. There were no words to describe this feeling. "Fuck. Fuck. Shane."

"I got you," Shane whispered. He pulled the earplugs from Shane's ears and gripped both cheeks. "Look at me."

Llew slowly opened his eyes. Even though he wanted to fall to the carpet with Shane under him and thrust against him in the worst way, he wouldn't behave like an animal. But oh, he needed so much right now. He just needed.

"Tell me what you want. Whatever it is, you can have it." Shane looked determinedly at him, and Llew knew he was telling the truth.

Llew couldn't respond. He was speechless. His head pounded with adrenaline-fueled lust. His body shook and he pressed himself closer to Shane, trying to hide his reaction to what was happening.

Shane didn't wait any longer. He yanked Llew's belt open, and in seconds, a hot palm was on his dick. Llew's knees gave way and Shane dropped to the floor with him. His decadent, comforting voice filled the small room while he nestled his soft lips against Llew's neck. "I know exactly what you need. It's okay, let go, Llewell." Shane's belt could be heard as he wrestled with unbuttoning his pants without taking his other hand off Llew.

"I won't fuck you right now. I-I can't. I'll be too rough." Llew didn't want to disclose this to Shane, especially right now, but he needed to know the truth. "I haven't come in years… e-eight years." He stuttered. The admission still sometimes shocked him.

"Shh. I know." Shane kissed Llew's mouth again, his tongue lazily swirling against his. "We don't have to have sex, but I am gonna make you come."

Jesus. Llew was guided back to lie on the floor. "I don't think it's gonna take long." He panted. It was there… right fucking there. His balls were engorged and pulled up so tight against him. He reached down, needing to feel it himself. To know he wasn't dreaming. His cock was throbbing and purple under Shane's touch. Llew ran his fingertips down the length and over his balls. *Fuck.* The sensitivity of his head was there… there to the twenty-fifth power. Shane lay on top of him from head to toe, his own cock out and pressing against him.

As Shane lifted up his upper body and arched, pushing his groin harder against him, Llew looked down between their bodies and gritted his teeth to keep from yelling like a madman. The feel of his own dick was foreign to him, but he was remembering now. It was all coming back to him, what he liked, what got him off. Something else that always helped was a rock hard body on top of him. He looked into Shane's eyes and was overwhelmed to see hope, truth, and desire all there in his sandy brown eyes. All just for him.

Llew wanted to spread his legs wider but his jeans were only down to his thighs. Shane reared up and slid Llew's jeans down to his boots, but didn't bother wasting time trying to get those off. He let Llew's legs fall to the sides and went back on his haunches to stare at him. He held their cocks in his hands, lightly rubbing the skin back and forth.

Llew's chest rose and fell rapidly while he watched the hypnotic motion. He fisted his hands at his sides; his resolve not to take control was waning quickly.

"You're fucking gorgeous. Everything about you is sexy, especially your quiet power. I can see you fighting not to throw me on the floor and fuck me through it. But that can and *will* come later."

Llew watched Shane's mouth move when he spoke. Mesmerized by him. Look what he'd done for him. He was smitten to say the least. *Shit*. He hoped it wasn't the white knight syndrome. Shane had rescued him more than once. What he was feeling looking up at him now, he knew it couldn't possibly be that. Shane had all the attributes he said he'd ever want in a man. Everything he'd dreamed of. That long, pale cock jutting out from his toned body was a very strong attribute. Llew imagined it inside of him. Long and not too thick. Oh yes, he'd bottom for his first time just for Shane.

"You keep looking at me like that and I'm gonna come on you, Llewell. All over your sexy body," Shane said huskily. His voice had gone from angelic to sinful.

Llew groaned low and rough when Shane began to stroke his thick length in time with his own. He wanted Shane's body pressed against him but he wanted it like this too. Shane spread his knees wider; pushing Llew's even further apart, putting their balls snug against each other.

"I'm gonna come on you, babe. All over you and I want you to come all over my hand. I want you to have a clear view of us coming together. Keep those dark eyes open." Shane bucked hard, his own words having the same effect on him that they were having on Llew. He felt him tighten his hold and start to work them both with purpose. Shane's shoulders hunched in as he embraced the feelings overwhelming him and Llew followed his hero. He stopped trying to shield his reactions and gave Shane all that he was.

"Oh god," Shane murmured when Llew gripped his muscular hips and forced Shane to move with him. He thrust up into Shane's palm while pulling him down on him. "Feels so damn good. I can't hold it anymore."

"Fuck. I'm coming." Llew huffed, already feeling out of breath. His eyes wide, and full of shock at what was approaching; he squeezed Shane's thighs with the power of his orgasm, not the least concerned about hurting this man. From the looks and sounds of it, Shane was getting off on Llew's strength. Instead of it doing a head-trip on him, the recognition that Shane wanted this sent a surge of dominant power through him that seemed to completely re-align his mind.

"Oh fuck! Fuck! Llewell." Shane jolted forward from the impact of his first shot, sending it all the way to Llew's throat. His naturally tanned body flushed a deep red, his eyes glazed over as he fought to keep eye contact with Llew. Shane stroked them both erratically in a punishingly tight fist, causing his own hips to lift up off Llew when he shot again and again, this time the creamy fluid coating the slick, dark hairs from Llew's navel to his cock. It felt so goddamn good; he'd never realized how much he'd missed another man's essence.

Llew growled and held Shane's ass tight against him. Fire seared his spine but a cathartic coolness brought him back to earth all at the same time. His back arched painfully as he shot in Shane's hand. Llew opened his mouth and let go of a guttural, pained, relief-filled moan as his balls released more than eight years' worth of pent up need.

"Yes, baby. Let it all out," Shane said, drowsily. Slowly milking Llew's cock with his slick hands. His eyes were hooded and satisfied as he watched Llew's body convulse through its erotic metamorphosis. "So good, Llewell."

Llew was coming down from the highest high he'd ever felt. Coming that hard from jerking off, he smiled inside, fearing for both of their lives when they had intercourse. He said "when" in his head with conviction. Shane said he was going to let him fuck him and Llew believed every single word Shane said. "Gaaawd. Shane."

"I'm here, babe. Just feel, don't talk. I'm there with you," Shane said softly.

Llew's cock twitched and jerked happily. He finally let go of Shane's hips, starting at the dark red hands prints he'd left behind.

Oh no.

"Mmmm. I like how those look on me, babe. Gives me something to jerk off to tonight. Your hands are strong, full of control and authority. It was you letting that part of you come back to life that allowed you to get an erection and come like that." Shane leaned in, pressing a tender kiss on his lips.

Llew held him close with one hand planted possessively on the back of his neck, while the other gently rubbed the bruise on his left hip. He watched Shane with irresistible desire. "*You* made me come like that."

"Well we can happily agree to disagree every single time, just like that." Shane chuckled against his throat, licking out his hot tongue to trace Llew's Adam's apple, and he'd be damn if his cock didn't jerk to life again.

"It's definitely you." Llew chuckled with him.

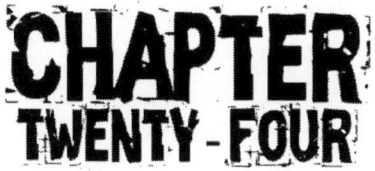

CHAPTER TWENTY-FOUR

Shane was speeding on I-95 heading into Wilson, NC. This was the last thing he wanted to be doing on a Friday evening. He had no choice but to be there to make sure his crew got their OSHA certs done. He banished work to the back of his mind and thought about what was on the forefront of his mind... Llewell.

Every time he thought about Llew's orgasm last night, he got rock hard. He'd done it. Well Llew said he'd done it. But all Shane did was let Llewell be who he was. He showed the big man that he wasn't afraid of him like so many in their town. Treating Llew like he was going to drag them into the closest alley and have his way with them. Idiots. Llew was so kind underneath all those muscles; and behind that guarded expression was a man that needed love, and companionship. Shane needed those things too. He hadn't shared much of his past with Llew because it was boring and typical. He did what all the country bumpkins did in Henderson, NC while growing up. He went to church like a good boy, and did everything to please his momma. He didn't go to college, his father said he didn't need a degree in kissing a professor's ass to run the family business. So there it was. All that spelled was boring. Llew was fascinating in so many ways. Not just being a survivor, but he was brilliant. Naturally brilliant, an artist.

Shane was now more determined than ever to show Llew that he was special; important to him now, and he could make roots here. They could work together; take Smith's Construction to new levels now that Shane had a master designer working with him.

Yes! That's it. Llew could submit some of his designs and Shane could corner an entirely different market. His company would provide an additional service. Not only bidding to construct already designed projects, but also bidding on sites that needed designing and construction. This was so exciting. He'd talk with Llew about what his future plans were, he wouldn't want to seem like he was using the man. Regardless, if Llew only wanted to work construction, that would be fine with Shane, as long as he stayed with Smith's.

When he pulled up to the Days Inn, he had to sit in his truck for a few minutes to will his erection down. He knew Llew was already in his room, having ridden down with Jack a few hours ago. Shane had to meet with the zoning director that morning and wasn't able to drive Llew himself, but he planned to spend more time with him tonight.

He stretched his back, grabbing his small backpack from the passenger seat and went to the hotel's front desk. Jessie was already there with the hotel manager specifying that no one had permission to make any charges to the room. God, Shane loved her, she was the best at her job. He kissed her on her cheek, knowing that she'd have everything arranged for them in the morning.

He dropped his bag off in his room, and went to check in with his foreman. He knocked twice on the door to the room next to his and Jack opened right up.

"You made it."

"Of course. How's everything going? Everyone here?" Shane asked quickly, not bothering to step all the way inside.

Jack laughed, and shook his head at him. "Yeah, Smith Jr. Everyone is here, including Llew."

Shane tried to hide his grin at the mere mention of Llew's name. God, if Jack only knew how hard he'd already fallen. "I wasn't just talking about him."

"Yeah, whatever." Jack sat back against the headboard and picked up the remote control. "He's not half bad, Smith. He's quiet as hell, gotta practically drag more than a one-word response out of him, but when he does talk he's very intelligent and interesting."

Shane stared at Jack, not quite sure what to say. He'd had a few conversations with Llew, but nothing too deep. He realized he wanted to get to know Llew a lot better than just knowing he wasn't a rapist. That was not enough to make a successful relationship.

"Smith Jr!" Jack yelled, waving his hand in the air.

"What? Huh?" Shane snapped back to reality. "Did you say something?"

"Uh, yeah. I said the guys are going to Buck's on Ward Blvd around eight, you coming?"

"Oh. Maybe. I'll see. I'm kind of tired, might turn in early."

"I bet. You gonna turn in early, alright." Jack laughed, throwing a pillow at him. Shane caught it and threw it back.

"Get your mind out of the gutter. I'm gonna have a talk with Llew about advancement in the company."

"What?" Jack sprang to his feet. "Are you serious? Advance him to what?"

"I'm not sure yet. What's the problem?" Shane sat in one of the chairs against the window. He certainly hoped his foreman wasn't thinking Llew should be held back because of his record. "I know you're not thinking like the other bigots in Henderson."

"Shut up. You know I'm not. But he's only been employed a week, man. You can't have him moving up to supervisor now or even anytime soon. How the hell do you think that's going to look? Especially once everyone gets wind that ya'll are sleeping together."

Shane shook his head, but stopped when Jack waved him off. "Smith Jr. I've been your best friend since pre-school; you think I can't tell when you've gotten laid? Jesus."

"Fine. But he's way overqualified to be some entry-level laborer. I've seen his sketches, his blueprints, fucking designs I've never seen made by architects with master's degrees. I don't want to lose him. He could be beneficial to this company Jack."

"Beneficial to the company or booty for you, Shane?" Jack said snidely, with his big arms folded over his chest.

"You know what? Fuck you," Shane snapped, standing up to leave.

"Wait. Smith Jr., wait. I'm sorry. That was out of line," Jack said, holding his palm against the door to prevent Shane from leaving. "That was fucked up. This company has been your whole life. I know you wouldn't stoop that low. I just don't want you to have to go through all that bullshit that'll surely come of you dating Llew, and then next thing you know he's practically running the company with you."

"I hire whoever's qualified, Jack. You know that." Shane rubbed the back of his neck, knowing that Jack was right to some degree. The guys would be in an uproar. Smith Jr. was known as being fair.

"No, *I* hire qualified men. The men are my responsibility. You handle the business side. If you want everyone to see what Llew can do for this company, then let me handle it. I can show them first; before you just go and shove it down their throats." Jack gripped his shoulder, opening the door for him. "Trust me. I've never let you down."

"No, you haven't."

"Alright then. See you in the morning."

"Yeah, okay." Shane walked a little ways. "Oh, and make sure the guys don't get trashed tonight, they need to be up by six and ready to learn a bunch of common sense rules that's gonna bore them to death in the morning."

"Got it."

"Thanks, Jack."

"Sure. Oh yeah, Llew's in room 425."

"I know."

Shane could hear Jack's boisterous laugh as he walked down the hallway.

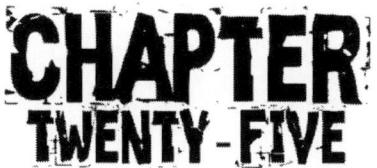

CHAPTER
TWENTY-FIVE

Llew dreamed about Shane all night long. They must've been newlyweds or something because they were in tuxedos. His brother was there, Jack, Ms. Pat, the crew from the job, even Ace and Jessup, everyone standing around clapping and congratulating them on something. Regardless, Llew was the happiest he'd ever been, he wouldn't be surprised if he was laughing out loud while he dreamed. They'd gone back to a room and made love all night. Llew taking Shane's body to a new high by tying him up and making him beg for Llew. The amazing part was Shane couldn't get enough of him and vice versa. He'd felt no shame in pleasing his lover the way they both wanted him to. It was absolutely perfect; just as it was supposed to be.

When Llew's alarm went off, he groaned, rolling over to silence it when he realized his cock was sticking straight up towards the ceiling. "Holy fuck." Llew gripped his shaft and bit his bottom lip to silence the deep moan. Groaning into his comforter while he writhed on the floor lost in the wonderful sensations. "Oh god, that feels good. Shit."

He stroked his dick at an easy pace, wanting to enjoy every single second. It was only a few more pumps before his large fist was flying up and down on his thick shaft. He watched with profound fascination. Morning wood, how he'd missed it. There was no other feeling. When he'd gone to bed, he wondered if his erection was something that would only happen if Shane was on top of him, arousing him, but obviously not. The thought of him was enough. He shot all over his abdomen, murmuring Shane's name as he came down from a very intense orgasm. Llew washed up with a huge smile on his face.

He'd taken Shane up on his offer to drive him to Henderson, but at the last minute, he'd sent Jack to drive him since he had an emergency meeting come up that morning. It was probably for the best, because he might've ended up staring at Shane the entire hour-long drive. Once Shane left last evening after their time together, Llew was on cloud nine all night, and miraculously, everyone noticed it. Ms. Pat said Llew looked different when she brought him some dinner after he'd finished repairing her steps with newfound energy.

Leslie was cautiously optimistic for him. Dating a boss could get messy, he'd told him. Nevertheless, Llew was hooked. He didn't care if he had to work on a completely different site from Shane, as long as he didn't have to stop seeing him. Llew was entitled to a modicum of happiness now.

Llew had already turned down Jack's invitation to go out and have wings and beer tonight, deciding to stay in. The guys were still not his friends… yet. So what was the point of going out to sit at a bar just to monopolize Shane and Jack's time because everyone else refused to socialize with him? He figured the boss man would be joining his crew, too, so he was surprised to hear a light tapping at his door as he got out of the shower.

Llew scrambled to hold the thin towel around his waist while he hurried to the door, dripping wet. When he opened it, Shane slowly caressed him from head to toe with those soft eyes, his mouth turning up appreciatively at the corners.

"Would you like to come in?" Llew said seductively, wondering where the hell he'd gotten that from.

"Puuleeez, let me in," Shane drawled, pushing the door with one hand and reaching for Llew's towel with the other.

He let the door fall closed behind Shane, backing up out of his hungry grip. Shane pulled off his windbreaker, letting it fall to the floor, advancing until the back of Llew's knees hit the edge of the bed. He let Shane push him back and climb over top of him with absolutely no resistance from him. Shane straddled his thighs and pushed his hard cock into him. Even though they were both gasping, they kept the touches light, grinding languidly against each other.

"Damn, you feel so fuckin' good." Llew hissed, meeting Shane's thrusts with his own. His cock was hard as a missile, and he loved it. He was still shocked when he got an erection, but it was like riding a goddamn bike, he knew exactly how to use it again.

"You feel good too. Too good," Shane answered back, kissing Llew's scruffy jaw. "I told myself I was going to come over and talk to you, maybe ask you on a date tonight, but you weren't supposed to answer the door naked, either."

Llew chuckled against Shane's throat, pulling his hips harder against him. "A date, huh."

"Yes. Jack said you were very interesting to talk to and I realized that I haven't had the pleasure of seeing just how interesting you are." Llew was watching Shane closely. "I've seen how passionate you are, but I don't want you to feel used, ya know."

Llew was amazed. Just when he thought he couldn't like Shane more, here he was; going out of his way to make sure Llew felt wanted, appreciated. "I don't feel that way." He tried to reassure his new friend. "I know you're not a user. I like what we're doing. If you want to talk, we can. I don't know what you want to know, I've been kind of sedentary the last few years."

Shane let out a loud laugh and Llew joined in, he'd meant for it to be funny. He didn't want Shane to be uncomfortable at the mention of his prison term. "I think you're amazing, Shane."

They watched each other, neither of them talking. The heat was building, and he saw the moment the fire ignited in Shane, his eyes turning a bright golden brown. "We'll talk more later." Shane growled, rearing up to yank Llew's towel off.

Not this time. Llew rolled on the queen-size bed, putting Shane underneath him. He gripped both of Shane's wrists and slowly brought them up over his head, kind of checking his reaction. His lover moaned his approval arching his back and tilting his head to lick at Llew's mouth. He rested his full weight down on him and pressed his forehead against Shane's, nudging him back down. The things he wanted to do to Shane were probably way more than he would be comfortable doing right now, but there were some things that it wasn't too soon for.

238

"I have on too many fuckin' clothes. Llewell" Shane snapped, fighting Llew's hold on his arms.

Llew glowered at Shane and dipped down to bite him on his neck. A little punishment to see how he'd take it.

"Ohh, fuck." Shane jerked, before going limp in Llew's hold.

Damn, his dick was so hard he could barely stand it. The way Shane submitted to him, the thought of burying himself inside his fiery boss was doing a number on his control.

"Please don't hold back, Llewell. I'm begging you. Don't hold back. I've waited so long for this, was waiting before you even came into to town, I fuckin' needed this." Shane panted.

That'll have to be good enough. Llew lifted himself up, pulled Shane's shirt over his head, and swooped down to take one of those flat, brown nipples into his mouth before his man knew what was happening. He sucked it hard. Bit it and sucked it again. Shane was getting loud, his hands out to the sides, pulling at the comforter.

"Touch me," Llew barked, moving to the other nipple to abuse that one too.

"Damnit." Shane groaned, digging his hands into Llew's hair. He didn't try to guide him, but the way he dug his fingers into his scalp showed how much he was loving everything Llew was doing.

He squeezed his eyes shut – he'd never thought he'd have the opportunity to think this again – but he willed his cock under his control and to not come now. Shane was his weakness, every bit of strength and resolve he had went out the window when he was with him. He pushed his naked cock against Shane's rough jeans, hissing at the fabric scraping against the sensitive skin.

Shane rubbed and massaged Llew's shoulders while he continued to scatter kisses all over his firm chest, licking eagerly at the smooth patch of hair in the center. He unbuckled Shane's belt and had his pants off quicker than he thought he could. Like riding a bike.

Shane had on tight black briefs instead of boxers. *What the fuck?* He wasn't expecting that at all. They were so sexy. That hard length straining against the soft nylon material. Llew squeezed the base of his dick with one hand while he rubbed Shane's rigid cock through the thin fabric.

"You like them? I took them out the box just for you, babe." Shane's voice was back to that throaty, wicked tenor as he watched Llew.

"I love them. You wore them for me."

"I've had them for years, never had a reason to wear them. Until… auuugh. God, Llewell."

Llew ran the flat of his tongue over the nylon-covered bulge, mouthing and licking at it eagerly. Shane smelled like his spicy cologne there too, and Llew buried his nose in his crotch, inhaling Shane's scent until he felt drunk. Shane anxiously reached inside his briefs, pulling on his cock, wanting way more than what Llew was giving him.

Showtime.

Llew grabbed Shane's hand, yanking it out of his briefs. He shot back up, pining Shane's hands back above his head in one fast, fluid motion. Sensual brown eyes watched him with excitement and want as Llew exerted his dominance over his lover. He put his mouth against Shane's ear, his voice coming out dark and husky. "Do you think you're controlling what's happening right now, Shane?"

A sexy moan escaped those plush lips before Shane finally responded, "No, babe."

"Good," Llew whispered, a second before he used his powerful muscles to flip Shane over with one move.

"Oh god."

Llew slapped Shane's round ass, those fuckin' black briefs making him wild. He wanted Shane in every position, he wanted to lick and taste every part of him simultaneously. Since that wasn't possible, he'd have to prioritize. First, he wanted Shane's perky, round ass. Llew pulled down the thin material just a fraction and nibbled at the top of Shane's ass. His tongue danced on the soft strands of fine hair.

Shane arched his needy ass in the air and moved to push down his briefs some more, but stopped before he did and put his hands back up on the pillow.

"Oh, good baby." Llew rewarded Shane's restraint by pulling his briefs all way off his ass and taking a long swipe with his tongue. It'd been so long since he'd enjoyed such a delicacy, and he was going to feast on Shane until he was good and ready to take him.

Shane spread his legs wider and Llew fully opened him up, rubbing his mouth around the dark, wrinkled bud. It had just the right smattering of hair, a manly hole, not some ridiculously waxed, baby-smooth skin. Llew circled his tongue around it a few more times, enjoying Shane's moans and curses, until he finally stopped tormenting the both of them and speared his tongue in for his first real taste. Shane's flavors exploded on his tongue, making Llew come alive again. He pierced that tight hole as deep as he could, until Shane was pushing back on his face and humping the polyester comforter. He ate at Shane's ass like it was a dying man's last meal.

"Fuck me, Llewell. Fuck me with your tongue."

Llew stopped long enough to take a much needed breath. "Taste so goddamn good, Shane." He slapped Shane's ass cheek again. The pale skin turning an exhilarating shade of red. "But, I'm gonna fuck you with more than just my tongue."

Llew crawled up Shane's back and brought his weight down on him again, grinding his thick cock against Shane's now-pink ass.

"Oh fuck, you're heavy. I love it. Fuckin' love it," Shane purred.

Llew turned Shane's face towards him so he could kiss those pretty lips some more. They tongued at each other hungrily while Llew continued to thrust and rut against him faster and harder until they were both on the verge of coming.

"Fuck me. Fuck me," Shane begged. "Llewell, damnit. I need to come with you inside me."

Llew's whole body shook from a need deep inside. He knew he'd never feel the same for another man after he made love to Shane. He rose up and aimed his cockhead at Shane's entrance. It was so slick and warm, ready and so damn inviting. He pushed at the tightness, his toes curling at the resistance. Oh how he wanted to thrust in all the way, feel that heat on his bare skin. Through the fervent haziness of their passion, Llew realized he needed to put on a damn condom. He was amazed that Shane was still pushing up to impale himself. Trust. Shane trusted Llew and he'd let him do him bareback if Llew believed it was safe.

Llew leaned in and placed a caring kiss on Shane's flushed cheek. "Let me get a condom, babe."

Shane didn't argue when Llew got up and went to his duffle to get the little brown bag. He'd bought a box of condoms and some lube at the convenience store when Jack stopped to use the bathroom. Llew knew it wouldn't be responsible to take Shane bare if they had the chance to be together. He turned off almost all the lights in the room, leaving on the bedside light so he'd be able to see his lover when they came together for the first time.

Shane was so still that Llew tapped his hip when he came back to the bed. "Are you okay?"

"I need you so damn much right now, I was willing to let you inside me without protection. I'm clean, I promise," Shane confessed tenderly.

"I know. I am too. I wouldn't lie to you," Llew said as quietly as his deep voice would allow in the dim room.

"I know you wouldn't lie." Shane turned over, looking him in his eyes. "I trust you."

Llew pulled on the covers and Shane rose up to let him remove the itchy comforter. Llew slung it on the floor and crawled on top of Shane. He tore off the wrapper and slid the tight latex down as far as he could, careful not to stroke himself too much. He squeezed some lube onto his head, gently easing it down his rod. He shivered at his own touch and again when Shane spread his legs wide and reached out for him.

Positioning himself again, he paused to kiss Shane with affection and adoration before he tilted his hips and pushed his thick head past the tight ring of muscle guarding Shane's entrance.

Shane groaned and squirmed beneath him, widening his legs even more.

"Am I hurting you?" Llew asked shakily. His muscles strained from holding his upper body while he fought his urges.

"I'm fine. Just been a while. Been wanting this for so long. Go slow, Llewell." Shane's wistful tone sounded like the song of angel as he said his name in the throes of passion.

Llew pushed in a couple more inches, going as slow as his lover needed, refusing to be anything but wonderful for him. The heat was sweltering, the tightness almost too painful to bear, the emotion... too potent to fathom.

Shane pulled Llew down so their chests were fused together, and thrust his hips upward, engulfing the last couple inches of him.

"Oh my —" Llew's eyes rolled in his head. "Shane, Jesus." The feeling was overwhelming him. He hadn't made love in... in... *oh my god.* Shane gave himself to him regardless of... *oh god.* Regardless that he was a convicted rapist. Llew tried to control himself. His breathing was getting out of control and his body shook from panic, not passion. *Not now, not now please.* Llew's chest heaved as he tried to take in some air.

"Llewell," Shane said softly. "Listen to my voice."

Llew gasped and choked on nothing. He felt strong sure hands caress his sweaty back, while Shane's tender lips brushed the sensitive rim of his ear. "You're okay, baby. Relax. Breathe for me."

He couldn't. He squeezed his eyes closed, moisture filling them behind his burning lids as oxygen refused to circulate. He could feel his erection going along with his pride. *Fuck.* Some dominant lover he was. Having a damn panic attack in the middle of sex, their first time at that.

Shane tightened his legs around him keeping him from pulling out. Shane held him tight but spoke so soothingly. "Easy. Easy. Gentle breaths, babe. Follow the rhythm of my chest, Llewell." He felt Shane's lithe chest rise and fall beneath him. "Do it with me." He coached him with that angelic voice. When he inhaled again, Llew took in a shallow breath, followed quickly by a ragged exhale. "Again, baby. Slowly." Llew's body rose with Shane's next breath and again he mimicked him, the air flowing a little easier. "Just like that." When Shane's chest rose up this time, he eased his hips up along with it, taking Llew back into his body. "Yeah, baby. Keep breathing." Shane kept up the languid pace of their breathing while he rotated his ass on Llew's quickly firming cock. His moans were real, his touch and the way he felt around Llew's dick was pure ecstasy.

Llew's body finally calmed and his breathing evened out enough to kiss Shane lightly on his collarbone. He couldn't muster a thank you yet, but he wanted him to know it meant so much to him that Shane didn't push him away.

Shane turned towards him, prodding Llew out of the crevice of his neck. "Look at me, lover. I need to see you're okay."

Llew lifted his head up slightly to look in Shane's eyes. He was scared he'd see regret or sorrow in them, but all that was there were beautiful sparkling eyes shining up at him. "You're okay, now." Shane smiled.

Llew took a deep breath and let it out slowly. Groaning loudly when Shane rotated his ass again, smiling wicked at him. "Yeah baby. I'm good now."

"Good. Now fuck me."

Llew leaned in and kissed Shane with all the appreciation he felt as he eased out of Shane's delicious confinement, snapping his hips forward, burying himself all the way back inside. They both yelled out together at the bottomless feeling. Llew wrapped his arms around Shane's neck holding him close to him while he plunged in and out of him powerfully, but in a deliciously unhurried tempo. Shane chased Llew's mouth, sucking aggressively on his tongue at the same speed that Llew fucked him. Llew cradled Shane's head in the bend of his arm and dragged the other hand down his side until he got to his hip. He squeezed one side of his ass, opening him up and pressing in deeper. He ground his pelvis into Shane's ass, growling at the primal urge he felt to claim him and make Shane his permanently. He hooked Shane's leg over his shoulder and thrust hard, watching Shane's gorgeous face contort in pleasure.

"Fuck, Llewell! I'm 'bout to come." Shane's legs trembled around him.

"Yes. Now, baby."

Shane's back arched erotically and a split second later Llew felt the heat spread between them. Llew was done for. He knew he was there. He pushed in and stilled; both of them yelling their release loud enough to wake whoever may have been asleep next door. "Augh god. Shane." Llew milked his dick inside Shane's heat, his stomach slick and sticky from the cum Shane had sprayed between them. They collapsed against each other both of them winded and sated. Llew peppered kisses on Shane's forehead, his cheek, his eyes. He brushed his lips back and forth over Shane's open mouth speaking against his labored breaths. "Thank you. Thank you so much. You are... you are...." What was another word for everything?

"So are you." Shane smiled, kissing Llew back. They watched each other again, which was starting to become a very expressive habit of theirs. So much could be communicated through looks; things they couldn't express with words. Shane smoothed his hand down Llew's cheek, digging his fingers into the length of hair on his chin. Llew watched Shane like he was a gift sent to him from god.

"Your eyes say things I may never hear from you, Llewell," Shane whispered in the darkness.

"You'll hear them." After a few more moments, Llew finally broke the eye contact and reached over to turn off the lamp. That was enough for tonight. They couldn't possibly say what was on the tips of their tongues. There was time for that... hopefully. He pulled Shane's back against his chest, burying his nose in the silky hair at the back of his head. Llew closed his eyes — and even though he was in a bed — he slept peacefully for the first time in more than eight years.

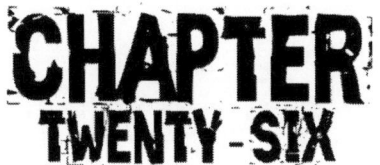

CHAPTER TWENTY-SIX

Shane's phone rang too loudly the next morning; interrupting him from one of the best sleeps he'd ever had. Llew's heavy arm was still around his middle and he could feel his hot breath on his neck. The phone rang again and Shane wanted to kill whoever was on the other end. He moved as little as possible and snatched the phone off the nightstand, noting that it was just a little after five in the morning. *Goddamnit.*

"Jack, what the hell do you want?" Shane hissed into the phone.

"Well good morning to you too, sunshine. I didn't interrupt anything did I?" Jack laughed loudly. Shane had always hated how damn chipper Jack was in the morning. True, they were used to getting up at the butt crack of dawn, but their class wasn't until seven. Sleeping in never killed anyone.

"Is this why you called?" Shane said, groggily.

"No. I wanted to see if you wanted to get a run in before the class but I guess you've had enough of a workout, huh?" Jack laughed again, so hard this time that he snorted annoyingly. He really was cracking his own self up this morning, but Shane wouldn't entertain him this time.

"Run with the cows, I'm sleeping in."

Jack was still laughing and trying to talk in between snorts. "Tell Llew I said, way to go big gu—" Shane pushed the end call button, cutting him off in the middle of another silly joke. He nestled back into Llew's large chest.

"I heard that," Llew said, from behind him. His voice sounded like Vin Diesel's in the morning.

"Ignore him. He's special." Shane yawned, and rolled over so he could face Llew. "We thought he'd grow out of his immaturity handicap, but we were wrong."

Llew laughed and pulled Shane closer, draping a heavy thigh over his hip, his hard, thick cock poking him in his leg.

"That's some hardware you got there." Shane grinned against Llew's pec, ducking down to lick at his nipples.

"Mmmm, feels good. Seems to get that way around you," Llew said, in that rough tone.

"Well then. I guess it's my responsibility to take care of it." Shane nipped and pulled at Llew's tight buds some more before reaching over for the supplies.

Llew stopped him before he tore open the condom. "You're not sore, Shane?"

Shane looked up at Llew, refusing to lie and say "Hell no," because his ass was actually sore as fuck. Llew wasn't a small man, and his cock was proportionate to his size, but Shane wanted him again; tender ass or not.

"Uh huh. Like I thought." Llew took the condom and lube from him and put them back on the nightstand.

"I want you. I need more," Shane whispered.

Llew ran his fingers through Shane's bed tousled hair, leaning in to kiss him teasingly. He scrubbed his beard playfully over Shane's cheek, making him laugh and push him off.

"Stop trying to distract me." Shane wrapped Llew's cock in a tight fist and began to stroke him while staring into his eyes.

"You want me, too. Don't you?" He hummed.

"Yes." Llew hissed.

"Then take me."

Llew scooted down some on the bed and cocked one leg up, letting the other rest on the bed. "Flip around and feed me that long cock, baby."

Shane's smile brightened like a hundred watt light bulb. Fucking sixty-nine. Shit, he hadn't done that since high school. Hell yeah, they could please each other at the same time. Shane whirled around and lined his cock up with Llew's mouth while he buried his face in all that sexy dark pubic hair around Llew's dick. Because of their height difference, Llew spread Shane's leg and tilted his hips forward, going right for his rim. Strong fingers spread him while a hot tongue gently lapped at his hole, soothing the burn left from their amazing night. It felt so damn good; Shane had forgotten he had a job to do, too.

He took as much of Llew's length into his mouth as he could, gagging when he got overzealous. Llew moaned, obviously loving the sound of him trying to take all of his hardness deep. After a few more tries, Shane finally focused on the head, groaning around the thickness, and flicking his tongue against the frenulum.

"Mmmmm, fuck. Just like that Shane." Llew stopped French kissing his ass just long enough to encourage Shane to suck harder when he was about to come. A big assed palm fisted Shane's cock and pumped it hard, once, twice, while that thick tongue continued to bathe his sensitive hole. Shane's eyes shut tight, and his cheeks hollowed as he shot his own load against Llew's chest. He was rewarded with his lover's essence before his own orgasm had finished. They were getting fuckin' great at this. After there was nothing else left in their balls, they split apart, both of them falling back across the length of the bed.

"Holy shit." Llew gasped, half laughing. "That was incredible."

Shane could only shake his head. His intelligence had apparently left his body along with his cum. Yeah, they were good together, incredibly good. Now that they knew they were definitely compatible in bed, he wondered how they'd be everywhere else.

"Have dinner with me." Shane panted the words out between breaths.

"Now?" Llew chuckled tiredly.

A wise-ass sense of humor. Nice. "Very cute, smart-ass. I mean when we get back to Henderson." Shane propped himself up on his elbow, gazing down at Llew. He was casually rubbing Shane's cum into his chest, staring back at him with that black, still-ravenous expression. Shane suppressed the urge to jump on top of Llew and ride his ass all the way to the sunset and back. He had a purpose and wouldn't be distracted by Llew, no matter how fuckin' hot he was. "Have dinner with me, babe."

"My brother will be in by noon today. He's bringing my furniture from his house."

"Oh. Okay, then." Shane didn't know what else to say. Did Llew not want Shane to meet his brother?

"If you drive me home and you're not busy, you can help us if you want." Llew stroked Shane's calf while he spoke. "Ms. Pat's making us a nice dinner; I know she wouldn't mind a bit if you joined us."

Shane smiled. "That sounds alright. Guess I could do that."

"Well I'm glad you're willing to grace us with your presence."

"Smart-ass." Shane dove on top of Llew, wrestling him all over the large mattress. Llew flipped and tossed Shane around as if he weighed nothing. Getting the upper hand was not easy for Shane. Llew's arms were huge and impossible to restrain; all Shane ended up doing was getting a good workout at six in the morning without leaving the bed.

"This is boring as hell man, and I'm hung over. I don't feel like taking no damn test."

Llew continued to ignore the obnoxious man beside him. He was one of Shane's new hires and it seemed the big man did nothing but complain for two solid hours during the class. Llew leaned back in his chair while he listened to the OSHA instructor explain how much time they had to complete the short, fifteen-question certification test. Even though he knew everything the instructor just told them, he still paid attention. Shane and Jack were taking turns coming to stand in the classroom, making sure no one was acting like the asshole beside Llew was. Why the guys went and hung out at a bar until two in the morning and got shit-faced was beyond him.

Hell, Llew had made love and had his man resting comfortably in his arms by two a.m. His phone buzzed in his shirt pocket and he pulled it out to check the text message while the instructor handed out the single sheet test to everyone. It was from Shane. He checked it quickly.

Stop smiling like that... you're looking like you got laid... the day before... last night... this morning. Lol... tonight

Llew barked a startled laugh at Shane's text, making the instructor and a few of the guys turn to look at him.

"No cell phones during the test," the man said, annoyed; dropping a test sheet in front of Llew.

He ran his hand through his hair, hiding his smile. He was going to get Shane when he got out of there. Llew skimmed over each question, rapidly circling each correct answer before standing and taking the paper up to the instructor. He was so ready to go. The man looked up at him, confused. Only three minutes had gone by. "If you don't take the test, I can't certify you."

"I did take it."

The man picked up the paper, going over Llew's answers. He guessed the guy saw that every one of them was correct, because he stamped the paper and put it in a folder on his desk. "Um. Your boss will receive the certifications; you can get it at his office." Llew smiled broadly, thinking that's not all he was going to get in Shane's office.

CHAPTER TWENTY-SEVEN

They were back in Llew's hotel room and Llew had Shane up against the wall ravaging his mouth. "You got me in trouble in school." Llew laughed, biting hard on Shane's neck and making his man laugh loudly as he struggled to get out of his hold.

"I didn't tell you to burst out laughing. I was just letting you know that you were sitting there smiling like a loon." Shane ran his tongue along Llew's beard, smiling cheekily. He sang his question teasingly, "What were you thinking about, Llewell?"

"I can show you better than I can tell you." Llew grabbed Shane's cock inside his jeans, groping it roughly.

"Fuck me," Shane murmured.

"I will."

Llew yanked at Shane's pants button, but his hands were grabbed in a tight, two-handed grip. "Babe. As much as I want that right now, we got forty minutes until your brother is supposed to get to your place and we got an hour drive ahead of us."

Llew towered over Shane, his bulk roughly forcing him back against the hard surface behind him. He gripped Shane's chin, turning it and jerking his head up so he could nip at Shane's ear. His lips aggressively brushed over his flushed skin while he snarled his words against the side of

Shane's face. "You're lucky, Shane. I was getting ready to show you what I do to my man when he misbehaves."

"Oh god." Shane squeezed between his legs; his face flushed a deep shade of rose. Someone liked the sound of that very much.

Llew stepped back and popped Shane once sharply on his ass. "Go get your stuff, let's go."

"Okay." Shane bolted out the door to his own room; which had only been used to house his duffle bag, and was back in less than ten minutes.

Fuckin' perfect.

CHAPTER TWENTY-EIGHT

"You sure finished the test quick," Shane said, merging onto the ramp to take them towards Henderson.

"I remember just about everything I read, and I've read OSHA regulations a million times," Llew responded casually. Shane loved how comfortable he looked in his big F-350. In a jet-black t-shirt and well-worn jeans, he looked good enough to pull over and fuck for a while. Damn having a time schedule.

"Um. Did ya'll have a big library in... in prison." Shane chanced a quick glance at Llew to see his reaction. He didn't appear to cringe at the mention of it.

He smiled to show Shane it was no longer painful to talk about. "No. The library was shitty as hell."

"Well how'd you have access to so much and blueprints?"

"Ace."

"What?"

"Ace. I joined his gang a few months into my sentence."

"You were in a gang?" Shane tried not to sound judgmental, but it was disappointing to hear. Did he want a gang member on his crew and in his bed? Did Llew hurt people?

"It wasn't that type of gang. Like East Coast, West Coast shit." Llew laughed. "Actually, Ace had a crew more so than a gang."

"Okay." Shane didn't know if Llew wanted him to know these things or not but if they were going to be together didn't they need to understand each other. "I understand if it's too painful to talk about."

Llew rubbed Shane's thigh soothingly, turning from his view of the outside world to look at him. "I just don't know how much you want to hear."

"Whatever you're comfortable with, but I promise you won't scare me away. Unless… well."

Llew continued to rub his leg, grinning at him. He loved that Llew's playfulness was starting to come out more and more around him now. "Unless what? Unless I tell you Ace was my boyfriend?"

"Was he?" Shane held his breath.

"Of course not. I was totally celibate in prison. I didn't even jerk off."

"I'm sorry."

Llew caressed the side of Shane's face. "Don't be sorry." Llew dropped his hands back to his lap, blowing out a long breath, as if girding himself for the conversation. "In the beginning, it was rough; to say the least. Un-fuckin'-bearable, to be honest. Everyone wanted to kill the so-called child rapist."

"Child rapist." Shane frowned.

"Moss was seventeen – a minor according to the Commonwealth of Virginia – a child according to the prison system."

Shane growled a little, but Llew kept going. The more he told him about what they did to him; the more he wanted to find this Moss and start a campaign to expose him for the fucked up piece of shit coward that he was.

"I finally joined up with Ace. Otherwise, I'd probably be dead. He and his crew; along with Big Waldo, protected me."

Shane barked a laugh. "Who the hell is that? His enforcer?"

Llew grinned mischievously at him. "Sort of. Big Waldo is the nickname for the warden or the guards' captain."

"Ahh. Got it."

"Actually, no you don't. Ace and Captain Jessup are a couple."

"Like couple, couple; as in me and you?"

Llew's hand was back on his leg again, and it took a lot of effort for Shane to concentrate on the road and keep up with Llew's story. "Exactly, but me and you to the one hundredth power. More in love than I've ever seen any two people before. Like they were talkin' marriage when I left."

"Holy shit."

"Yeah. No one knew how Ace had so much power. Most likely never will. He had any and everything in his cell, from a DVD player to a cell phone and everything in between. If he wanted it for himself or a member of his crew, he got it. Jessup would ask me what books I wanted and he'd bring them within the week. I got to eat all kinds of take-out in his office, while everyone else was working. I worked out when I wanted, worked in whatever department I wanted. No one ever fucked with me again, because if they did; they ended up in the hole, that's solitary, or worse; they were transferred. After a while, best part was I got to visit with my brother in Jessup's office. Somehow, Ace knew that I needed him to see that I was truly alright. Les needed me to be able to hug him. I needed a fuckin' hug from him just as bad. In the regular visitation room, there was no physical contact allowed, so no hugging. For a while, I didn't want him coming there; seeing my bruised face, and busted lips, me looking depressed as hell. It tore both of us up. So it was a whole year before Ace called him to come back to visit me. The next thing I knew, I'm walking into Big Waldo's office, and there my brother was; waiting for me with two large pizzas and a *Transformers* DVD."

"Wow."

Llew chuckled. "Yeah, I was wowed too. Jessup was the meanest SOB walkin' in that place, but behind closed doors, he was a lovesick puppy and he'd do anything Ace asked… and vice versa."

"You got very lucky I guess."

"Heck yeah, I did. Ace's crew didn't do bad stuff. Ya know what I mean? Most crews were about violence and dominating the entire inside. Ace did mentoring and counseling. I helped with tutoring for the GED classes, and I ran the carpentry workshop department with two of Ace's other guards. Hell, that's what kept me sane, still being able to design and build."

"Why'd Ace even let you in his crew if everyone hated sex offenders as much as you say?" Shane deliberately didn't say rapist. He'd never say that word.

"I wondered that at first. It's why I turned Ace down a few times; I thought he might be setting me up. I had no clue how he was so damn influential in there. It scared the shit out of me, seeing the power he had. But he said I reminded him of someone. He never said who; just someone he lost years ago. Something about I had the same eyes as that person."

"Oh my god, well yeah, that'll do it. I'm still caught up on your eyes. Never met someone else whose eyes tell it all." Shane put his hand on top of Llew's where it still rested on his thigh. The slight blush on Llew's cheeks was heart-warming. "So where's Ace now?"

Llew dropped his head, sighing sadly. "Still in there."

"How long does he have?"

"I don't know. I write but... well. He's supposed to be up for parole soon. I don't know when. It's kind of a thing not to talk about release dates in there. Might get you popped in the mouth by a big fist if you ask a man how much longer he has."

"Man, there's a shitload of rules to remember."

"Yep, and you gotta follow them, cause your life depends on it."

"I'm glad you made it out of there, Llewell. I'm really glad you made it to Henderson."

Shane pulled on to Ms. Pat's street, feeling like he really knew Llewell. Knew him better than anyone except maybe his brother. He'd gained the trust of the giant, hard man. That had to be the only reason Llew would tell him about the most traumatic experience in his life.

"There's the big dope." Llew laughed.

Shane saw a medium-built handsome man leaning against the back of a large pickup with an attached trailer, full of furniture. The logo on the truck bed was an image of a group of shrubs with the name Gardner Boys written across it.

As soon as Shane came to a stop, Llew jumped out the truck and ran up to the man who was a smaller version of himself. They eagerly hugged each other, Llew lifting his brother's feet completely off the ground. Llew beamed with excitement and Shane loved seeing him like that. Llew beamed at him, too, but in an entirely different way. After the two Gardner men exchanged handshakes and another hug, Llew turned and waved for Shane to come over.

He couldn't believe he was nervous. Llew said that Leslie raised him since his parents died while he was in high school, and was the most important person in his life. He sure hoped the man would find him worthy of Llew's affection. As soon as Shane was in range, Llew spread his hand on the small of his back and guided him in front of his brother.

"Shane this is my big brother; Leslie, Leslie Gardner. Les, this is Shane Smith Jr."

Leslie's smile was genuine when he shook Shane's hand. "You're his new boss right?" Leslie's eyes were just as dark as Llew's, but not as revealing. Leslie's black irises twinkled with mischief.

"Yes, I'm his new boss and—" Shane looked up at Llew, silently asking for permission. It surprised him when Llew leaned down and kissed him chastely on his lips.

"And my boyfriend," Llew finished.

Leslie's smile was bright and beautiful. It was clear how happy he was for his brother, and hopefully he could see how happy Shane was to be with him, to be given the title of "Boyfriend."

"You always did wear your heart on your sleeve, bro." Leslie jabbed Llew in his arm, but he paid no attention, his eyes still locked on Shane. Leslie laughed, teasing his brother. "Yeah. You got it bad already, man."

He did have it bad. Leslie had no idea. Shane had been the soothing balm his blistered soul needed. He finally felt like he was recovering, living, breathing again. It was the worst feeling in existence to be suffocated by life.

"Llewellyn, you're home." Ms. Pat stepped out onto the porch, letting the screen door slam behind her. She hurried down the steps, wiping her hands on her brown-and-pink flowered apron. Llew let her hug him and kiss his cheek; she turned and did the same for Shane before turning to Leslie. "You must be the brother. You two could be twins fo' sho' if you was just a smidge bigger." She held her two fingers an inch apart, laughing loudly. Leslie would need to grow way more than a smidge to be as big as Llew.

Leslie leaned in and kissed her cheek. Schmoozing her immediately. "Yes, ma'am, I'm Leslie. He may be bigger but he still can't whup me."

"Well when I was in jail, I put on a few muscles myself. I was really a piece of work in my younger days," she boasted, laughing again when Leslie's eyes widened.

"Jail." Leslie shook his head like he didn't believe her.

"You got it." She took her dishtowel and swatted Llew's shoulder, winking at him. "Me and this one are like two peas in a pod, huh, Llewellyn?"

"You got it," Llew said right back, unconsciously pulling Shane into his chest.

Ms. Pat covered her mouth, while she stared at them. "Oh Llewellyn, Shane. You two. I knew there was something about ya'll. I could see it in the both of ya. I'm so glad. Lord knows. Llewellyn, Shane is a good boy, ya'll look great together." She looked between them excitedly.

"He better be good," Leslie piped in, his arms crossed over his chest.

Here we go. Llew knew Les would turn on the big brother act sooner or later.

Ms. Pat turned with her hands on her hips, feigning anger. "I know he's good because I helped raise him. So you just get off your high horse, mister."

Leslie put his hands up in surrender. "Yes, ma'am. I'm just doing my job."

Llew let go of Shane. "Okay everyone relax. We're fine, I'm fine, Shane's fine, everyone's fine. No one has any job to do."

"Actually yes ya do. Ya'll got a big job to do. Go on and get this furniture moved so you can eat this nice dinner I'm fixin'." She turned to go back in the house, stopping when she remembered something else, like she always did. "Oh, and Llewellyn, Shirley say she is coming by to bring you something. She was too pleased about the job you did on her benches."

"Oh, okay," Llew said, already dropping the bed on the truck and climbing inside to see what his brother brought him. "Come on guys. Les, Shane's gonna help us."

"Cool. Llew, I brought you most everything from your room except your bed."

Llew saw a queen-size mattress and bedframe against the left side of the truck bed. "Where'd you get this?"

"Um… donation," his brother said sheepishly.

Llew knew his brother had bought him a new one thinking that Llew might've slept on the floor because his other bed wasn't comfortable. But that wasn't the case. Instead of giving his brother a hard time, he simply nodded and thanked him. The shocked look on Leslie's face was priceless.

It only took them an hour to get the bed, full-size futon, a brown leather recliner, one dresser with a mirror, corner desk, and the black entertainment stand up to his room. They were extra careful with the fifty-inch television. Llew looked around the room, liking the setup. It wasn't overly cluttered, and he had someplace that Shane could sit when he came to visit. Shane left to get Llew a bookshelf he'd made while Leslie and his brother hooked up the cable and entertainment system.

"He seems nice, Llew."

"He's great. And yes, he's really nice. One of the nicest men I've ever met," Llew said, tacking the cable to the baseboard.

"Hmhmm," Leslie said nonchalantly. "Are you and him, um —"

"Les!" Llew looked up in shock, his face feeling warm.

Leslie threw his arms up. "I just want you to be careful, Llew, is all."

Llew dropped his hammer, stomped over to his refrigerator, and yanked out a bottle of water.

"Llew, calm down. You know I'm only looking out for you."

"I know. I got it. But he knows everything, okay. And he believes me. He's knows who I am and what I'm not," Llew said, stabbing himself in his chest with his thumb. He realized his hands were shaking. "He's the only goddamn person besides Ms. Pat to actually give a damn about the truth. He believes me," Llew said harshly, coughing hard to get air into his lungs.

"Llew calm down." Leslie gripped Llew's shoulder, a pained look on his face. "Llew relax, it's okay. I didn't mean—"

"Why would you try to throw shade on this, man? Try to make me doubt him?" Llew gasped for air, holding his chest. "I know he believes me."

"Yes. I do." Shane came through the screen door, and raced over to him, wrapping him tight in his arms. Whispering softly in his ear, "Calm down, it's okay. It's okay, babe. Breathe."

Llew draped his large body over Shane's and held him close, burying his face in Shane's neck, breathing in his strong scent. It was like a gift from the heavens to hear his lover's voice right at that moment, because if he hadn't, he was sure he would've had a full-blown panic attack. He couldn't let those thoughts fill his head. Shane believed in him and wanted him for who he was. There was no ulterior motive. Llew had had enough deceit in his life to last him two lifetimes. He refused to allow himself to believe Shane would hurt him. He needed to trust and have faith in love again or he would turn into some crabby, bitter old man.

"Look at me. Let me see that you're okay."

Llew unhooked his arms and stood to his full height to look down into Shane's eyes. Yes, he was okay... now. They kissed each other; exchanged the kind of kiss that was confirmation of how they really felt about each other. He ran both hands through Shane's hair, cupping the back of his head. Moving him until he was in exactly the position Llew wanted him. Until his mouth was slanted perfectly over his. Llew's shirt was clenched in Shane's tight fist while he kissed him long and deep, moaning into his mouth. Llew could feel Shane's erection pressing against his thigh; he reached down and squeezed it a few times before delving even deeper to cup his balls.

"Yes. God, Llewell."

"I need you, Shane." Llew's own cock was solid and leaking in his jeans.

"Let me stay with you tonight, please. Let me take care of whatever you need," Shane whispered into his mouth.

Llew groaned and captured Shane's mouth again. God, yes. How he needed to be taken care of. Every single burning hot need.

"Llew are you okay? Is it okay to come in now? Have ya'll stopped?" Leslie yelled from outside. The two of them had been so caught up in each other, they hadn't heard Les leave. "I'm coming up with the bookshelf! Coming in; in three, two, one... stop what you're doing!"

Llew and Shane both laughed, still holding on to each other. Yeah, he was okay now. He was better than okay. He nibbled on Shane's rosy bottom lip. "Yes, stay with me tonight. Let's test out my new bed."

Shane's moan was the perfect answer.

CHAPTER TWENTY-NINE

"Llewellyn, your brother is such a sweetheart. Just like you. I really enjoyed him the other day." Ms. Pat was making a cake for her elderly neighbor. She rambled on and on, while Llew replaced her pantry door. "When's he coming back to see you? I'll make his favorite. Didn't he say pot roast? Yepper. That's what it was, pot roast. I got a great recipe passed down generations. My great-great-nanna started it. We've all added our own ingredients over time. I added cream of celery soup. Did you know cream of celery tastes good in 'bout any stew? Well it does. I wonder why it's so rarely used."

Llew kept working while Ms. Pat yammered on about nothing in particular. Asking him meaningless questions and answering them for him, too. Barely taking a breath in between. Llew loved that about her, he found it charming.

"So what are you doing tonight? Is Shane coming over? This coupling of ya'll's is just a win-win for everyone. You've never looked happier and I get to see my godson a whole lot more. Yes, thank you Lord. Everything is working out just fine. That boy's been right lonely these past few years, too. So what you doing tonight?"

He waited a beat to see if she was gonna let him respond this time. "Um. Just gonna relax in my room. It was a long day at work. I'll probably work on my computer until my eyes cross."

She laughed at his answer. He was exhausted. Jack had him doing all types of extra work on the site this week. Fixing equipment, dissecting blueprints. He even asked Llew for his opinion on laying the foundation on a job in the middle of one of their meetings. Everyone was floored when Llew stepped up front with Jack and Shane while the architect pointed out some more specifics the owners wanted to add to entrance of the building. The figures and calculations swam around his head, and strategically fell into place like magic. He'd slid the pencil from behind Shane's ear and drew in the new lines, not even needing computer software to make the additions. The architect couldn't thank Llew enough for saving him from having to draw up completely new blueprints. Everyone thought the additional layout would have them working mandatory overtime this weekend. Llew made it so not only did they not have to work the weekend, but Jack promised everyone they would be knocking off early on Friday. Shane showed Llew just how impressed he was with him that night back at his place.

"And what are you smiling about over there?" Ms. Pat's knowing smirk told him she already knew the answer to that question, too.

"Nothing. Just thinking is all."

"Mmhmm. Where's Shane tonight?"

"At his parents' for dinner."

"Oh. That's nice. I gotta call that lady. It's been ages since we had tea. Since Big Daddy retired they just been all over the country."

"Must be nice," Llew said absently. He wondered if he'd ever meet Big Daddy Smith.

"How's the new site coming, son? Ya'll broke ground yet?"

"Yes, sir." Shane popped off another piece of asparagus, hopping that Queenie would quickly serve dessert; making it all the sooner he could leave.

"Smith Jr., are you going to sulk all evening or are we going to enjoy dinner? We don't get to see you much, darlin'," his mom said. Her graying blonde hair was swept up into a loose a bun, showing off a very expensive set of pearls. She sat with one hand clutching a cloth napkin in her lap that only made a brief appearance to wipe the corners of her mouth before disappearing again. The other perfectly manicured fingers held her fork delicately while she ate tiny bite-sized morsels of her Chicken Florentine.

"I apologize. I'm just a little tired Momma, is all. Been putting in a lot of hours in the office this week." Shane quickly ate another few bites.

"I heard that ain't all you been putting in work on." His father glared across the formal dining table at him.

Shane dropped his fork, leaning back in his seat exasperatedly. *Here we go.* He knew it wouldn't be long before his father brought up Llew. Gossips in this town were worse than a damn soap opera.

"Don't sugarcoat, Big Daddy. Coyness doesn't become you. Spit it out." Shane huffed.

His father put his own fork down, leaning in intimidatingly. "Watch it boy. You not gon' smart-mouth me in my own house. I just want to know if it's true. Have you hired a rapist to work for my damn company, and gone and started dating him, too?"

"I hired a qualified contractor to work for *my* company. It is mine, right? I'm pretty sure I was there when we signed the papers. To address the next part of your question; that shouldn't concern you at all. I started dating a man that I'd taken an interest in and who I sincerely like. And for the record, he's not a rapist. I've never known you to entertain gossips, Big Daddy. This family has always been a supporter of, and participant in, equality in the workplace. I wasn't going to turn away one of the most talented designers and hardest working laborers I'd ever encountered just because years ago some guy he dated didn't know how to stand up to his daddy and took the bitch way out."

"Shane," his mom gasped, clutching her pearls. "Language at my table, young man."

Shane just refrained from rolling his eyes. This is exactly why he didn't think Llew would be able to meet his parents anytime soon. Llew thought Shane was worthy to meet his only family but Shane was ashamed of his. They were all from Henderson, so why his parents acted like some pretentious, pompous aristocrats from Bel Air really baffled him. Llew might have taken one look at the way his parents behaved and high-tailed it away from a serious case of déjà vu.

"Honey. We just don't want you to get hurt," his mom said quietly, trying to calm them both down.

"Llew would never hurt me. Ever. He's never hurt anyone."

"You don't know that," his father barked. "He's only been in town a few weeks."

"So what? I do know him, and I believe him."

"Son, I swear you're bout as sharp as a cue ball sometimes," his father said, shaking his head sadly.

Shane got up, throwing his napkin down on the table. He hated when his father insinuated that he wasn't intelligent or knowledgeable. It drove him crazy. He never should've listened to him about not going to college. Now he had this fucked up complex anytime someone called him stupid; corrected a word he misused, or figured something out before he could, making him feel like he was just some hick contractor.

"Shane honey, don't go. Sit down. Big Daddy don't mean nothing by that."

His father sat there looking unfazed. "Let him go Meredith. If all he knows to do is tuck tail and bolt, then go on; cover your balls, and skirt on out of here. Or, if this man's so important to you already, then sit your sensitive ass down and defend him."

Shane stood there seething, looking down at his father. His father stood, slowly coming to his full six foot two height. Although he was almost sixty, he was still strong and well-built from his years of hard physical work. His skin was sun-worn and he had more than a few wrinkles from years of yelling and barking orders, but he was still handsome and the older ladies of their town often flirted with him.

"Stop standing over me, boy. Sit. Down," his father said through clenched teeth. "And apologize to your mother for disrespecting her at her own dinner table."

Shane took a couple of deep breaths and pushed his chair back. He walked over to his mother's side of the table and lightly kissed her cheek, taking her small hand in his. "Momma I apologize for raising my voice. I didn't mean to ruin dinner."

She patted his hand where it held hers. "Nonsense. It's okay, darlin'. Go on now and sit back at your plate, and let's have an easy conversation about this new fella. We want to hear all about him. Don't we, Big Daddy?" His mom glared across the table at his father and that was his cue to sit down and stop his part in ruining dinner as well. He may have been the head of the house but they both new who the real boss was, so unless his father wanted to be sleeping in the dog house he knew to tone it down and not run her only son off.

His dad grunted and picked his fork back up. They ate the rest of their dinner while his mom talked about what she looked forward to on their latest cruise, coming up next week. His father had bought a new forty-five foot sailing yacht to explore the east coast. It was a dream they'd had since they were newlyweds, and his mom beamed when she talked about it. They were taking the yacht down to Florida at the end of the week. Shane remembered all the fishing trips he took with his father as a kid, and how he talked and laughed about building a boat big enough to live on. His father's dreams had come true for him and his spouse, why didn't he want the same for his son?

Shane waited until Queen brought out their desert. He told their long-time maid and cook how wonderful everything was, and asked her a few questions about her family before letting her go back to the kitchen. Queen was like a grandmother to him. His mother's mom had lived in Wisconsin his whole life, he had only seen her three times, and his father's parents passed when he was still in grade school.

"Big Daddy. Llewellyn Gardner is a fine man. He's accepted every challenge life threw at him, got back up, and kept fighting. You taught me to respect men like that." His father nodded his head as Shane told them about what happened to Llew at such a young age. His mother was almost in tears by the time he finished. He hoped Llew wouldn't mind him telling his parents his story, but he wouldn't let those slack-mouth nosy hounds of Henderson taint Llew's image, not for his parents. They needed to know why Shane was already in love with him.

"He's a brilliant architect. He lost his scholarships when he went to prison but he didn't let that stop him from continuing to teach himself for eight years. That's more education than architects have that get to earn a degree." Shane left out the information on how Llew had access to all the latest technology. His parents didn't need to know about Ace and Big Waldo. "Hell, yesterday the architect kept coming back to Llew to amend the blueprints, saving us from having to stall for production of new prints."

His father's eyebrows rose almost into his hairline, and Shane knew he had him. Anytime money could be saved on labor, his father loved it.

"Well he sounds like some guy. Huh, Big Daddy?" His mom smiled. She added more rum sauce to her bread pudding, encouraging Shane to keep talking.

"Mom, Ms. Pat gushes over everything he does. He really has her house coming along. Making all the repairs she's been needing."

"That ole good for nothing son of hers still making excuses?" his dad grunted.

"Of course."

Shane continued to win his parents over while he told them about how hard Llew worked, and how well the bidding and plans were going on the current and future sites. By the end of the evening, he was exhausted and ready to leave.

"I'd like to come by the site before we head out this weekend. Take a look around," his father said, walking him to the door.

"I got everything under control Big Daddy. I don't need you to come in overruling my decisions." Shane stood his ground.

"I'm not coming in to overrule anything. It's your company now, Shane. I just miss the sound sometimes, son."

Shane noticed the thoughtful expression on his father's face, knowing he couldn't refuse him. It probably wasn't easy for a man like his father to not have a specific purpose when he woke every morning. Shane didn't think days filled with long breakfasts, afternoons of golf at the country club, and evenings of sailing were all that bad. He could sure live like that for a while instead of waking at five a.m. every day and getting to the daily grind.

"Missing hard work and manual labor, that's just crazy." Shane smiled before adding, "Sure, Dad. Why don't come by on Thursday?"

His dad patted him on the back, opening the large double doors of their large Kerr lakeside home.

"But if you give my guys a hard time... especially Llew, I'll forbid you from stepping foot on my site again. It'll be so long, you won't know a tractor from a trailer, old man." Shane laughed, taking a few jabs at his father's midsection to show he was kidding him.

His father grabbed him, ruffling his hair like he used to when he was kid. "You forbidding Big Daddy? You the one that's crazy, boy."

Shane jumped out of his father's hold, springing down the steps from the large, wraparound porch. He felt so much lighter now that his parents knew the truth. They may still be hesitant about Llew but once they met him, they'd be able to see it – see his man's goodness just like he could.

CHAPTER THIRTY

The week went by quickly, quicker than Llew wanted it to. Shane said his father was coming by the site that afternoon and to say Llew was nervous would be a gross understatement. He'd worn his work pants that didn't have any holes in them and a blue flannel shirt. He made sure to trim his beard so he didn't look as rugged as usual. He was glad the guys had warmed up to him some, especially since he'd proven himself on the job. They knew he wasn't just a guy with no experience who had weaseled his way into a position via the boss' pants. He'd even eaten lunch with a couple of the guys this week instead of going off to sit by himself with Shane's iPod playing in his ears.

"Llew do you wanna check with the boss and see if he wants us to go ahead and pour this concrete today or if he wants to wait until tomorrow morning?" One of the cement masons yelled over the engines of the tractors digging up the soil a few feet away.

Shane and Jack were in the trailer and it'd become kind of the consensus on the new site this past week that when someone had a question, they came to Llew since he seemed to know most of the answers. Llew looked at his watch. It was a couple hours before quitting time. "Go ahead and pour, Rick. We got time."

The man gave him the thumbs up, trusting Llew's judgment, and began directing the truck to back up to the large slab. He had been watching them for a few minutes when Jessie ran up to him, out of breath. "Llewellyn. You need to come to the office, now."

Llew looked at her, wondering why the hell she was on the site in those heels and no hard hat. He yanked his off his head and put it on hers, smashing down her ponytail, and almost completely covering her forehead. "Jess are you crazy? You can't be out here like this. Does Shane know you're out here?" he said, while half-dragging her away from all the machines, piles of cement blocks, suspended boards and raised scaffolding. Way too dangerous a place for a lady or a man for that matter; not dressed properly. Shane would lose his permit right quick if a zoning officer drove up at that moment.

As soon as they cleared most of the active site, he turned to look at her. "Don't let me see you out there like that again."

"Llew, listen to me." Jessie huffed out in between breaths, since Llew had practically made her run behind him.

"Jessie, it's way too dangerous for you to go out there like that, Shane would have — "

"Llew, shut up and listen," she yelled, yanking the hard hat off her head and shoving it at his chest.

He stood there staring down at her, wondering what the hell was going on.

"You need to get to the trailer Shane is going crazy on some guy and Jack is trying to hold him back and Big Daddy Smith will be here any minute," she said, all in one long breath.

Llew took off towards the trailer, not bothering to wait for the rest of her explanation. If someone was messing with Shane, he was going to kill 'em: end of story. He cleared the parking lot with long quick strides, barely registering the black Mercedes with the Virginia license plate right outside the door.

He took the four stairs leading up to the trailer in one jump and threw open the door to the sound of the loud voices. Jack was yelling, and so was Shane. *What the fuck?*

Llew shouldered past the man in the charcoal gray suit standing with his back to him and went straight for Shane. His face was crimson and sweat poured down the sides and into his shirt collar. Jack looked just as angry, but he didn't know at who. He could be mad at Llew. *Fuck*. Llew took hold of Shane, and Jack looked more than happy to let him go. He bent at the knees putting him eye to eye with his lover. "Baby, what's going on?"

"Llewellyn."

Llew stiffened instantly at the sound of that voice. A voice that had invaded his thoughts, his nightmares for more than nine years. *No fuckin' way. Impossible.* He didn't turn yet, his body wouldn't do it. The look Shane was giving him was doing a number on him. His lover looked like he was in so much pain, like he couldn't stomach the feelings waging war inside of him. Understandably so. Shane had an easygoing spirit, a light carefree life; the last thing he wanted Shane to do was hurt for him. When Shane spoke to him, his voice was hoarse and strained. "I tried to get him to leave, Llewell, but he said not until he saw you."

Even being held in Llew's arms, Shane's body shook with rage. He looked over Llew's shoulder, his voice raised to an all-new high. "I told him he doesn't deserve to see you! Ever! Get out of my goddamn trailer!"

"Shane, calm down," Jack said, from beside them.

"Llewellyn, please. I just want to talk to you for a few minutes."

Llew stood up straight and slowly turned around, his heart hammering in his chest. "Why are you here Moss?"

Moss cleared his throat, a very thin and bony throat. He looked nothing like the athletic young man Llew had once loved. Hell, he looked even worse than when he'd seen him right before he left Emporia. Moss' suit was clearly too big, like he'd lost a shit-ton of weight over a very short period of time. His eyes had sunken in and were surrounded by dark shadows, like he'd been awake for many nights running. *Jesus*. He looked like walkin' death. Was Moss here to tell him he was dying?

"Llewellyn if we could just go somewhere and talk," Moss said quietly, his murky eyes pleading as clearly as his words.

"Fuck no," Shane spat from behind Llew.

"I wasn't talking to you. Stay out of our business," Moss snapped back, and that was all it took for Shane to unleash all the pent up fury that was raging inside him.

"He is *my* fuckin' business, not yours!" Shane barked. Before Llew or Jack could react, Shane was around Llew and charging at Moss full speed, his face contorted with rage, and his hands out-stretched, locking around Moss' narrow throat. There was no time for Moss to raise his guard. He was pushed backwards until the both of them went flying out of the trailer door and down the stairs, hitting hard and rolling across the dirt.

"Shit!" Jack yelled, running behind Llew.

Llew bounded down the steps and pulled Shane off of a still-choking Moss. Those once beautiful green eyes were now wild and terrified. Though they quickly returned to dull and pain-filled... or could that be sorrow Llew was seeing in them? Llew didn't know and he didn't care. All he cared about was Shane. He got Shane to his feet, pulling him away from Moss. "Shane, please calm down. I don't want you fighting him."

Shane's chest heaved up and down, and the look he shot Llew had him quickly clarifying what he meant. "He ain't worth you hurting yourself or getting into trouble. He ain't shit to me, my only concern is you. Please calm down." Llew turned back around, noticing that several of the crew had run over to see who the hell the boss was fighting. Great, he didn't need this right now. Things were actually starting to look okay for him, now this.

The pathetic specimen that had completely turned his life into a shambles was still lying there in the dirt, like he hadn't even the energy to get up. "Moss, just go. Don't ever come back here."

"Llew I just... I'm so —"

Llew put his hand up, closing his eyes at the absurdity. "Don't you fuckin' dare say sorry, don't you even think about it. Go! Now!" Llew growled.

Moss moved like he wanted to get up, but couldn't. One of the younger laborers inched over to help him but Jack barked at him to back away.

"Get your ass back, Mark. Leave him there. There on the damn ground where he belongs."

Moss' eyes lit with fire. He frowned at Jack, at the men that had rallied to stand with him. "You all don't know me. I came to speak with Llewellyn, not you." Moss stood shakily. "All of you need to mind your business."

"You little shit," Shane yelled, struggling against Llew's hold on him. "You're trespassing on my site; I can kick your ass if I want to."

Moss brushed some of the dust off him. "Llewellyn, just a second please. In private."

As if things couldn't get any worse, a dark sedan pulled up close to them and Llew had a sinking feeling that he was getting ready to meet his man's father for the first time in front of the man who claimed Llew had raped him. *God take me now, I'm ready.* Llew dropped his head and pinched the tension building in the center of his forehead.

A tall, well-built man wearing dark navy slacks and a white Polo golf shirt stepped out of the driver's seat. He lifted his sunglasses and pushed them back into his full head of salt and pepper hair as he strolled over to his son. He was no doubt Big Daddy Smith. He commanded attention as he approached and he had the booming voice to match the persona. "What the hell is going on here, Smith Jr.? Is everyone on break right at the end of the day?"

Jack came over first. "Smith Sr., why don't you come on inside and I'll catch you up on the new project as —"

Big Daddy sliced his hand through the air, effectively cutting off Jack's weak attempt at covering up what was going on. "Hush up, Jack. Tell me what's really going on, here." He looked back towards Llew and his son, no doubt noting his wild hair and dirty, disheveled clothes. "Smith Jr., are you out here fighting?"

Shane paced back and forth, nodding his head. "Yes, sir. I was fighting a piece of trash that won't leave my property."

"Who are you?" Big Daddy walked towards Moss, who stood there, still seething.

Shane came around from Llew, lightly touching him on his shoulder, indicating he was calm enough now. "Oh, please; allow me. Everyone, this here is Moss McGregor the sixth. He's here because he just wanted to see how Llewellyn here was doing," Shane said, calmly. He spread his arms wide as he continued. "Most of you have read Llew's criminal history about what he did to get put in prison but you all might *not* know Mr. McGregor the sixth because his name was sealed. Yes, this is the man who said Llewellyn raped him in his own home and sent him to jail for eight motherfuckin' years!" Shane yelled again.

"Shane, please." Llew tried to stop his lover but he was too far on a roll.

"Tell me people. How many rape victims do you know would make a point of tracking down their attacker to tell them they're sorry and they just wanted to check on them and make sure they're okay?" Shane turned his venom back towards Moss. "I'll tell you if you don't know. The kind of so-called victim that lied about an innocent man and ruined his life, because he was too much of a sissified-no balls-havin'-punk-ass-bitch to tell his daddy the truth when he got caught fuckin' a man."

Moss looked a wreck, like his whole world had crashed down on him. His body sagged from obvious

285

depression and malnutrition. He had a bruise forming on his cheek were he'd connected with the ground, and now tears ran down his dirty cheeks; leaving ugly track marks down his hollow face.

"Smith Jr. that's enough," his father ordered.

"No Dad, it's not." Shane approached Moss in a few long steps, standing so close to him that their foreheads touched. "You see him? That's *my* father. I'm not too scared to tell him that Llewell is *my* man!" Shane barked emphasizing "'my" with a hard poke at his own chest. "And I'm standing out here in the middle of my *own* business, fighting for him because *I* love him, and anyone that tries to hurt him; I'm gonna beat the shit out of them. I'm *not* too scared to stand up for him or to stand up for what is right."

The amount of pride Llew was feeling right now was enough for his chest to explode. Damnit. Even Smith Sr. looked proud.

"Now, I'm gonna say it one last time. Get your useless, weak ass off my property before the sheriff gets called on *you* this time."

"Okay, okay," Moss cried. "I just wanted to say that I never meant to hurt you, Llew. I swear. If I could take it back, I would. I think about it every day, every damn day. I can't sleep, I can't eat, I can't work. My wife, she, she l-left—"

"You expect someone to feel sorry for you?" Shane cut Moss off, no amount of tears the man shed softening his attack.

"I don't know you. I don't want *you* to feel sorry for me. I'm just glad he finally has someone to love him like I couldn't. I really am sorry, please, Llew." Moss sobbed some more. "Please forgive me, Llew. Please."

When Moss tried to look around Shane to see if Llew was going to say anything, Llew turned his back on Moss, just like he'd done to him all those years ago.

"That's all the answer you need, now get the fuck out of here," Shane said, sounding even angrier. The guys started to join in with Shane, mumbling loudly. The words "coward" and "scared punk" could be heard over all the other murmuring.

Llew didn't see, but he heard the purr of a luxury car engine start up and the sound of tires departing slowly over gravel. Jack's loud voice made Llew jump since he'd been unaware of what had actually just happened behind him. "Show's over. Get it shut down and get on out of here, before I find something more for you to do!"

As the guys departed, a few of them stopped to shake Big Daddy's hand and to tell him how great a boss Smith Jr. was. Llew was nervous to go back inside that trailer, but it was inevitable. He felt Shane's presence before he put his hand on his shoulder. "Llewell. If you're mad, I-I'm sorry. I just. He was here acting like you two were old friends and demanding to see you. It was so fucked up and he… it was like he wanted you back. I couldn't even think after that. Please don't be mad. I know I caused a scene but—"

Llew turned around and pulled Shane into his arms, regardless that his dad was somewhere watching. "No one has ever stood up for me like that. Thank you." Llew rested his head on top of Shane's. "God. You were wonderful."

Shane looked up at him with a slow smile spreading on his face. "Yeah?"

Llew chuckled softly, wiping some dirt off Shane's cheek. "Yeah."

"I can't believe you said all that in front of your dad and your crew," Llew whispered.

"I still apologize. I know you prefer your business to stay your business, but someone needed to put that arrogant prick on blast. Coming here in secret like no one would know. He had no right to try to clear his conscience on the hush, while no one knows that he'd fabricated the entire case against you. We should go to the sheriff. We have witnesses now. He basically admitted it."

"Hey, hey. Shh." Llew bent and whispered against Shane's ear when his man started to get amped up again. "Calm down my little spit-fire, it's over. I don't want to relive a trial or sue Moss McGregor. I did the time, it can't be taken away, and money sure as hell won't compensate for it or give me back the life I lost. Now I'm ready to move forward, okay? Believe me. Moss will suffer every day for what he did. He already is. Can't you tell?"

Shane nodded and hugged Llew tight to him. After a few moments, he lifted Shane's chin so he could look into those soft eyes. "Hey. I love you too." He leaned in and gave him a couple gentle kisses before ending it far too soon, but they'd put on enough of a show for now. Llew released him and stepped back, helping to right some of his clothes.

"Introduce us, son." Big Daddy's stern voice cut into their bubble and Llew straightened, turning to meet one of his lover's parents.

Shane stepped back and looked his dad in his eye. "Big Daddy, this is Llewellyn Gardner. He doesn't mind being called Llew. Llewell, this is my father, Shane Smith Sr."

Llew reached out and shook Big Daddy's hand. His grip was strong and assertive. He held it there for a moment, looking Llew in his eyes as if he recognized something.

"You got a strong handshake, son. They say a man's handshake is but an inkling of his soul's strength."

"Indeed," Shane chimed in.

"Thank you, sir. You got a pretty tight grip yourself." Llew looked Smith Sr. in his eye when he spoke. The man looked pleased with his response, and Llew instantly relaxed upon seeing that his man's father was not disgusted by what he'd just witnessed. He actually looked damned proud of his son.

"Well it looks like you boys have had enough excitement for one day. I'll check out the site some other time. I'll let you boys get yourselves situated." Llew had a feeling that was father talk for get your emotions under control. Fuck the testosterone out of each other. "Smith Jr. Why don't you and Llewellyn come on by the house before me and your mother head out this weekend? I'd like to hear more about your new vision for Smith's Construction and those designs Llewellyn made that's going to bring it to fruition."

Smith shook his dad's hand. "Yes, sir."

Llew looked at him with surprise. Shane hadn't exactly had the chance to tell Llew about wanting him to design a model for him to pitch to a company that wanted to bring a new mall to Wilson. But the look on Llew's face said he liked that Shane believed in him and had talked about his drawings to his father.

After everyone had left for the evening and the sun was setting, leaving a gorgeous orange glow across the sky, Llew waited for Shane to finish his e-mail so they could go back to his place. He was in desperate need of a shower, a good meal, and some really good loving.

Shane turned off his monitor and stood, stretching like a big cat. "Ugh. I think I pulled a couple muscles in my back."

Llew laughed at him. "You probably did John Cena."

"Shut up." Shane blushed, walking up to him and putting his arms around his waist. He tilted his head up, and Llew knew that was his man's way of saying he needed a kiss.

Llew bent down and dragged his tongue over Shane's plump lips, moaning at the soft feeling. "Exactly how hurt are you?" He spoke into Shane's mouth while kneading his fist into the base of Shane's spine.

His man groaned and squirmed in his arms. "Mmmm. I'll live. I just won't be diving out of trailers any time soon."

"Good. Because I was thinking we'd go back to your place and have some food, a hot shower and…." Llew dropped his voice, his deep baritone rumbling in Shane's ear. "Something else," he murmured suggestively.

"Oh, yeah. I could use a lot of 'something else', babe."

"I could use some of you inside of me." Llew licked the shell of Shane's ear while he ground his thigh into Shane's rock hard cock. It looked like his fighter loved the thought of his suggestion. His own cock was hard and aching too. Watching Shane fight for him like that was like taking ecstasy.

"Oh, my god. Are you teasing me?" Shane shamelessly ground himself wherever he could reach on Llew's lower body.

"I'd never tease about that. I need you, baby. Inside me; deep inside me. Your long, pale cock making me crazy. I've been thinking about it for a while. I want it to be you, Shane. The only one to top me. The only one to ever top me. I want to know what everything feels like with you."

"Let's go, now. Before I come all over myself right here."

Llew laughed, swooping down to capture Shane's delicious mouth one more time. He tasted deep inside his mouth, his tongue fucking him the way he wanted Shane to fuck his ass. He walked them backwards until Shane was pressed up against the wall. "Just a quick taste, baby." Llew hissed, sliding down Shane's compact body.

"Oh fuck. Llewell."

Llew quickly opened Shane's pants, burying his face between his legs, inhaling his strong fiery scent. *Fuck. All mine.* He swirled his tongue around the head, gathering the fluid that was already there and waiting for him. He moaned around the deep purple head, sucking hard, sucking with the anticipation he felt at knowing this sexy cock was going to be inside him soon.

"Oh, babe. I won't last at all," Shane moaned.

Llew was only going to take a quick taste but the way Shane was squeezing his shoulders, he greedily needed more than just a taste. "Come in my mouth, baby," Llew said, lapping at Shane's tight balls.

Llew cupped Shane's ass, the taut globes tightening as his orgasm took over. Shane thrust his hips a few more times, shouting out Llew's name. He stilled a second before Llew's mouth was flooded with his seed. He swallowed it hungrily, pulling and stroking his cock for every last drop. Llew pressed his own dick, his eyes rolling at the torture of needing to come but making himself wait.

Shane lovingly caressed Llew's cheek while he rubbed his face back and forth over Shane's deflating cock. "That was so good. God, I needed that."

"I know," Llew whispered, rubbing his scratchy cheek along Shane's sack, liking the way he jerked from the sensation on the sensitive skin there.

"Fuck."

Llew tucked Shane back in his pants, since he was limp against the wall. His own knees popped as he kissed his way up Shane's body. Licking him under his throat. "I'm getting old." He groaned, making both of them laugh.

"You and me both, then. I feel like I been working on a chain gang today."

"Come on, champ. Let's get out of here. I'm starving and that snack I just had is making me even hungrier."

"Yes," Shane hissed, giving Llew one final kiss.

CHAPTER THIRTY-ONE

They decided to stop at Shirley's for the special instead of trying to cook anything when they got back to Shane's house. Both of them were too exhausted and horny to waste time on dinner preparations.

When they walked in, they saw a few of the crew sitting at a large table by the window eating dinner. One of the field supervisors called out to them. As they approached the table, Shane noticed that their eyes were all locked on their joined hands before finally meeting their eyes.

"Hey, uh. Just wanted to say that was pretty badass what you did today boss man. Didn't know you had it in ya." The other guys laughed, nodding their heads in agreement.

"Thanks Joe," Shane said, boldly. He wasn't the slightest bit ashamed of what he'd done. He noticed the young guy on the end that had tried to help Moss up out the dirt was looking longingly at their joined hands. *Hmm. Interesting.*

"Llew. We heard you were a big deal in high school on the football field, man," Joe smiled broadly, wiping his mouth again with his napkin before continuing. "I'm the assistant coach for the high school team and the rec league team. We could sure use some help on our offense. We ain't made the playoffs in a few years. Our defense is the truth but our offense just can't get it together. If you're not busy sometime, why don't you come on by and take a look at a practice or two."

Shane felt Llew squeeze his hand. He hoped it was from happiness and not something else.

"I wouldn't mind that at all."

Joe smiled again. "Alright. Sounds good, bro. We practice every day at six on the athletic field behind the city park."

Bro.

"Alright, I'll come by. I've still got a few tricks on the field."

Joe perked up. "Oh yeah?"

"Yeah. Gotta play dirty in the penal leagues," Llew said, the hint of a smirk playing on his face.

Joe almost spit out his sweet tea as the other guys busted out in laughter. Shane loved this. He was glad they were getting to know the man that Llew really was.

"We're gonna get some food, we're famished," Shane said in between their laughing.

"Alright. See ya'll on Monday," Joe said, going back to his meal.

Llew gave a slight wave, turning back with him.

They both ordered the special and Shane drove them back to his house.

They ate at Shane's table, both of them stealing quick, lustful glances at each other. It was as if they were both psyching themselves up for what was coming.

Shane was the first to get up and throw his plate away, still chewing on his last bite. "I'm going to go shower."

Llew's voice was a pitch past husky. "Okay. I'm going to shower in the guest room."

Shane nodded his head, backing up into his room. Llew stood and began inching in the other direction to the other bathroom. Evil smiles crept onto their faces that quickly changed into exiting laughter as they each bolted into the bathrooms. Llew didn't know if they were racing or just acting like wild, horny kids. Probably both. But it was sure fun as hell. With a huge smile on his face, he stripped his clothes off, leaving them in the middle of the floor. The shower wasn't even fully hot before he was inside, scrubbing crazily at the dirt and grime caked to his hair and skin. He paid extra special attention in certain areas, making sure he was right for his lover. He hoped he'd gotten all the soap off, turning off the taps and wrapping a towel low around his waist.

Leaving wet footprints across the wood flooring, he hurried into Shane's room, chuckling when he heard the water still running. He felt so silly for thinking that he'd won. Ditching the towel, he pulled back the soft white cotton sheets on the large bed and settled in the center. He could hear when the water stopped in Shane's bathroom, the thought of the man he loved behind that door, dripping wet and squeaky clean had his cock standing straight up in the air. Only Shane could do that to him.

Damn. What you do to me, baby. Llew stroked his hard dick, his neck arching from the blissful feeling.

"Starting without me, babe?" Shane's beautiful voice somehow made his cock even harder.

Llew's hand gripped his rod tighter, trying to tamp down his enthusiasm. Of course it wasn't working. He could smell that wonderful soap Shane used from all the way across the room. The one that smelled like an erotic blend of vanilla and spiced musk. He watched Shane close the bedroom door and light a couple candles that sat on his dresser. The romantic lighting was perfect. His lover was so thoughtful, wanting to make Llew's first time sweet and special.

"Com'mere, baby." Llew held out his arm, and Shane came to him like a moth to a flame. That light-colored cock bobbing heavily in front of him.

As soon as he settled on top of Llew, the temperature spiked to a sweltering degree in the room. They probably were both hoping to take things slow but neither seemed to be able to stay calm enough to slow their hands down. Their lips roamed everywhere they could reach. Tongues licked frantically, while teeth nipped aggressively at each other. Llew's hands squeezed and rubbed all over Shane's perfect body. He reached between their bodies and stroked Shane's dick, pulling so that it rubbed against his aching balls.

"Llewell," Shane groaned like he was in pain. "If you keep doing that, I won't be fucking you until I can recover, cause you're about to make me shoot."

"Mmm. No, can't wait. I want you so fuckin' bad right now."

Shane kissed Llew passionately, rubbing his calloused hands all over his chest. "Turn over, babe."

Llew's body shook from excitement, not panic. He wanted this, needed this to make him whole again, to heal him completely.

Shane reached over to his nightstand but Llew caught his wrist and pulled it back. Neither of them said a word. The action spoke volumes. They didn't need any barriers between their union. Shane eased his weight back on top of Llew and began to grind against his furry ass. "You're so perfect, Llewell."

"No, I'm not," he said softly.

"Perfect for me, babe. Perfect in every way that I need."

Llew turned and let Shane kiss the side of his mouth, peppering honeyed kisses down his face to his neck. Murmuring quietly in his ear. "Gonna make love to you, Llewell. Make you mine, forever."

All Llew could do was moan in agreement. There were no words powerful enough to respond to Shane's promise.

He felt Shane snaking down his body, kissing and licking a wet path on his way. Llew had been eagerly anticipating this part too. He knew his man was going to do it, knew he was going to – "Oh my fuckin' god." Llew groaned, raising his ass up wantonly at the first long swipe of Shane's hot tongue against his hole. He felt his ass clenching, wanting more, so much more. "Oh, baby. Damn. Like that," Llew begged, spreading his legs wide, until each foot was hanging off the side of the bed.

Shane settled between those hard thighs and spread Llew's ass open for the taking. Shane swirled that talented tongue against the hot wrinkled skin surrounding his hole. "God, you're making me crazy." Llew's voice was a mere throaty whine. After Llew began to grind his aching dick into Shane's mattress, his man kicked it up another degree and slid his tongue deep inside Llew's hole, making him shout out his name.

"Fuck, Shane! Fuck!"

He could feel his little spitfire smiling naughtily against his ass as he slid his tongue out and back in again just as slowly as the first time. "Goddamnit. Gonna make me come, baby."

"Yessss," Shane hissed, fucking Llew's ass with his tongue. A hard palm landed on his ass and spread it open again. Shane's movements were becoming more demanding and dominant, and Llew loved every bit of it. Loved that Shane felt free to express this side of himself.

Shane's weight left him for a second, and Llew felt strong hands grip his hips and pull him up higher in the air. His cock hung neglected between his legs, missing the friction of the mattress. While Shane continued to eat his ass raw, he spit in one hand and reached between Llew's thighs, pulling his cock back, alternating between licking his hole and licking his balls and cock too. *Shit*. Llew was dripping wet. His lover's spit had him slick from cockhead to the top of his ass. Shane sucked Llew's entire sack into his mouth when he felt the tip of a blunt finger at his entrance. His legs began to shake with the effort to stay upright and take all the pleasure flooding his system at once. Shane hummed with Llew's balls in his mouth as he slowly slid one finger inside him, not stopping until Llew's eyes crossed. "Fuck!" He couldn't see behind him, but with his eyes clenched tight he could see in his mind's eye; his lover crouched behind him, his long cock hanging hard between his legs. Llew trembled with intense desire, that visual had his orgasm streaking up his spine, slamming into his balls that were encased inside Shane's hot mouth. "Jesus Christ." Shane hummed louder and pushed two fingers in, rubbing firmly against Llew's gland. His body jolted forward, his nuts drawing up tight and Shane's mouth squeezed them until Llew shot his load beneath him. God, did Shane force his cum out? *Fuck*! Llew's ass was clenched around the intrusion of his man's long fingers while his cum flowed from the tip of his cock in long streams. All he could do was murmur Shane's name repeatedly. Seconds felt like minutes by the time his orgasm released him from its clutches. Llew was limp and useless.

"I'm gonna fuckin' come any minute." Shane groaned, anxiously shoving a pillow under Llew's pelvis and pushing him back down. Shane draped his hot body over top of his, connecting them from head to toe. Shane raised his hips and pushed inside Llew's ass in one fluid motion, not stopping until his wiry hairs were flush against Llew's ass.

Llew let out a long, deep groan as his body was filled. It was the sweetest pressure. There was no pain, no nervousness, only a love that ran deep. Shane's slick chest lay heaving against his own back, panting shallow breaths across the back of his neck. "Llewell, fuuuuuck," Shane cried, slowly pulling out a couple inches.

Llew felt drunk. There was no other word to describe this. His man's cock was absolutely delicious. Not too thick, simply long, and wide enough to make him feel full. Long enough to press against his gland and drive him to the brink of insanity with each moment he stretched out the withdrawal of his marvelous cock.

"I'm not gonna last, babe. Fuck, Llewell, I gotta come." Shane huffed against the side of his face. "You are fuckin' perfect. So damn tight and perfect."

Llew's voice didn't sound like his own when he spoke. Gruff and slurred, crooning as Shane fucked him with long, slow strokes. Dicked him good while he sought out his own release. He could hear himself but he couldn't control what left his mouth. That was what good cock did to you. Made you whisper hushed nothings in between each deep stroke. Sexy talk of lustful abandon especially for your lover uttered into the darkness.

"Sweetheart, you're fuckin' me so good. Don't stop. Don't stop. Deeper. Mmmm. Fuck, yeah. Deeper, Shane."

"Yeah, babe. Only I can make you feel like this," Shane whispered back to him. He drew out to the tip, and instead of easing back in; he gripped Llew's shoulders and pulled him back into his pelvis while he thrust forward.

"Augh! Fuck!"

"That's what I want to hear," Shane said, in the most erotic sounding voice Llew had ever heard. "Want to hear you curse me, baby."

"Fuck! Fuck!" Llew yelled between every hard thrust. The sound of skin slapping angrily echoed off the walls of Shane's bedroom. God, he didn't know Shane held this much power in those usually submissive hips. But he was proving to Llew that although he was so much bigger than Shane, he could be made to scream and beg like a needy slut. And he damn sure was. A strange, but amazing prickle moved through Llew's groin; his cock not fully hard, but he could feel the throbbing inside it, as Shane forced him to rub repeatedly into the pillow. Light danced behind his lids.

Everything inside him felt euphoric. Every part of him felt so damn good, like an orgasm for his soul. He felt at one with Shane. For the first time in his life, he felt alive. "Ahh god. Shane."

"I'm here, Llewell." Shane's hips sputtered and faltered, slamming in hard, one final time. He plastered himself to Llew's back, holding him as close to him as two people could get. Llew groaned, as his ass was flooded with a comforting heat that spread deep inside him. Shane hissed and cursed with each shallow thrust, emptying himself completely. He rubbed Llew's hips, kissing and licking at the sweat on his neck while his orgasm receded quietly.

"So good, babe." Shane kissed him some more. "Love you so much."

They both lay there for an unknown amount of time, neither one eager to break their connection. Llew was the first to squirm when Shane's cock slid out of him. "Augh. That feels weird."

Shane chuckled lazily. "I know." He rolled over, his hand resting on his chest. "Damn. I have never felt like that before."

"Me, either. God you did things to me, made me feel things that I didn't know existed." Llew propped himself up on his elbow, staring down at the man he loved. "Do I make you feel like that when we make love? Like everything in the world is right."

Shane looked into his eyes, lightly caressing Llew's face with his fingertips. "Yes. You make me feel like that every day, not just when we make love."

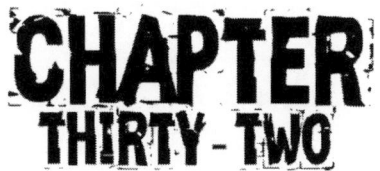

CHAPTER THIRTY-TWO

Their wash-up was quick. They were both so tired they could barely keep their eyes open to brush their teeth. Llew flopped down on the bed face-first, while Shane made sure everything was turned off and the doors were locked. He smiled, easing into Llew's side and burrowing under his large arm. He couldn't remember a single thought after he closed his eyes. He fell asleep that quickly.

The loud ringing of Llew's phone had them both starting in their sleep. Llew leaned over Shane's body, smashing him down into the mattress, and all that weight pressing into him made him whoosh out a rushed breath.

"Fucker," Shane muttered lazily.

Llew chuckled at Shane as he answered the phone with a groggy, "Yeah."

"Bro. What are you doing?" Leslie said breathlessly on the other end.

"Les, it's three in the morning what do you think I'm doing?" Llew stretched, groaning at the delicious ache in his ass.

"Oh god no. Eww, don't tell me," Leslie said, dramatically.

"Les, you idiot. I was asleep, man."

Shane obviously heard his simple-minded brother, because he started laughing, pulling the covers up over their naked bodies.

Leslie's good mood was obvious. "Are you with Shane? Is that him in the background? Tell him I said hi."

"You're fuckin' acting high, Les. Is this why you called me at three a.m., dude?"

"Oh, no. I called because you are not going to believe this."

Llew sat up against the headboard, running his hand through his hair. Damn, he hated when his brother did this. He always had to try to build up to a story with anticipation instead of just telling him. "Les, spit it out."

"It's all over Emporia, bro."

"What is?" Llew yelled in exasperation.

"Moss held a press conference. He resigned as CEO of McGregor Enterprises, and came out to everyone."

"Good for him," Llew said drily. "Now if you don't mind, I was having a really good dream."

"That's not all." Leslie paused.

Llew huffed. "Well, are you gonna tell me the rest? Damn, you tell a story like a high school cheerleader."

Leslie laughed. "Fuck you."

"Les, I'm hanging up."

"You and your brother are really weird." Shane chuckled beside him, his face buried in Llew's hip.

"No, *he's* weird," Llew mumbled.

"Llew are you listening?"

"Yes! But you're not saying shit, Leslie."

"Okay. Well not only did he resign, but he was arrested."

Llew sat up higher. "For what?"

"You wouldn't believe." Leslie laughed.

"Oh, my god. Les, just finish the fuckin' story!"

"Okay, okay." His brother paused again for affect. "Moss McGregor the sixth was arrested for perjury."

Llew's mouth hung open, Shane's did too. He leaned against Llew's chest and put his ear closer to the phone.

"He. I quote, 'Admitted to lying during sworn testimony given in the Commonwealth of Virginia versus Llewellyn Mark Gardner, resulting in Mr. Gardner being sentenced to ten years in prison for a crime he did not commit. Due to my overwhelming sense of guilt and the need to do the right thing by Llewellyn Gardner and his family, I can no longer in my distressed mental capacity continue to run McGregor Enterprises'."

"Holy shit," Llew and Shane said in unison.

"Bro, do you know what this means?" Leslie's loud voice was barely registering as Llew held the phone limply in his hands. Moss had told everyone. He told the truth.

"You should sue the hell out of them, Llewellyn. That whole damn family, man," Leslie said eagerly. "Use it to put yourself through college and get the degree you were robbed of, man."

"No," Llew whispered, talking to himself.

"No! Llew are you crazy! They put you through hell. That whole fuckin' family. Hit their asses where it hurts. In their damn pockets!"

"Leslie. Thank you for telling me. I need to talk to Shane now." Llew's voice was still low and distant. He couldn't believe this. After all this time. He didn't know if he should be happy, or if he wanted to find Moss and rip his fucking head off. The whole "too little too late," ringing in his mind.

"Shane if you can hear me, talk some sense into my crazy brother. He's still trying to be the nice one. Always the damn good guy. It's time to bust some heads, Llew," Leslie yelled.

Llew pulled the phone from his ear. "Leslie. I love you. I'll call you later." Leslie was still yelling when Llew disconnected the call. He dropped the phone on the bed and pulled Shane into his arms.

"Llewell, are you okay?" Shane hugged him back, affectionately rubbing his shoulders and his arms.

"Yeah, baby. God, I love you so much." Llew's voice was shaky when he spoke.

Shane looked at him with concern. "I love you too, babe. What's wrong?"

"Nothing. I just don't want to sue anyone. I don't want a dime from him. Moss' big-time lawyers will get him off on a mental insanity plea or some shit, but his life was already wrecked before he confessed."

"I thought you'd be happy."

"I'm not happy at anyone's misfortune, baby." Llew sighed.

Shane looked at him in wonder. "You are such a good man, Llewell. Always considerate of others, no matter what. But, this is still good, everyone will know the truth now. You can win this in the end."

Llew scooted back down under the covers, taking Shane with him. He held him in his arms, sighing at the inherent sadness in what he'd just said. "Yeah. They'll know the truth *now*. But I can't be happy about it, Shane. Because they should've known all along. I grew up in Emporia, so did my parents. They *all* knew me.

306

Classmates, teachers, guidance counselors, even the damn sheriff. But when it came time for trial, not one person testified on my behalf."

"Oh Llewell. I'm so sorry." Shane kissed him gently over his heart.

"Shhh. Don't be." Llew pulled Shane up to him. Kissed him with all the love he felt for him. "I have you, Shane Smith Jr. Out of all of the deceit that plagued my life… I still came out on the other side of it with you, baby." Llew ran his hands through the beautiful golden brown strands, cupping Shane's face. "I'd already won before Moss decided to tell the truth."

Llew gently rolled Shane onto his back and made slow, adoring love to him again. Their eyes and bodies sealing their very promising future. From that moment on, he vowed not to give Moss McGregor or Emporia another thought.

EPILOGUE

Llew, Leslie, and Shane sat at Ms. Pat's table eating slices of sweet potato pie as their compensation for coming over to install a stove into the room above the garage. Since Llew had moved out three months ago, she'd been slow to rent it out again. "You boys want some more?"

"I do," Leslie and Llew said. at the same time.

Shane leaned over and pinched Llew's midsection. "All this pie is making you soggy around the middle, babe." When Llew did odd jobs around town, he was most often paid with money and baked goods. The women couldn't get enough of his charm, now that word of what a wonderful guy he was had quickly spread.

Llew swatted Shane's hand away. "No it's not."

Actually it wasn't. Llew was as rock solid as the day Shane had met him and fallen hard in front of the movie theater. Shane would watch Llew work out prison-style in their backyard. Sweat pouring off him while he bicep curled cinderblocks and did pushups and pull-ups until his muscles were too tired to move. It was so damn bad-boy erotic; Shane would quickly jump him as soon as he finished showering.

"Babe, we got to get going. We're pitching to Holly Farms in the morning," Shane said, standing to put his plate in the sink.

"Yeah, okay." Llew picked up his plate and Ms. Pat's. He leaned down to kiss her rosy cheek. "I'll be back on Wednesday to cut your grass, okay?"

"Okay, dear." She patted his cheek, standing to see them to the door like always.

They walked out at the same time Jim Sr. was walking up the porch stairs. Llew and Ms. Pat's son still weren't best friends but at least he was civil to him now, had even been man enough to apologize for being such a dick.

"Hey fellas," he said, stepping aside and letting them come out first.

"How you doing, Jim?" Llew shook his hand on his way by.

"Good. Thanks, Llew."

Shane rolled his eyes when he walked by. "Jim," he said, with zero enthusiasm.

"Smith." Jim rolled his eyes right back.

Ms. Pat huffed. "You two. I tell ya. Worse than brats on a playground."

"He's always starting stuff momma," Jim Sr. grumbled, walking through the door.

"Whatever." Shane threw over his shoulder.

"Augh. Ya sound like spoiled little chaps too." She waved to them one last time, closing her front door.

Llew climbed into the driver's side of his only slightly pre-owned Chevy Blazer. Shane got in on the other side, settling in for the short ride home. Their home. It was only a few months after they'd said, "I love you" that Shane wanted Llew with him twenty-four seven. Now that Llew was doing more of the design for Smith's Construction, he was in the office in town most of the day, only on the site when Shane was shorthanded. It worked out well for them, made it easy not to drive each other crazy, giving them a little distance from each other during the day. Llew also coached a couple nights of week, giving Shane time to hang out alone with a few of his friends or just him and Jack. Just because he and Llew were in love, didn't mean they didn't have the same issues any other couple had. Llew could drive him crazy, and vice versa.

"Leslie are you getting on the road or you gonna come to the house for a while?"

"Naw, bro. My girl's coming over tonight." Leslie winked.

"Cool. Tell Melissa I said hi. Why don't you both come back in a couple weeks, we'll put some stuff on the grill, invite a few people over."

"Will do." Leslie hit the top of his truck and Llew pulled off. Even though they were a little over an hour apart, he and his brother visited often. Either he and Shane were going up there, or Leslie was coming down to see them.

Llew rubbed Shane's leg while he drove through town, raising a hand here and there waving back as people acknowledged him. He turned down Dupoint, winding up the road to their house. Llew pulled his truck into the wide driveway, beside Shane's Ford. He looked at the sleek addition attached to the back of the house. It was still new and very special to him. Shane had his converted garage that housed his woodshop and Llew had the large add-on room suitable for the amazing architect that he was. A room that inspired his innovative work. Tall textured walls, wide drafting tables dominating the center, his own executive-style desk, a study corner, everything he needed to create his masterpieces. Regardless of his lack of a degree. Once people saw his designs and his immaculately drawn blueprints, any concerns about education went right out the window.

"Baby, I'll be in my office. I'm gonna go over my blueprints for tomorrow again," Llew said, climbing out the truck.

"You always do this. You over-plan and over-critique, every time we have a meeting to pitch your work. Your design is beautiful, there's no way they'll say no. You've designed three buildings already; has anyone said no to you yet?" Shane came around the truck to wrap his arms around Llew. "You're amazing, and you're going to wow them at that meeting."

"I'm not gonna be cocky. I need to be prepared."

"You are prepa—"

Shane stopped midsentence looking over Llew's shoulder. He didn't even have a chance to turn to see who was approaching before he heard the suave voice.

"So I heard if I wanted to have my dream house designed, I should find a great architect to design it."

Llew's face split into one of his biggest grins at the sound of the super-composed voice. He turned out of Shane's hold, his lover's brow furrowed in curiosity at the two big men walking up their driveway. "No way." Llew's voice held the same awe that his face showed. He shook his head in absolute disbelief.

"And I heard that a kick-ass architect lives in Henderson, North Carolina. So, I told my husband, 'pack a bag, gorgeous, we're going to Henderson'. Because not only is the man that's going to design our home there." Ace stood in front of Llew, looking as handsome as ever. "But my best friend lives there, too."

"Fuckin' Ace," Llew said, so quietly, his voice choked up with emotion. Ace looked like he struggled as well. They threw their arms around each other in a strong hug. Llew couldn't stop the tears that flowed down his face. The man who had saved his life so many years ago, when he was contemplating hanging himself in his cell with his own bed sheets, and countless times after that, was standing in his driveway. Just as free as he was. He squeezed Ace one more time, making sure he was really there before finally releasing him. "You son of a bitch," Llew gasped, laughing and wiping the tears from his eyes.

"Llew. Damn. You look great, brother. I knew you'd thrive when you got out of that hellhole. You sure as fuck wouldn't fit in on D-block now looking as beautiful as you do... not that you ever fit in, anyway."

Llew blushed under Ace's approval, like always. He reached back, wanting Ace to see his most precious accomplishment. "Ace, this is my heart, Shane Smith Jr. Shane, baby, this is Ace."

"You can call me Robert if you want. Only Llew still calls me that." Ace winked. Shane reached out and shook Ace's hand.

"It's a great pleasure to meet you, Robert. I've heard such wonderful things. I can't thank you enough for what you did for him. Without you he never would've found his way to me."

Llew loved what Shane said. Loved that Shane could show Ace so much respect, regardless of where he'd just come from.

"I like him, Llew. He's fitting for you." Ace's smile was genuine, like it'd always been.

Llew looked behind Ace smiling, reaching his hand out only to be pulled into a hard chest for a bone-crushing hug. "How you been, Gardner? You look good, buddy."

Llew gasped when he was released. "I'm damn good, Jessup. How are you?"

"Happy, can't you tell?" The big man grinned a megawatt smile, tucking Ace into his chest.

"Yeah, I can tell." Llew chuckled, beaming at his best friend with his new husband.

"Damn. I guess congratulations are in order." Llew caught the gleam of the gold bands on Ace and Jessup's fingers. Made him nervous and excited at the thought of making Shane his husband when the time was right.

"Yes, definitely. Congratulations," Shane added, reaching around to shake Jessup's hand; introducing himself then adding, "I reckon you're Big Waldo."

Everyone laughed at the mention of the nickname, especially Jessup. "I always hated that fuckin' name," he growled, making everyone laugh even harder. Damn, that felt good.

"Where are my manners? Come on inside. No need to stand out here in the driveway to catch up. I believe a toast is in order for the newlyweds," Shane said, waving everyone towards the front door.

They did a couple shots of Patròn while Llew filled them in about his record being expunged and his name being removed from the sex offender list a couple months ago. Ace almost teared up again. Hugging him and congratulating him over and over again. He'd always believed Llew, from the moment he'd seen him, he knew he wasn't a rapist, that's one reason why Llew loved Ace so much.

They settled in the living room with beers, Jessup pulling Ace up close to his side. Llew was simply elated. They looked so happy. Ace deserved some happiness, too.

"So how long you been married, man?" Llew asked. Shane sat down next to him, propping one boot up on his knee, resting his palm on Llew's thigh.

"Four days." Ace winked, bright blue eyes gazing up into Jessup's face. The big man leaned down and kissed his husband passionately. A thick tongue delved deep into Ace's mouth, greedily tasting him until they were both breathless.

"Wow. You guys are hot as hell," Shane said boldly, making them all laugh again.

Ace was flushed when he looked back at them. "I got out last Wednesday. The first thing I did after I was released was I got a real haircut." Ace rubbed his hand over his short blonde hair. "Then we were off to Vegas, baby."

"You guys drove to Vegas and got married?" Llew said, in shock.

"Yep. Been planning that for seven damn years," Jessup said, sadness just beneath the surface of the relief in his voice.

That was a long time to wait for what you wanted. But Llew knew that all too well. It wasn't until he met Ace and became his friend that he'd learned how to hope and dream again. It wasn't until he met Shane that all his dreams finally came true. He stared across the small coffee table at the happy couple, realizing just how much he owed them. Damn, he'd missed his friend so much. He'd had half a mind to go and visit Ace after he hadn't heard back from him. It was driving him crazy to know.

"Why didn't you write me back, man?" Llew asked, seemingly out of nowhere.

Jessup and Ace looked back and forth between Llew and each other. A concerned expression crossed Jessup's face. He leaned in and kissed Ace on the forehead, urging him to talk. "Tell him, honey."

Ace turned back to face him, his eyes filling with moisture. "I'm sorry, Llew. I got every letter, brother. I read 'em every day. When you finally got out of there, I didn't think I'd make it, man. I missed you, dude. You leaving was like me losing my best friend all over again." Ace wiped the tears that began to fall again. This was the most emotional Llew had ever seen him. "I just wanted to get the fuck out of there and come see you. It was like losing Jeremiah all over again."

"Is that the guy I reminded you of? You never told me."

Ace smiled through his tears. "Yeah. I did eleven years for manslaughter, Llew. I killed the bastard that took my

316

only friend. Me and him had been friends since elementary school. Ever since he started giving me half of his small lunch because my mom was too hung-over to make mine. A man that was as innocent and pure as love, who would take from what little he had, to give to stranger. Never hurt a soul." Ace looked at Llew as he remembered his friend. "With dark dramatic eyes that told a beautiful story if you took the time to look at him. A man that god created and broke the mold after." Jessup held his husband close as he struggled to talk about his loss. "He was on his way home from work. Headed back to the shitty apartment we shared, when he saw a woman being dragged into an alley by her pimp. He tried to intervene and the bastard shot him in cold blood and left him there on that filthy street, like he was trash. He was all I had, the brother I took care of. The one night I didn't walk home with him… one goddamn night."

Ace tucked his head into Jessup's arm and cried quietly against his strong husband. Shane held Llew's hand while his body shook from the emotional impact of Ace's story. He could feel his friend's pain. He remembered all the times Ace had held him when he was losing it, all the times he told Llew to keep fighting. Now he knew why Ace didn't give up on him. Even thought he'd sought out and administered street justice for his friend, he was still trying to make up for the guilt he felt over not being there for Jeremiah by being there for Llew.

Llew said a quiet prayer for Jeremiah before standing and coming over to his brother. Llew squatted and put his hand on Ace's shoulder. This wasn't Ace, this was Robert. They no longer had to wear the tough armor required to survive in prison. They were out of that hell and both had men that loved them; they could be who they were meant to be now. He respected Ace very much, he'd always be his best friend, but Robert; he loved him, that man would be his brother for life.

Robert stood and let Llew hug him to him. "I can't replace him, Robert. But let me love you like he did. Like a brother." Ace squeezed him back, hugging him for a long time, purging all that pent-up guilt. After a few more moments, Jessup stood and Shane followed, going to join them. The comforting touches of their lovers' hands on their backs made them both sigh and relax in each other's arms. When they finally all moved apart, Robert looked like a weight had been lifted off him and Llew only hoped he'd helped with that. After pulling themselves together, Llew clamped Jessup on his shoulder. "Tell me about this dream house. I'd be honored to design it for you." Shane squeezed Roberts's hand, and added with all sincerity. "And I'd be happy to build it for you."

Robert laughed, hugging Shane to him. "You're alright, brother-in-law." They grabbed a few more beers from the fridge and headed to Llew's brand new drafting office.

The End

COMING SOON

Blue Moon III: Call of the Alpha

Excerpt

Chapter One

Call crouched low and pressed his back against the rough bark of the tall tree and trained his ears to any possible movement within his vicinity. It was too damn dark to see anything. *What I wouldn't do for some night vision goggles right now.* But he didn't have that luxury. He was trying to focus on using his natural senses. He took in a deep but silent breath. Held it and closed his eyes. He heard the suave, lightly accented voice in his head.

Don't underestimate man's ability to use the earth as his cover, his weapon and his shield. Call glided back into the indent of the dense bushes and bunkered down, practically belly crawling to lower ground. He had to stay out of sight. Had to wait out that perfect opportunity to switch from being the hunted to the hunter. Right now. He was the prey. He'd taken a different, jagged route into the vast acres of wilderness in hopes to throw his hunter off his game.

He heard the sounds of the Thompson River. Its smooth trickling sounds, different from the other lakes. *Damn. Have I already gone this far? Fuck.* Call stilled, his eyes widened at the sound of movement to his left. *Goddamnit.* Could be an animal, plenty of deer, bear, various other small rodents in the Jocassee Georges. He wished those clouds would break so he could get a little moonlight.

His heart beat frantically and he slowly pulled his Ka-Bar from the sheath buckled on the side of his camouflage fatigues. He listened some more. The sounds of crackling leaves on the forest floor reached his ears. Snaps and crackles of fallen twigs. The steps were measured. Calculated. They were not the steps of a four-legged beast...they were of a two-legged man. A stealthy man. *Fuck.*

Call was up on his feet in a millisecond and sprinting back towards the river. A searing pain hit his left leg, the feeling didn't have a chance to filter that he'd been caught before a split second later another shot hit him in his back. Hit in a major organ. A kill shot. He'd bleed out in five minutes or less. "Fuck!" Call screamed to the wildlife flittering around above him. He was so close to making it this time.

He turned around and looked down at his leg then back up at the dark forest behind him. He didn't see his hunter. He squatted down and pulled his canteen from his tactical backpack. He took a long swig of the water and listened to the sounds of the night. He didn't hear him approach, but he heard his smooth voice.

"You're dead commander."

"No shit, Alpha. How'd you do it this time?"

Alpha stood directly behind him, squatted and put his arms around Call's thick neck. "I can smell you." He whispered.

Call chuckled deeply. "Get the fuck outta' here." He could feel Alpha's sexy grin against the base of his neck.

"No really. You're wearing my favorite aftershave. It's fiery and strong. A scent like nothing else out here." Alpha gently kissed Call's now evenly beating pulse under the damp skin on his neck.

Call pulled Alpha around to his front and the sleek man didn't hesitate to straddle Call's large lap. He gripped the back of Alpha's head. The black, wool skull cap he wore kept him from running his hands through the dark strands of his lover's hair. Call gently kissed Alpha's soft lips. They placed languid kisses on each other's faces. Call knew Alpha loved him more than anything in this world. He never knew a love like this could exist, especially for a damaged man like him. The way he looked. He shouldn't be with a man as beautiful as Alpha.

"I can taste your thoughts, John." Alpha murmured in his Persian accent against Call's scared cheek. "Why do you think these things when I'm touching you? Licking you. Fucking you."

Call leaned back and rested his elbows in the soft soil, staring up at his man. The moon had emerged from behind the dark clouds, just in time for him to feast on Alpha's beauty. He shook his head. He had to stop doing this to Alpha. They'd been together two years now. How many times did he need to be reassured that Alpha wasn't disgusted by his marred skin on the entire left side of his body? He was in love with the man within him.

When the almost mythical, legendary assassin breached Call's headquarters and showed himself to him and his team, Call had never thought he'd seen anything more stunning. But just like there was more to his lethal assassin than his outward appearance, the same applied to him. Call was one of the Navy's most elite and decorated SEALS. Commanding the country's elite team, The Beastmasters for fifteen years. His life had been dedicated to his country, just like his assassin's had been dedicated to his order. They both fought for justice and equality, sometimes putting them up against the same criminals and terrorist. Only Alpha did it a little differently. He had only the laws of his order to follow. Call had the military. So when they encountered each other face to face for the first time two years ago while Call and his team were backing up Pierce's – Code name Backhander – mission, Alpha had showed himself to Call. No one having ever laid eyes on the world's deadliest man.

Alpha had put his trust in Call before the man even knew him. Only knew of Call's reputation. That'd been enough back then. Alpha's words and actions should be enough for Call now, certainly after all this time. Call snapped upright and gripped Alpha's forearms and yanked him into his solid chest.

"Yes." Alpha growled, letting himself be handled by his big Commander. "That's right. I'm all yours."

Call rolled them and positioned himself on Alpha's hard body. The man may be three inches shorter then Call's 6'4 and under-weighed him by almost forty pounds, his lover was all firm muscle. A body trained by the order of Imuma Aga Khan from birth. He dug his hands in Alphas thin black pants that enabled him to move so freely, it sure as fuck was a convenience when Call quickly needed to get to Alpha's thick cock. His lover was already hard for him. Aching and throbbing. Damn they had it bad for each other. Alpha tilted his head to the side and let Call bite him on his throat. A surge of power rolled through Call anytime he had Alpha pinned under him. Fuck, the man's name alone was an aphrodisiac to a man like Call.

"Let's go to the Wright Falls." Alpha hissed as Call continued his assault on the man's finely tuned senses. "The temperature will be dropping soon, not much time left to swim."

"Can't." Call licked his way to Alpha's ear, chuckling softly. "You shot me in the leg."

Alpha grinned back at him. "How many times do I have to tell you to stay down? Stand your position. I knew I was close to you, but I didn't know exactly where you were." Alpha nipped Call's lip. "Until you got up and ran."

"If the enemy is closing in then you…."

"You make him come to you." Alpha cut off Call's standard military style procedures. "Pull him *in* to your trap. You're thinking that you're out here with your team and you have eight men watching your back. Hawk and Shot are not in a tree one hundred yards away ready to snipe anyone getting close to you. It's me and you. One on one. Skill against skill. Mind against mind."

"You're too wise, Alpha. I wasn't trained like you. You'll always best me." Call looked down at Alpha admirably.

"Only a wise man can understand wisdom."

"Oh no. You're talking in proverbs again. Come on lets go." Call laughed and got up to pull Alpha with him.

"Fuck you." Alpha laughed waiting for Call to pick up his backpack. "I'm just saying. You're just as smart as I am in many aspects…smarter."

"You stroking my ego now?"

"That's one part of you that doesn't need stroking. I'm saying I've only had to keep myself alive. You had an entire team to command. Assassins are groomed to work alone. They only put me with my brother when they noticed how well he responded to my presence. He could mimic me, anticipate my moves and follow them. We did more good together than separated."

"So your brother worked alone at one point? All I ever heard were stories or theories on Alpha and Omega, never of you two apart." Call footsteps were heavy as he trudged through the dark woods, since they were no longer playing their game. Alphas' always silent. He knew no other way to move.

"Yes. He did work alone for -"

Alpha's mouth snapped shut. Both men stopping at the sound of leaves rustling behind them. Silence. Call moved for his knife but Alpha's glare told him not to move. *You never make a sound, never a movement. Until you absolutely must.* Call remembered Alpha's teaching. He could pull his knife or his weapon fast but since he'd been learning from Alpha... he was even faster. After another few seconds of them standing motionless, Alpha released a soft sigh.

"It's a deer."

"Where?"

"About three hundred twenty feet." Alpha said coolly, continuing their journey.

"Jesus." Call shook his head. He could see about a quarter of that distance in front of him in the darkness, even with the moon's help.

"Night vision goggles spoiled you. You never had to use your eyes that way." Alpha reached back for Call's hand pulling him closer behind him as they walked.

"Very true. But I'm making another alteration to our game." Call sneered. "I'm getting rid of the rock salt shells. Those shits hurt babe, especially if you're only twenty feet away."

Alpha laughed at him. "I don't even like guns. But you insisted. Soon, it won't be an issue anyway. You're getting better every time, Commander. It's taking me longer and longer to track you."

Call didn't say anything. But that was a helluva compliment. The first time they'd started playing their hunting game, Alpha had caught him in less than five minutes. Now they were up to three and half hours. They called it a game, but Alpha was serious when he hunted. He told Call to take it seriously as if Alpha was really his enemy. It was Call's favorite activity to do among other things.

It was nothing but beautiful, mountainous landscape around their secluded lake house on Lake Jocassee. Only accessible by boat. There spacious home sat on five acres, tucked into a private cove. They were in their own environment. Separated from the world the way his lover needed to be right now. Call was more than fine with it. His entire team had retired after their last very deadly mission with Backhander. If it wasn't for Alpha, he'd be dead. He'd lead men for over half his life. Now, he was happy to follow Alpha anywhere in the world. When Alpha had took one look at him two years ago and told Call that he could see his weariness, he'd been right. Call was tired of the wars and strife. Now he had the best of both worlds. Trying to elude Alpha on the days they played, kept his skills sharp and helped him cope with his new calmer lifestyle without fully losing himself.

Call dropped his back pack on the ground and stared up at the waterfall only a mile from their home. A different four hundred foot portion of the falls was only accessible to them.

"Strip."

Call quirked one side of his mouth. Damn his man was something. Call pulled off his fleece that was caked with dirt and grime from crawling on the forest ground. His army green t-shirt was drenched from his sweat. Once he was bare-chested, he watched as Alpha's mouth literally watered at the sight of Call's thick hair that lay slick to his skin. Call slowly unbuttoned his fatigues and pushed them down along with his briefs. "Come take off my boots." He commanded.

Alpha was in front of him on his knees before Call could blink. He watched his man unlace his boots and pull them off one at a time. Like he had the highest level of respect for this menial act. Alpha removed his pants for him and looked up at Call in all of his naked glory. His cock was right there, pointed at those pretty lips. God how he wanted to thrust forward, but he'd wait, wait until they were in their spot. Alpha stood and removed his clothes. Neither of them speaking. Call turned Alpha and led him to the edge of the water. It was already chilly but they were going to heat up pretty quickly. Once fully submerged in the rippling water, Alpha trembled in Call's arms.

"Cold." Call pulled him to him.

"Yeah. Colder than I thought." Alpha groaned as Call lifted his legs around his waist, walking them to a romantic area behind the waterfall.

"You can make your body stop trembling, can't you?" Call held Alpha tighter, careful not to stumble on the flat rocks on the river's bed.

"Of course I can. But, why would I do that, when I got you to make me warm?"

Call licked Alpha's chin before he dipped them under the waterfall into the dark cave. The moonlight streamed in through the water making the water droplets sparkle like crystals. He pushed his lover's hot body up onto the smooth, cool surface of the rocks. His skin glistening in the darkness. His cock was hard and begging for attention. A fine rod jutting out from a trimmed bed of dark hair. Call opened his mouth and took his lover in, loved to give him pleasure with his mouth first. Starting out intimate and loving before they fucked and growled like the badass men they were.

Coming in Fall of 2015

ABOUT THE AUTHOR

A.E. Via is still a fairly new author in the beautiful gay erotic genre. Her writing embodies everything from spicy to scandalous. Her stories often include intriguing edges and twists that take readers to new, thought-provoking depths.

When she's not clicking away at her laptop, A.E. devotes herself to her family—a husband and four children.

While this is only her seventh novel, she has plenty more to come. So stalk her – she loves that - because the male on male action is just heating up!

Go to A.E. Via's official website http://authoraevia.com for more detailed information on how to contact her, follow her, or a sneak peak on upcoming work, free reads, and where she'll appear next.

BLUE MOON SERIES

Blue Moon II: This Is Reality

You Can See Me   (STANDALONE)

NOTHING SPECIAL SERIES

Nothing Special (Nothing Special #1)

NOTHING SPECIAL SERIES (CONT)
Embracing His Syn (Nothing Special #2)

Here Comes Trouble (Nothing Special #3)

14369978R00184

Printed in Great Britain
by Amazon.co.uk, Ltd.,
Marston Gate.